DESIRE
UNBOUND

THE DUFORT DYNASTY
BOOK FOUR

JULIETTE N. BANKS

COPYRIGHT

Author: Juliette N. Banks

Editor: Cozy Nook Editing

Cover design by: Elizabeth Cartwright, EC Editorial

ABOUT THE AUTHOR

Juliette is an indie steamy romance author who has taken the paranormal romance genre by storm with her popular vampire series, The Moretti Blood Brothers. Not all of her sexy and powerful heroes are supernatural—Juliette now has a series of hot, page-turning contemporary romances readers can't get enough of.

Juliette also has a vast background in consumer marketing and previously published with Random House. She lives in New Zealand with Tilly, her Maine Coon kitty.

www.juliettebanks.com

ALSO BY JULIETTE N. BANKS

Visit www.juliettebanks.com to get all my books!

THE MORETTI BLOOD BROTHERS
Steamy paranormal romance
The Vampire Prince (**FREE**)
The Vampire Protector
The Vampire Spy
The Vampire's Christmas
The Vampire Assassin
The Vampire Awoken
The Vampire Lover
The Vampire Wolf
The Vampire Warrior
The Vampire's Oath
The Vampire's Fate

THE DUFORT DYNASTY
Steamy billionaire romance
Sinful Duty (**FREE**)
Forbidden Touch
Total Possession
Desire Unbound
Dark Surrender
Ruthless Temptation

THE MORETTI BLOOD WOLVES
Steamy paranormal shifter romance
The Claimed Wolf
The Alpha Wolf

REALM OF THE IMMORTALS
Steamy paranormal fantasy romance
The Archangel's Heart
The Archangel's Star

DESIRE
UNBOUND

CHAPTER ONE

Never in a million years did Jackson Wiles think he would be sitting at a table full of billionaires in a restaurant in New York City.

A table full of Dufort's.

There was more Tom Ford *this* and Armani *that* at the table than most people saw in their lives. Their women boasted diamonds the size of rocks, and discrete personal security hovered nearby.

Six months ago, this would've felt like the furthest thing likely to happen to Jackson. Not that he wasn't an extremely rich man himself. He was.

Now.

His hand lay casually along the back of Kristen's chair, and he mindlessly drew little circles on her shoulder while everyone chatted easily around them.

There was nothing mindless about it, though. He was highly aware of Kristen's sexy body. Every damn inch of it.

If only he'd seen more of it.

One kiss.

That's all they'd had, and she didn't even fucking remember it. But it had been the best goddamn kiss of his life. His entire body had burst into flames. It had been way too tempting to take advantage of her drunken state, but he wasn't an asshole.

Then he'd found out she was Harper Dufort's best friend, and Jackson quickly realized what an asset the sexy green-eyed, blonde beauty could be.

Fine, maybe he *was* an asshole.

Kristen was only in the United States on vacation, so his plan had been simple. He'd wine and dine her and enjoy some mind-blowing sex while she inadvertently provided him access to the Dufort family.

It was a good plan.

Except, so far, it wasn't panning out at all.

The three dates he'd taken her on before Kristen had disappeared last weekend to the Hamptons—where Daniel and Harper had married—had been nice.

Nice.

As in, non-sexual nice.

As in, not-one-fucking-kiss nice.

But two things *had* happened. During those dates, he'd visited Daniel's penthouse and spent time talking to the man. And…he'd found himself enjoying Kristen's company.

She was interesting. Funny. Beautiful.

He'd been eager to see her again.

When she'd agreed to another date, this family dinner wasn't exactly what he'd been expecting, but Jackson had reminded himself this was why he was dating her.

Wasn't it?

Was it really dating if, in a week, Kristen was returning to the other side of the world? To New Zealand.

Could you live further away, you sexy thing?

He had realized, when he walked into the restaurant and saw her gorgeous eyes on him, he wanted to see her as much as he could before she left.

Jackson liked her.

A lot.

He was also determined to break down whatever walls she'd put up since that kiss and unearth that sexy tiger underneath.

Kristen had shared her father had warned her off falling for anyone while on holiday, but Jackson wasn't asking her to marry him. He did, however, want a few delicious days exploring the sexual tension that swirled around them when they were together.

Jackson was skating on thin ice. If she found out who he was, she'd be pissed, but he had no intention of revealing that just yet. He had a few things to tick off his list before he did. Until then, and while she was still in the country, Jackson wanted to get his hands on the petite, sexy little kiwi and fuck her on as many surfaces as he could.

But not hurt her.

The way she was looking at him tonight, glossy green eyes full of hunger, he was feeling pretty damn confident she wanted the same thing.

About time, gorgeous.

Damn, she made him hard, blinking beneath those lashes, giving him a hint of what she'd look like when she submitted to him.

He wasn't a dom, but Jackson was a dominant lover. When it came to pleasure, he always took the lead. Consensually.

Kristen turned to him and blushed, as if reading his thoughts. "You shouldn't be doing that," she said, quietly leaning into him.

"Touching you?" Jackson asked.

She nodded. "This isn't a date. We're just friends, I told you."

Liar.

"So you keep saying." He winked.

"And keep those dimples to yourself, mister. I'm not falling for them."

Oh, yes, you will, sweetheart.

He smirked.

"Oh my goodness," Kristen suddenly whispered, as Hunter Dufort arrived with a woman Jackson recognized.

Jackson frowned, confused about what the big deal was. He looked around the table and found everyone smirking or grinning.

"Can I please have everyone's attention?" Hunter said, pulling out a chair for the woman, who was glowing.

The table quieted.

"This is Addison. My girlfriend. End of story. Great, okay, so what else is happening?"

The girls all gasped, then clapped. Fletcher laughed, and Daniel rolled his eyes. They were clearly all friends, and everyone knew her.

"They've been dancing around this attraction for each other. Long story," Kristen whispered.

"Oh," he said, not really understanding at all.

"Girlfriend?" Addison asked, staring up at him with mischief in her eyes. "I agreed to *one* date."

Well, at least she was admitting it was a date. Jackson glanced down at Kristen, who poked her tongue out at him.

Do that again, sweetheart, and I will bite.

Hunter sat and laid his hand on the back of Addison's chair, mirroring Jackson's pose.

"Oh, they're adorable together," Harper said, clasping her hands at Hunter and Addison.

"Wow," Kristen said. "So happy for you."

"Nice to meet you, *Hunter's girlfriend*. We met at the bar that night," Jackson said, reaching out to shake Addison's hand once he'd connected the dots in his head about who she was. "The bachelorette night. I'm Jackson Wiles."

"Oh, hey," Addison said. "Nice to see you again." Then she grinned at Kristen, who blushed.

"Yeah, that was a random coincidence," Hunter said, giving him a dark look.

It had been.

Despite Jackson's motivations, stalking the women around this table was not one of them. The night he'd bumped into Kristen and her friends *had* been a pure coincidence. He'd been having a drink in a random bar in Manhattan, and they'd shown up.

Drunk.

Harper had apparently wanted to escape her bachelorette party and gone wandering around Manhattan, then chosen the bar he had been in. Like the universe wanted him to meet Kristen.

He'd recognized Olivia from a meeting he'd had with the Dufort Group a few days earlier. Jackson owned *Forbes 500* company, Appopolis, and was there presenting a proposal to them for a guest app. That wasn't a coincidence. He'd manufactured it so he could meet Hunter and Fletcher.

But that night, when Kristen's green eyes had captured his attention, he'd crossed that bar like he was a thirsty man in a desert.

Their chemistry had been electric.

Even now, his body burned to pull her onto his lap and claim that mouth of hers.

As the conversation continued around them, Kristen smiled up at him. "That was some night."

Jackson winked at her. "My favorite part was the cab ride."

The flush on her cheeks deepened. They both knew he meant the kiss, but she refused to acknowledge it.

Soon, little kitten. Soon, I will bring out the tiger in you.

"So, happy honeymoon, or whatever we're here for," Hunter said, lifting his glass to Daniel and Harper, the newlyweds.

Jackson began to lift his, when Daniel held up his hand. "Let's wait for Dad," Daniel said.

Jackson froze.

What?

Oh my fucking God.

Johnathan Dufort was joining them…Shit.

"Your father's coming?" Jackson asked, feeling the blood drain from his face.

"Yes." Daniel narrowed his eyes. "Why?"

"Ah—" Jackson began, and his chair shifted, making that God-awful noise on the polished floors. He'd have to make an excuse and get out of here.

Now.

"Sorry I'm late," Johnathan Dufort said as he walked up behind them. "I got…"

Jackson turned and stared at the salt-and-pepper-haired man who was built just like his sons.

Broad, tall, and strong.

Power and confidence rolled off him.

Dressed in black designer pants, a black shirt, and a button-down cardigan, which was done up, he had a light dusting of facial hair and a thick head of hair. At fifty-five, he was still in great condition.

And was staring right at Jackson.

The senior Dufort clearly knew who he was. Jackson figured he had photos of him, but to recognize him this quickly was a surprise. Jackson wasn't sure *how* much the senior Dufort knew about him, but he *was* aware of Jackson's existence.

After all, he'd paid for his education at Brown University.

"*Don't go digging up ghosts,*" his mother had said, when he'd later asked how she'd paid for his education. The one everyone, except the two of them, believed was a scholarship.

Curiosity had gotten the better of him once he'd graduated. And boy, what a surprise he'd gotten.

Not only had he found out who his sponsor was, he'd found out the man who had spent his life hating him, Trevor Wiles, wasn't his father.

Johnathan Dufort was.

CHAPTER TWO

"**W**hat's going on?" Kristen asked, looking around at everyone. Johnathan Dufort was staring at Jackson in a very odd way, and it was freaking her out. Not that she knew Harper's father-in-law well, but the usually controlled man had frozen on the spot.

And kept staring.

At Jackson.

Her date.

"You know who I am?" Johnathan asked, his voice low.

What?

Jackson nodded. "Yes. I know. Are you going to tell them, or should I?"

"Jesus," Fletcher cursed, shaking his head. "I can't fucking believe this.

Believe what?

Hunter glanced at her with pity in his eyes, then glared at Jackson, muttering, "Jesus."

"What's going on? Who are you?" she demanded, her head swiveling from Hunter to Fletcher to Daniel.

They were shaking their heads and rubbing foreheads.

Kristen's heart pounded. She looked across the table at Harper, who seemed just as perplexed as she did. They glanced at each other, and her friend shrugged.

Johnathan took his eyes off Jackson, quickly looking at Kristen, then took in his sons sitting around the table.

Suddenly, like a lightbulb going off, Kristen saw it.

Oh my fucking God.

How had she missed this?

How had they all?

"Jesus," she said, her stomach dropping.

All the Dufort men were tall and powerful looking. Their chests broad, square jaws, and they oozed confidence and charm with that same slightly arrogant but sexy smirk.

The same one she'd been trying to resist for weeks. On Jackson.

Thank God she'd resisted because it was quickly becoming obvious why he'd been interested in her. And it wasn't her sparkling personality or that drunken kiss.

Shame and anger fought for dominance as she sat staring at him.

How dare he?

"Who the hell are you?" Daniel growled, but Jackson was no longer looking at them.

He was staring at Kristen.

For a deep, impenetrable moment, he held her eyes in what looked like an apology.

Fuck you.

Jackson's eyes ripped from hers. "I'm your brother. Half-brother," Jackson said. "Johnathan Dufort is my father."

For a moment, there was silence.

Then, as gasps let out across the table, Kristen jumped to her feet and cried, "You bastard. You used me to get to them. How dare you!"

Jackson tried to grab her, but she shoved his arm away. "Kris—"

She slapped him.

As his hand went to his face, Kristen threw her napkin on the table and bolted from the restaurant.

She heard Jackson say, "I deserved that."

Kristen pushed open the doors, and seconds later, Harper, Olivia, and Addison surrounded her.

"HOLY shit," Harper said.

"Did anyone know about this?" Addison glanced from one to the other.

They all shook their heads and looked to Olivia.

"Don't look at me. I may've known them for longer, but I was just an employee, until recently." Olivia shrugged.

"You okay, babes?" Harper said, rubbing Kristen's arm.

"No. Yes. I don't know." Kristen's heart still pounded. "I feel like an idiot."

They all nodded and began shaking their heads, as the reality of what they'd just learned sunk in.

Jackson was a Dufort.

Or, at least, related to them.

Johnathan had a love child. And he didn't seem surprised. He clearly knew who Jackson was.

"God, listen to me. I'm sorry. This is a much bigger deal for all of you. He's related to your men." Kristen wrapped her arms around her middle.

"I'm still processing that," Harper said. "Jesus, I have three brothers-in-law now."

Olivia was rubbing her swollen stomach and shaking her head. She was engaged to Fletcher and pregnant with his child. "Same. Well, nearly."

"For what it's worth," Addison added, "I saw the way Jackson was looking at you before Johnathan arrived. He's totally into you."

So had Kristen. *What an actor.*

It all made sense now.

He'd been insanely patient with her, despite their chemistry. They'd kissed the first night, and he'd never mentioned it or acted like it had happened. He'd been a complete gentleman on their dates after that.

Why?

Because it wasn't her he wanted; it was the Dufort's.

Kristen had thought he was trying to save her from embarrassment. It had been one of those miscommunications. The one where, in her drunken state, his delicious masculine lips had lowered, and she'd thought he was going to kiss her.

When he'd started to speak, she'd kissed him.

Without missing a beat, as she tried to recover from her utter shame, Jackson had taken over.

Taken complete and utter possession of her mouth.

Pleasure had rocketed through her. Nothing in that moment had existed outside of them. Not the cab. Not the people, the noise, the lights of NYC.

Just his mouth, his tongue, his body.

And the promise of pleasure way beyond what Kristen was prepared for. Their eyes had locked as they'd parted. The dark desire she'd seen reflected matched the ache between her legs.

It had freaked her out.

So, she'd said the first dumb thing that came to mind. "Damn it. Now I owe Harper twenty bucks for kissing an American."

His expression had shuttered, and the moment disappeared. She'd thought she wouldn't see him again after that, but then he'd texted her.

Kristen didn't recall giving him her details, but she'd been pretty drunk. And she was stupidly excited to hear from him.

How could she not be?

Jackson was gorgeous. Nothing like the men she dated in New Zealand. For one, she was a sucker for the American accent, plus he was tall—six foot something to her five foot four—and charming.

Did she mention hot?

After their first date, Kristen knew she really liked him, and it had given her pause. She had to be careful. The last thing she wanted was to fall for a sexy man who lived halfway around the world. One who was clearly charming and probably had a different woman every week.

When Jackson had dropped her back at Harper and Daniel's afterward, he'd placed a kiss on her cheek and said, "Sweet dreams, little kitten."

Kristen didn't know why he called her that, but it had sent shivers down her spine.

Yet, the kiss had felt chaste.

And yet, not.

Now she understood.

Each date, Jackson would show up a little early and chat with Daniel before they headed out.

"He used me to get access to your husband. God. I'm such a stupid, stupid idiot," Kristen cursed. "I have the worst taste in men ever. In every single country on Earth."

"Two countries, babes. Just two," Harper said unhelpfully.

Olivia cleared her throat. "Did you, umm…?"

Kristen stared blankly until Olivia added, "Have sex?"

Oh.

Kristen shook her head. "No. Thank God."

Tonight, she thought they might have. Things had changed when she was in the Hamptons. Their connection seemed to have gone to the next level, and Jackson had been eager to see her again when she'd returned.

Kristen hadn't been able to stop thinking about him the day they arrived in the Hamptons, and then he'd texted. Then again. One day, he'd Facetimed, and they'd talked long into the early hours of the morning.

When Daniel's helicopter had landed back in Manhattan, delivering them home, she couldn't wait to see Jackson again.

So, Kristen had invited him to the dinner tonight.

She'd been teasing him about this not being a date because she did have to go home in a few days. It was her way of keeping an emotional distance between the sexual energy, which had felt explosive, and how she was beginning to really like him.

Or so she'd thought, until a few minutes ago.

Clearly, he'd only seen her as a means to an end, and all his flirting was innocent fun so he could have access to the Dufort family.

Except, it wasn't innocent.

Not to her.

Kristen didn't appreciate being made a fool of, or used.

Fuck him.

She drew in a breath. "It's fine. He's the asshole."

"Totally," all three of the women said together.

She let out another long breath.

Kristen wasn't going to waste her last few days in this magical city being sad over yet another shitty guy. Harper and Daniel were leaving for their honeymoon tomorrow. Now all the wedding activities were over, Kristen had plans to be a tourist and check out the Big Apple.

Then, she was going home to New Zealand.

With her heart intact.

And her pride.

An hour ago, she had been worried about two things: where she'd find the perfect navy-blue handbag, and how to sleep with Jackson without falling for him.

Now, she knew it had all been a lie.

Jackson hadn't wanted her at all.

TEN minutes later, Daniel bundled them into his black Rolls Royce and instructed the driver to take all four of the women home.

"Sorry, Kristen," he'd said, shooting her an uncharacteristically caring look. Then he kissed Harper and promised to be home in a few hours.

Kristen leaned back into the soft leather and closed her eyes, letting the city streets and all the chaos of Manhattan pass her by.

She'd fall back in love with NYC tomorrow.

Tonight, she needed her best friend and a stiff drink.

And maybe some ice cream.

CHAPTER THREE

"My wife's pissed, which means *I'm* pissed," Daniel ground out. "So you need to keep the hell away from Kristen."

Jackson stood with his arms crossed, leaning against the back of the sofa in Johnathan Dufort's penthouse. He stared at Daniel and then glanced away.

Keeping away from Kris?

No, that wasn't happening.

Unless she never spoke to him again. But that was her choice, not Daniel's. Nor anyone else's in this room.

Those big angry green eyes, which did nothing to hide her pain, were stuck in his mind, and on repeat.

Jackson had wanted to go after her, but he couldn't. Not with the three Dufort men staring daggers at him, while all the women went flying outside, following her.

Jackson had thought it wise to give them time to digest the news. He was still trying to understand it all himself.

Despite wanting to meet his father, he'd planned to do it on his terms. Not announce it in one big family dinner.

God, what a clusterfuck.

Yet, as important as this moment was to him, he couldn't help worrying about Kristen. He hated the way she looked at him, like he'd completely deceived her.

Hadn't he?

Jackson clenched his jaw and focused back on his father. After all, that was why he was here.

"Ditto. Olivia is pregnant. I swear to God, if this stresses her out, heads will be knocking," Fletcher said, crossing his arms.

Christ.

They were all wound up like coils, so he might as well let them get it off their plates. Jackson turned to Hunter. "And you?"

"I've always wanted to punch your lights out, so it's just another day at the office for me." Hunter shrugged.

Jackson glanced down to hide his smile.

Despite the threat, he liked Hunter. The younger of the Dufort brothers had been clear he distrusted Jackson from the moment they'd met. In fact, he was surprised Hunter hadn't worked out his secret already.

Then again, suspecting someone of being your brother wasn't a natural train of thought. Hunter had known something wasn't right, and Jackson had to admire the guy for that.

"Having brothers is fun so far," Jackson said, lifting a brow.

Fletcher let out a slight snort, while Daniel growled. "Half-brothers."

Hunter just continued to stare directly at him, like there was a risk he was going to pull a gun on them or something.

Trust issues much?

"All right, let's sit down," Johnathan said, handing out glasses of whisky to them all.

No one sat.

They all remained perched against tables or leaning against walls.

"Excellent," his birth father said and sat in the furthest armchair, letting out a sigh. "God gave me stubborn children as a punishment, I swear."

Jackson took a long look around the penthouse apartment, at the opulent wealth. Luxury furniture, a stunning view of Manhattan, and high ceilings.

His own home in Los Angeles was hardly a slum. Jackson had made his first ten million dollars by the time he was twenty-three, and life had opened up for him.

It was a far cry from what he'd grown up with.

"First, Dad, you're not religious, so give that up. Second," Daniel said, "let's discuss your *children*."

Here we go...

Johnathan ignored Daniel and turned to face Jackson. "When did you find out?"

"A few months ago," Jackson replied.

"Does your mother know you're here?"

Ah, no.

There was no way she could either.

That was vitally important.

"No, and it needs to stay that way," Jackson said firmly.

Johnathan took a sip of his whisky before responding. "You have questions."

Of course, he did.

Jackson had dozens of questions, and he wanted answers. Now the cat was out of the bag, Jackson wanted to know exactly how he'd been conceived and why his parents weren't together.

Why his mother had stayed with Trevor, the asshole, and who he was.

Finding out the man, whether an asshole or not, wasn't his birth father had been a shock. Jackson had framed his whole life and identity on being Trevor's son. An unwanted son at best.

Thinking he was like Trevor, and trying really hard not to be.

So yeah, Jackson wanted answers.

But there was more to it than that. Things he wasn't going to share with anyone in this room.

"Wait a damn minute," Hunter said, dropping his glass on the table beside him and pointing in Jackson's direction. "Are we just going to accept what he says? How do we know Jackson is who he says he is?"

"He's my son," Johnathan said firmly.

"Clearly," Daniel growled. "Look at him. Fucking hell, Dad. First the senator blackmailing us, now this. Jesus, what other secrets do you have? Actually, don't tell me. I can't deal with this right now."

Jackson stayed quiet.

"I'd still do a DNA test." Hunter shrugged.

And in three, two, one...

"So you want in on the family wealth?" Fletcher asked. "Is that why you are here?"

Bingo.

Jackson rolled his eyes. "How predictable."

"You might have money, Jackson, but not *this* kind of money," Daniel said darkly. "If you've done your due diligence, you'll know that most of the Dufort Dynasty is now owned by the three of us boys. You can't touch it."

"Jesus, the app proposal. Dating Kristen," Fletcher said, shaking his head. "Fuck man, that's low. Why didn't you just man up and—"

"Stop," Johnathan ordered, and Jackson was surprised when they all did.

Jackson crossed his arms.

"Leave Kristen out of this. And if you don't want my fucking app, that's your call. You know it's the best on the market," Jackson said arrogantly.

Because it was.

He hadn't hit *Forbes* by creating crappy products. Jackson had the best team, the best tech, and the best customer service.

Hunter shrugged.

Fletcher raised a brow.

"Little bit of advice, Jackson," the old man said. "These boys have spent nearly thirty years asserting their alpha status by pounding each other to an inch of their lives. The pack status is firmly in place. Before you go riling them, maybe make friends first."

Friends? They hated him.

As if on cue, the comments started flying.

"Nah, I'm good," Hunter said, shaking his head, all *nooo*.

"Clearly, I'm the alpha," Daniel added.

"We let you think that," Fletcher quipped.

"How did you find out?" Johnathan asked.

"I got curious about why Mom never told Dad about my college education being paid for. She asked me to tell him I got a scholarship to Brown," Jackson said.

Daniel shook his head.

"You knew about him? His entire life?" the eldest Dufort son moaned, rubbing his forehead. "Jesus."

"It's not that straightforward," Johnathan said. "So, your father knows?"

Jackson shook his head.

His father, Trevor, had passed away suddenly six months ago. Jackson hadn't shed a single tear.

Still, he wasn't sharing that piece of information just now. In fact, he wasn't sure what to share with the man. First, he needed answers to his questions. Then he'd decide what he told Johnathan Dufort.

If anything.

Don't go digging up ghosts, Jackson. Please. His mother's words—the ones she'd say to him whenever he asked about the scholarship payment—ironically haunting him as he stood in the one place she didn't want him to be.

But why?

Had it been a great love affair, or had Johnathan hurt her? He was known for his philandering, so it wasn't a stretch.

"No. He doesn't know," Jackson said. None of which was a lie. Trevor might be dead, but it was true, he hadn't known.

At least, as far as Jackson knew.

If Trevor did, it would explain his cold, judgmental behavior toward him all his life. Jackson had read somewhere that fathers were important in developing a sense of security, both physically and emotionally. And that it was natural for kids to want to make their dads proud. It built confidence and personal power.

Perhaps that was why Jackson was seeking out his real father, now he'd learned the truth.

"I hacked into Mom's computer and found some correspondence between you," Jackson added.

Johnathan cursed.

"Obviously, I knew who you were. The Dufort name is plastered across the top of major hotels in every city in the world."

Johnathan nodded, staring into his whisky.

"Great. And you wanted to give this goon access to our business systems," Hunter said to Fletcher, who just shook his head.

Jackson pressed his lips together to stop from smiling. He could have hacked into their company with or without access, but he wasn't going to announce that.

"I'm not sure I can tell you any more than that. Once these three have finished pounding their chests, we'll talk," Johnathan said, ignoring Hunter.

Jackson nodded once.

His heart was thumping despite his outward appearance. These men were his blood family, whether they liked it or not. There was no guarantee of a relationship with them, but he hoped they could accept him.

Trevor had been a poor role model, as far as men in Jackson's life. He'd criticized and, in reflection, bullied him. Even humiliated him at times.

When Jackson had made his first hundred million, Trevor had picked up the *Forbes* magazine—Jackson's face was on the cover—and chucked it across the table. Then scoffed, "They couldn't find anyone else for this edition?"

Asshole.

Jackson was proud of his tech business, Appopolis. He'd built it from the ground up. Now he had huge plans, including a potential contract with the U.S. government him and his team were negotiating.

Jackson didn't want or need the Dufort billions.

What he wanted was a family.

Both sets of grandparents had passed away when he was younger. Not that he saw his paternal grandparents, or rather, Trevor's parents. They must have known Jackson wasn't a blood relative.

And now, his mother was sick.

Really sick.

It felt to Jackson like he was facing a future alone. It was, if he was honest, the driving force to finding his father.

Johnathan had answers and possibly wanted to know him now.

Or not.

Only time would tell.

The wounded boy inside of him wanted to know there was a man he could respect and share his success stories with. Hell, it was normal to want your father to be proud of you.

Jackson had never had that. Even before learning Trevor wasn't his father, he had felt very little grief at his passing.

Daniel, Hunter, and Fletcher continued bickering about whether they could trust him and how their father was the cause of so many dramas these days, so Jackson slid his phone out of his pocket.

Something else was nudging him for its attention.

Or rather, someone else.

Kristen.

No missed messages. Well, at least she hadn't texted to say she hated his lying ass.

Her silence was loud enough.

Except, he'd be happy to take her anger, if he knew she was okay. He wanted the opportunity to tell her this wasn't entirely about the Dufort's. That he genuinely liked her.

And he wanted her.

Even for just one night.

The way her eyes had lifted to his, as his fingers circled over her silky skin in the restaurant tonight, told him she wanted it too.

Was he arrogant?

A little. But he knew women. The sparkle in her eyes had told him a million things. Kristen liked his touch. She wanted his touch.

She *needed* his touch.

Jackson wondered, if he'd slid his hand between her legs in that moment, if he would have found her wet. Tasting her was right at the top of his list.

She would forgive him.

He'd make sure of it.

Harper and Daniel were leaving for their honeymoon tomorrow, which meant less barriers in his way to reaching her.

Plus, a part of him didn't like the idea of Kristen in Manhattan on her own. Not that she was his responsibility. But he felt…protective of her.

Something unusual for him.

"I'm not leaving," Daniel said loudly, pointedly breaking him out of his spell. "We all deserve to hear this. Start talking, Father."

The muscle in Johnathan's jaw twitched.

"Daniel, you may be in charge in the boardroom these days, but I will warn you about crossing the line with me outside of it."

Ouch.

Watching the power dynamics between all the men was incredibly interesting, if he took away the fact they were arguing about him.

"This is between Jackson and me," Johnathan added.

Fletcher moved to sit on the sofa, and their father shot him a dark look, his patience clearly running thin.

"I'm out," Hunter said, lifting his glass and tossing back the last of his whisky. Then he glanced at Daniel. "You still going on your honeymoon?"

Daniel turned to his father. "Is anything going to explode if I leave the damn country?"

Johnathan shook his head.

They all turned to Jackson. As they stared at him, like he was about to drop another bomb on them, something inside of him snapped.

"For fuck's sake. I'm not here to destroy your life *or* business. I just found out the man who raised me wasn't my birth father," Jackson growled, leaving out the part about the man now being dead. "I've got plenty of money and don't need yours. And by the way, as for who I date, that is *my* business."

While he was on a roll, he figured he'd cover all the odds and let them know he wasn't going to be pushed around when it came to Kristen.

Or anything.

Alpha status, and all that.

Jackson might not have grown up with brothers, but he was a businessman and hadn't reached the top by being a fucking pushover.

He wouldn't with these men either. They could choose to have a relationship with him or keep being assholes. It was their call.

At the heart of it, they had to realize he, too, had Dufort blood running through his veins. Jackson was a powerful, intelligent man with his own influence in this world.

"I'd be surprised if Kristen wanted to see you again," Fletcher said, watching him. "Why lie? That's what I don't understand."

Fletcher meant to them all, not just to her.

Wasn't it obvious, though? Or perhaps he just needed to spell it out.

Jackson held out his palms. "It's not like you're the Smiths from Chicago. I couldn't exactly rock up, knock on the front door, and announce I'm your fucking brother. You're the goddamn Dufort's."

Owners of a global hotel dynasty.

Billionaires.

Renowned playboys…now a thing of the past, as they'd all partnered up. Or at least, he assumed, after seeing Hunter with Addison tonight.

"He has a point," Johnathan said.

Daniel watched him for a moment, the air tense. Then he turned to Hunter and said, "Yes. Harper and I will still be going on our honeymoon."

Good.

He needed to see Kristen.

"If I have to return home early to sort out any shit, God help you all," Daniel said, planting his hands on his hips.

"Goodbye, Daniel," Johnathan said, swirling the liquid in his crystal glass. "Give Harper my love and tell her I'm sorry the dinner didn't go to plan."

Daniel snorted, then slapped Fletcher on the shoulder before following Hunter out.

Yeah, see you, bro.

Fletcher stared from across the room, then got up and slid his hands into his pockets.

"Honestly, I have enough annoying brothers to deal with, but, *Jesus*, welcome to the family, I guess."

CHAPTER FOUR

"It was Jackson texting when we were in the Hamptons for my wedding, wasn't it?" Harper asked after they had dropped Addison and Olivia off. They were now heading to Daniel and Harper's penthouse.

Despite her mood, Kristen watched the high rises, tourists, and cars whish past as they drove through Manhattan.

The view from their luxury penthouse was incredible. A girl could get used to this lifestyle pretty easily.

Kristen loved New Zealand, but NYC had a magic about it she hadn't being expecting. Nor did she expect to love it as much as she did. Sure, it was a bustling, chaotic energy, but she felt alive here. After nearly three weeks, she still hadn't scratched the surface.

The Hamptons had also stolen her heart. Those big, beautiful houses. The beach. Fletcher's house, where Harper and Daniel had gotten married, was enormous. Talk about dream home.

Kristen wasn't envious of Harper's new life—although it was hard not to feel some envy when she stopped to think about the magical life Harper was living.

A gorgeous husband who adored her. More money than they would ever need. A successful author career and living in a magical place on Earth.

Kristen knew better than anyone the challenges Harper had had to overcome to be with Daniel after meeting him in Hawaii, but now, they were married and doing that happy ever after thing.

Kristen wanted that.

She had a great career, but more than anything, she wanted a family of her own. A man who loved her, and to create little babies.

It might be an unpopular goal in a world of independent woman striving to succeed alongside men, and she was. Kristen managed a popular florist in Auckland, which allowed her to be creative every day. She'd had to learn management skills, including people management.

That part wasn't her favorite.

Kristen enjoyed her work, but deep down, now she was twenty-nine, she had been hoping to have found a nice man to settle down with.

Instead, she seemed to attract men who had no interest in committing.

Why?

She had on idea.

Guy after guy, she fell for their bullshit lines as they were trying to get her into bed. Then, the communications slowed down. Or they'd show up late on a weeknight with some excuse, and, like the idiot she was, she would let them in.

The next day, or middle of the night, they were gone.

Some of them were better than others. One guy, Greg, she'd taken home to meet her parents, but after a year, Kristen had found herself so bored she'd half hoped he wouldn't call her.

She had broken it off with him.

Kristen didn't know why she was so annoyed about Jackson. They'd had a few dates, and obviously, she'd had no expectations. He lived here. She lived in NZ.

The end.

Kristen had to get home to her parents, not fall for a sexy American, like Harper had. They were elderly and had told her she was not to meet one of those *yanks,* as her dad called them.

"That's not PC now, Dad. You have to say 'Americans'."

"I'm seventy-eight. I'll say 'yank' if I want. They call us Australians," he'd replied.

Kristen had snorted, shared an eye roll with her mom, and left him to his rigid beliefs. She figured when she was seventy-eight, she would have a few herself. He wasn't hurting anyone from his armchair.

The truth was, she had fallen a little for Jackson. She'd been looking forward to seeing him tonight, and as she'd expected, their chemistry was growing.

Those calls over the weekend of the wedding had done nothing but build the tension between them. Then, when his fingers had touched her shoulder—a ridiculously chaste move—her body had shuddered and felt like an inferno was swirling inside her stomach.

Okay, fine. Her damn pussy had clenched, as if holding on for dear life. She'd never wanted to throw herself at a man so much.

It hurt that a part of her was wondering what a wealthy, gorgeous man, who was at least five years her junior, would want with her. His designer suits, flashy big watches, and charming smile were not what she was used to. Except for Harper's in-laws.

Daniel, Hunter, and Fletcher were dripping in Armani and Rolexes. She had no idea if those were brands they wore. It wasn't Gap, she knew that.

Kristen turned to Harper. "Yes. Jackson was texting me. Mom did once, but mostly, it was him."

"Well, at least we can both keep your promise to your parents."

She frowned. "Which one?"

"The 'not falling in love with an American.' Your parents phoned me when you were flying over. They threatened to come and bring you home if I tried to matchmake you with anyone."

Kristen let out a short laugh. "They did not…"

Harper nodded.

"Oh, Jesus. That's embarrassing."

Harper giggled. "I get it. They saw me move to the other side of the world and leave my mom. She's not nearly as old as your folks."

True.

They'd been in their early forties when Kristen had been born. A surprise third child, her brother and sister fifteen years older than her.

Despite the age gap, she was close to her sister. Karen had her first child at twenty, when Kristen had been five. So she had grown up with her cousins and sister around.

Karen was now the main caregiver to their parents. Both had survived one round of cancer each already and recently celebrated their seventy-first birthdays. Every extra year was a bonus, as far as Kristen was concerned.

Still, she was embarrassed to hear they'd rung Harper.

Her dad, Terry, had made himself clear. "I don't want you coming home with no damn ring on your finger, girly."

Kristen had snorted. "Says the man who's always telling me I need to get married before I turn thirty."

She had one year.

"I said marry a good *kiwi* man," her father had continued. "Isn't that right, Sharon?"

Her mom had nodded. "I don't want my little girl disappearing, like Harper has on her mom."

Kristen had pressed her lips together. Harper's mother was a serious control freak. She had major trust issues because, as it turned out, her husband had been hiding another family in Hawaii.

But still.

Daniel was the best thing to ever happen to her best friend. Living a distance away from her mother was good for them both. It was different for Kristen. She loved her parents, and they didn't have much more time on this Earth. They all knew that.

"Stop worrying. I have no intention of falling in love or marrying anyone in the U.S. So, settle down."

She'd meant it.

She still meant it.

Jackson's deceit had made it that much easier after she had found herself falling into *like* with him.

WHEN they got home, Kristen had poured herself a glass of Macallan, Daniels top-label whisky, and hopped onto Harper's bed, watching her pack. After her third glass, she had a nice little buzz going on.

Harper threw a yellow bikini into her suitcase.

"How many boobs do you have?" Kristen asked, having counted at least seven bathing suits so far.

"Funny, ha, ha." Harper glanced over at her. "The better question is, how many of those whisky's have you had?"

"Five trillion and seven," Kristen replied, taking another gulp. "But it's not taking away any of the memories of *you know who*."

Harper snorted.

"He who shall not be named. Is that what we are doing?"

Kristen nodded.

"I know you're upset, but tomorrow will feel worse if you don't drink some water," Harper said.

Kristen let out a sigh and slid down the bed, staring up at the ceiling. Getting blacked-out drunk wasn't on the cards. She had tours booked tomorrow, and there was no way she was letting that lying piece of handsome crap ruin the rest of her holiday.

Kristen was tipsy but would be fine.

If she stopped now.

"Jackson was an ass, Kris," Harper said for the tenth time. "And apparently, he's my new brother-in-law. Or half. How do these things work?"

Kristen shrugged. "He could be dead by now. Daniel looked furious."

"Oh, that's just his resting angry face. He won't commit murder before our honeymoon," Harper said, straight-faced. "I think," she added, and they both giggled.

Her laughter faded away. Kristen didn't want Jackson hurt. Not that she believed Daniel would do anything to him.

Mostly.

She couldn't help but wonder how it was going. Facing his birth father for the first time must be daunting. Especially this powerful family.

Kristen was angry and didn't plan to speak to him again, but that didn't mean she didn't care. Or wasn't curious.

Over and over, she wondered if she had imagined their chemistry. Perhaps he'd been attracted to her, happy to get sex out of it and use her?

Things weren't always black and white.

It didn't make her feel any better, though.

God, what an idiot she'd been.

Despite how ashamed she was, she hated how much she wished he would burst through the door, yank her up against his gorgeous muscular body, and kiss her face off.

Who could blame her?

Jackson had Dufort genes. Those round, muscular shoulders, his towering six-foot-three height, and stunning cheeky eyes.

Not to mention his smirk.

The only thing she found sexier was when his smile and charm faded away, when he thought she wasn't watching, and she'd catch the rich lust in his eyes. Eyes which reached deep inside her and demanded she submit.

A shiver snaked through her.

Was he a dominant lover?

God, she craved that.

Now she would never find out.

"Blue or black?" Harper asked, holding up a beach coverall.

"Both."

"Good point. Thank God, we're not flying commercial," Harper said, tossing it into the second large suitcase, then gasped. "Oh God. I've turned into one of those rich people."

Kristen snorted. "You *are* one of those rich people."

"Yeah, but, like, I'm a nice one," Harper said.

"Not all rich people are horrible. That's a dumb thing to say," Kristen said. "Following that theory, it means all poor people are nice. They're definitely not."

"Sorry. I'm still adjusting to this life." Harper sighed, then sat down on the end of the bed and tucked her feet under her. "Am I different?"

"You have way more bikinis now." Kristen grinned.

Harper let out a laugh. "No, but tell me. Am I?"

Kristen sat up and finished the last of the whisky in her glass, then put it on the bedside table.

"Yes," she said, ignoring her friend's horrified face. "You're happier. You're in love. You're glowing. And you're loved by a huge, kind of scary man who protects you like you're the world's greatest diamond."

Harper's expression softened. "He does, doesn't he."

"That. What you did there. It's both sickening and beautiful," Kristen said, pointing at her face. "I'm happy for you, Harper, but being with Daniel has changed you. As it should. You were miserable in New Zealand with whatshisnametheasshole."

Referring to Harper's ex-boyfriend, who had cheated on her.

Harper let out a sharp laugh. "God, I really was."

"It's okay to change. If we stay the same in life, it means we aren't growing," Kristen said, feeling all wise and a little drunk. "Look at me, attracting just another asshole who used me."

Harper frowned at her. "You only went on a few dates. Don't beat yourself up. In a few weeks, you'll have forgotten Jackson Wiles."

Would she?

She had a feeling she wouldn't.

Those late-night calls in the Hamptons had stirred a sexual need within her, as his voice purred through the phone. She'd ended up touching herself, craving the feel of his strong talented hands on her.

Tonight was supposed to be the night he did.

Damn it all.

"I get it. I'm pissed too. He lied to everyone. Even me," Harper said.

Kristen slid down the bed again and stared at the ceiling for a long moment.

"Imagine finding out your dad is not your dad, though," she finally said. "That must be horrible."

Daniel chose that moment to step into the room.

"Ladies," he said, tugging off his tie. Harper leaned back as he gripped her face, and they sucked lips.

"Ugh, can't wait for you two love birds to leave," Kristen said, fake gagging. "Too much happiness. I can't stand it."

Daniel laughed and walked into the master bathroom. "Keep away from Jackson while you're still in the States, Kristen."

Why?

What had happened?

Not that she was planning to see him again.

When she sat up, she and Harper simply stared at each other, then Daniel took a step out of the room. Shirtless, with a toothbrush in his hand.

Jesus.

Damn bloody Adonis Dufort's.

It wasn't the first time Kristen had seen him or any of the Dufort men half naked. They'd spent a week at the beach in the Hamptons, after all, but it was still hard to ignore their utter muscular perfection.

What finally caught her attention, when she drew her eyes away from Daniel's pecs, was the way he was staring at her so forcefully.

Oh right, he was waiting for her to agree.

Daniel believed everyone should do as he said. It was lucky Harper was so strong and he adored her so much, or Kristen would be concerned he would completely dominate her.

She was sure he did in the bedroom, but in life, she'd seen Harper hold her own quite impressively.

However, in this instance, Daniel was right. Jackson was not to be trusted. Even if she had to let go of her heightened desire to be ravished by him.

Stupid body. Stop wanting him.

"I have no intention of seeing that liar again," she finally said.

"Darling, put a shirt on," Harper suggested.

Her husband ignored her. "Good. Remember, once a liar, always a liar."

Harper coughed and patted her chest dramatically.

Daniel quirked a brow. "Our situation was different."

"Was it?" Harper asked, lifting a brow back.

He stabbed his toothbrush in the air in her direction. "Yes!"

Harper turned and gave Kristen a wink. When Daniel disappeared back into the bathroom and the shower turned on, Kristen climbed off the bed.

"Before your caveman comes out with less clothes on and destroys my eyeballs, I'm going to bed. What time do you leave?"

Kristen slid her feet back into the powder-blue Prada slippers Harper had bought her.

They were gorgeous.

Kristen had squealed when she'd seen them, and moments later, Harper had snuck off and bought them for her. This had gone on every time they went shopping. In the end, Kristen had begun saying she didn't like things—her friend might have a ton of money now, but it still felt wrong.

"Nine in the morning. I'll pop my nose in and say goodbye. I doubt you'll be awake after all that whisky." Harper grinned.

"Are you sure it's okay if I stay here?" Kristen asked, glancing around the kabillion-dollar penthouse.

It was the fanciest home she'd ever been in, with the exception of Fletcher's Hamptons house. Not only was it huge, but the wraparound porch with floor-to-ceiling windows gave breathtaking views of the bay. The open style of the huge white house was cozy, modern, and she had never wanted to leave.

Harper nodded and climbed off the bed.

"Yes. I wish you would stay forever," Harper said. "I can't believe you will be home in New Zealand in five days."

They both made sad faces and hugged, squeezing each other tightly. Kristen had kept her emotions pretty close to her chest about that subject. She hadn't lost her best friend, as such, but it felt like she was.

They were now living half a world away. Even the time zones meant one of them would be waking as the other went to sleep.

"You said you'd visit," Kristen said. "Make sure it's soon. And we'll do weekly video chats."

They both knew that was a huge commitment with their busy lives.

"Absolutely," Harper said as they walked downstairs to the living area. "So, are you going to see him?"

She meant Jackson.

Kristen had had no intention of meeting anyone in the United States during her holiday, but the truth was, Jackson was unexpected.

She hated how much she'd fallen for his lies.

Those heated looks across the table.

The way he'd taken her hand, placed his in the small of her back, winked at her when silly things had happened.

"I was going to sleep with him," she confessed.

"Oh, babes."

He had fooled all of them, not just her. Except Kristen couldn't stop feeling like there was more between them. Was it just wishful thinking?

Or lust?

She flashed back to when he'd walked into the restaurant tonight. Jackson had beelined straight for her. A hand on her hip, the other on her shoulder, he'd leaned in and kissed her cheek.

Butterflies had fluttered around her stomach, like they were in a hurricane. Warmth hit her cheeks, and she had to stop her eyelashes fluttering like a silly teenager.

Kristen shrugged. "I'm angry with him, but I deserve answers. Or at least the opportunity to give him a piece of my mind."

"I'd get that apology from him, at the very least. It will help you move on when you get home," Harper said.

Daniel had been very insistent she keep away from him. Perhaps she should just get on with her holiday and forget Jackson Wiles.

She flopped onto the sofa, and Harper leaned her hip against it.

"I did like him, Harper. I was trying not to, but he's so damn hot, and there seemed to be a connection. Stupid me for falling for it."

"Maybe it would be better to ignore his messages, then. Otherwise, you're just going to leave America with a broken heart. Trust me, I have some experience with that, and it is not fun."

Broken heart?

No, she liked him, but she wasn't falling in love with him.

Whoever Jackson Wiles truly was, she deserved an apology and explanation.

And perhaps one last kiss.

Then she would tell him to take a hike.

CHAPTER FIVE

"**W**here are you staying?" Johnathan asked, topping up their whisky's.

"At the Waldorf-Astoria," Jackson replied, taking a seat now Fletcher had gone home.

He specifically hadn't booked one of the Dufort Hotels. For some reason, it felt wrong.

"You've done well in your business."

"You know about Appopolis?" Jackson asked.

"Yes. I followed your grades at Brown and then watched the development of your company."

He had?

Jackson tried to imagine what it would be like knowing you had children in the world and not being in touch.

Which just made him mad.

But then again, Johnathan was a powerful and influential man in the United States and around the world.

Jackson narrowed his eyes. "Please tell me you didn't interfere," he said darkly.

Johnathan shook his head. "No. Your accomplishments are all yours. I'm proud of you."

Jesus.

While he'd longed to hear that all his life from someone, it just sounded condescending right in this moment.

"You don't have to be all fatherly. We're DNA related. I'm not your son," Jackson said, shaking his head.

Johnathan sat forward. "You *are* my son. Despite how things unfolded, Jackson, you are my son."

"Tell me what happened."

Johnathan shook his head. "As you know, I assume, your mother was a famous singer. An artist. She was at an event I attended in Los Angeles."

Jackson nodded. He did know that about his mother.

Jenna Stone. Lead singer of the same name band, with two platinum records.

"We instantly connected," Johnathan said. "The night we met, everyone had cleared out, and we carried on, drinking late into the night. She told me about her marriage. I told her about mine."

"You were unhappy, even then?"

The Dufort family history was online and no secret, along with Johnathan's many indiscretions. Jackson was prepared to hear Jenna, his mom, was nothing but a fling.

But he had to hear it.

"Yes. All three of the boys were born, and my wife was drinking heavily. Look, I'm not going to lie. I had been sleeping with other women by that point and working long hours in the business. Neither of us happy."

Jackson crossed his legs. "Why not just leave?"

Johnathan let out a dry laugh. "Come back to me when you have kids and ask."

Jackson lifted a shoulder.

Fair response. Kids did change things.

"And the short answer is, I did, eventually. We spent the night together, and I thought we'd never see each other again. Except, I found myself calling her each time I was in town."

Jackson lifted his eyebrows in surprise.

They had a relationship?

So, it wasn't just a one-night stand.

"Worse…I found myself going to L.A. for no other reason but to see Jenna."

Oh.

"We had to be careful because we were both known to the media. In the nineties, the media was a different beast. Think Princess Diana."

Jackson cringed. It was a good example of the media, but neither his mother or father were as famous as the English royal princess, who had been hunted by the paparazzi and died in a car crash in Paris.

Then again, no one was.

In his head, it was all piecing together.

"So, Mom got pregnant, and you walked away?" Jackson asked. "Because you had the house, the kids, the wife, and your thriving business and didn't want the media to expose you and destroy any of it?"

"It's not that black and white. Your mother made choices of her own. Remember, she was married too."

"If you were both unhappy, why did she stay? Why did *you* stay?" Jackson pushed.

"You need to speak to her to get those answers. They're not for me to say," Johnathan said firmly.

Really?

What the hell.

Jackson had come all this way for answers, and that was all he was getting?

"But she called you about my college tuition? You stayed in contact?"

"She did." Johnathan nodded. "But that was the first time I heard from her since she emailed me the photos of your birth."

Jackson froze.

"Photos?"

Johnathan lowered his brows. "Baby photos. She thought I would want to see you."

Me?

Just me…not my twin sister, Jessica.

"So, that's it. That's all you're going to tell me?" Jackson growled.

Johnathan got up and walked back to the bar, pouring himself a slow whisky while Jackson watched him.

"Why haven't you told your mother you're here?" he asked.

"I have my reasons," Jackson replied. Such as the man he'd believe to be his father suddenly dropping dead, and then his mother getting cancer.

She was dying.

The last thing he was going to do was stress her out. When he'd asked about his scholarship, she had gotten quite distressed.

"Don't go digging up ghosts, Jackson. Let them stay dead."

Johnathan had answers and could tell him.

"I only know my side of the story, son. You need to speak to Jenna and let her tell hers."

"You mean, like finding out the man who raised me isn't my father?" Jackson said, letting out a short angry snort. "And that my real one didn't want anything to do with me, even though he knew about my existence for twenty-four years?"

When Johnathan turned, he nodded. "Yes."

When Jackson glared back at the man, Johnathan let out a long sigh.

"Listen, matters of the heart are straightforward. There was much more to it than just sleeping with each other, then getting pregnant." Johnathan twirled the golden liquid around in his glass.

Heart?

"How long have you been dating Kristen?" Johnathan suddenly asked.

What?

He glared at his father. "What does that have to do with anything?"

"You like her." Johnathan placed his glass down beside him.

Of course, he did. She was fucking gorgeous. Funny. Interesting.

Goddamn him.

"Yes, I like her. She's a beautiful woman. However, she's leaving the United States in a few days and thinks I've used her. The end."

Johnathan's lips twitched. "Ignore Daniel's threat. You need to speak to her. To apologize."

Jackson frowned. "I'm sorry, did I miss something? Are you close with Kristen?"

His father shrugged. "We met at the wedding. She's a nice girl."

"I've known you for less than three hours, and you're trying to matchmake?" Jackson said, shaking his head. "Wow."

Johnathan let out a short laugh and sat down.

"She deserves an apology, and while she's here, you need to give her one. Unless you *were* only using her," he replied, the question in his tone.

"No. I wasn't."

"No, I don't think you were. I saw the way you looked at her," Johnathan said immediately. "Don't live with regrets."

Ah. So that's what this was about.

"Like you have about my mother?" Jackson asked.

The silence hung between them, heavy.

"Yes," Johnathan said finally. "Before I tell you any more, I want you to ring your mother and tell her we've met."

No can do.

She was grieving her husband, and…not in any condition to be dealing with this. Especially as she had warned him away from digging into said ghosts of her past.

Johnathan put his glass down when he saw the reluctance on Jackson's face.

"Jenna needs to know we've met. Speak to your mother and then call me."

Jackson let out a sigh. He could tell by the man's stiff jaw he wasn't getting any more out of him tonight.

Neither was he going to ring his mother.

CHAPTER SIX

Kristen climbed off the bus and walked into Macy's. The Manhattan store was the largest department store in the world, spanning four blocks.

How hard can it be to find the bathroom?

She stood looking around, when an employee asked if she could help.

"Yes, where would I find the ladies' room?"

"Down there and turn right," the Macy's woman said.

"Thank you." Kristen clenched her muscles, knowing relief was in sight after the four-hour long tour bus ride around Manhattan.

But she'd been wrong.

Four more times, she had to ask for directions. Each time, she only got so far before standing around, looking like a lost tourist.

Which she was.

It was like a damn treasure hunt.

One her bladder was getting very impatient with.

"Bathroom. Now. The entire goddamn map. Please," she said to the next Macy's employee.

"Two lefts, and a right," the man said.

"Thank you. Thannnk you," she cried, this time nearly powerwalking in the instructed direction.

Please don't let there be a queue.

Please don't let there be a queue.
Please don't let there be a queue.

Kristen spotted the restroom sign ahead. Ten minutes later, she was washing her hands, when her phone beeped.

She smiled.

It was probably Harper. While she missed her friend already, she was looking forward to doing some normal shopping.

In shops she could afford.

Harper, Addison, and Olivia had all been middle-class girls before hooking up with their Dufort men. It had been exciting at first, being part of the billionaire world, but very quickly, Kristen had found it daunting.

Now she could be a real tourist and shop at Zara and Gap. Maybe she'd splash out on a Michael Kors handbag, if she found one she loved.

Kristen slid on her lip gloss, pulled her bag onto her shoulder, and walked out of the restroom. She pulled out her phone to read her text message.

Jackson: I want to see you.

Shit.

Kristen put her phone back in her pocket as her heart thundered.

No apology. Just a demand.

Bossy. Just like his brothers.

His masculine dominance might have a ton of sex appeal, but surely, Jackson was self-aware enough to realize he'd fucked up royally.

She expected an apology. Until then, she wasn't going to reply. If that meant leaving the country and not seeing him, then she would.

He had four more days to figure it out.

Carrying a handful of Macy's shopping bags on her arm, Kristen stepped out onto the sidewalk. Feeling confident, she decided to try hailing her first New York City cab.

How hard could it be?

Chewing her lip, Kristen stood watching to see how it was done. Life with Harper and Daniel had been very different. They had luxury cars and drivers, which seemed to appear magically whenever they exited a building.

It was for security reasons, Daniel advised. Kidnapping of the wealthy happened far more often than the media reported, he'd told her.

Yikes.

That was not something she was envious of. But she did worry about Harper. Still, with Daniel protecting her best friend, she needn't worry.

Kristen watched a woman, who appeared to be local, hail a cab. The woman reached out her arm as she stepped off the sidewalk, then a yellow taxi just swooped in.

Got it. Easy.

Kristen sucked in a breath, waiting for the lady and her driver to move away. She spotted another one heading her way. Taking a step forward onto the road, she lifted her arm into the air.

The yellow cab zoomed past her.

The hell?

"You need to put your arm out, not up," a familiar rough voice said from behind her.

Kristen swung around.

Despite her reaction, Jackson slid an arm around her and guided her back onto the sidewalk, as if her body was his to do with as his pleased.

Yes, please.

No!

"You," she said accusingly.

He released her but didn't move far away. Instead, he stared down at her, his eyes blazing. They were so close she could barely breathe.

"Me," Jackson said thickly.

God, why was he so handsome?

As they stood staring, people weaved around them, but neither of them cared. She felt locked in his gaze, his woody scent enveloping her with all its masculine magic. The breadth of his shoulders blocking out the world as his dark curls kissed the collar of the blue shirt tucked into his deep blue jeans.

Probably Gucci.

He might be worth less than his billionaire brothers, but Jackson was still a very wealthy man.

Kristen might have Googled.

Money aside, all three men had the same sexual confidence, and right now, his was dialed up to full. And directed at her.

"This isn't a coincidence, is it?" Kristen asked, trying not to look at his lips.

"God, I've missed your accent," Jackson said, his eyes roaming her face like he hadn't seen her for a decade. He looked...hungry. "And those beautiful eyes."

Despite the way her body was reacting, she let out a scoff. She was still mad. "You can cut the act now."

He frowned. "Kris, I never wanted you to feel like this."

She didn't want his pity; she wanted an apology.

"I'm walking away in ten seconds. If you plan to say you're sorry, now's the time. Otherwise, adios," Kristen said, dropping her hip.

Jackson smirked. "Can I take you to dinner?"

The gall of this man.

"No apology. Got it," she said, shaking her head. Tugging her shopping bags over her wrist, she added, "Goodbye, Jackson Wiles."

Then Kristen turned and walked away.

JACKSON watched as Kristen swung that sexy ass of hers like she owned Manhattan.

God, he wanted to drag her over his lap and slap it until her pussy was wet and dripping.

He bet she was a screamer. Jackson was determined to find out. But first, he needed her forgiveness, and then he had to break down her walls.

In less than four days.

Jackson jogged up behind her and fell into step.

"Gah," Kristen said, rolling her eyes at him. "Don't bother. Go away."

He placed his hand on the small of her back, the need to touch her beyond his ability to stop. So he didn't.

Kristen slowed.

"Truly, can you not just apologize, and then we can say goodbye."

Jackson ran his hand up her arm and stopped her. She turned, sighing dramatically.

"I want to explain and apologize, but you deserve more than just a simple sorry out on the streets. Kristen, please let me take you to dinner. Or—"

"The Plaza," she said firmly. "Take me to The Plaza tonight, or nothing."

His brows shot up, and he let out a laugh.

She was testing him.

Fine, little kitten, I can play this game.

"You know very well it can take months to get a table at The Plaza." He smirked. "You leave in a week."

He knew she was going to dig her heels in, could see it in her eyes. The green fire, swirling like she was out for blood.

Jackson knew he deserved it.

So how the hell could he get…

"Four days," Kristen corrected him. "Dinner at The Plaza tonight. Otherwise, you can email me your apology, and I will read it on the plane."

He smiled.

Challenge accepted, kitten.

He leaned into her neck, breathing in her scent.

"Done. I will pick you up at seven," Jackson said. Then more darkly he added, "Wear a dress."

Placing a slow kiss along her jaw, he smirked at her gasp. Straightening, he cupped her face.

"I promise you won't regret it."

Fighting the urge to scoop her up and toss her in his waiting car, Jackson walked backward for a few steps, his eyes holding hers.

Then he swiveled and sent out a prayer to the table reservation gods.

Because one way or another, he was getting that fucking booking.

CHAPTER SEVEN

"*Wear a dress. Wear a damn dress,*" Kristen muttered over and over, as she pushed the coat hangers back and forth.

She didn't like living out of a suitcase when she traveled, and because she'd been in the States for a few weeks, she'd made herself at home.

As Daniel had pointed out twice. Harper commenting, "she may as well just stay," as she'd hung up her clothes.

Kristen felt for her friend. Falling in love and marrying your soulmate was wonderful, but having to leave all your friends and family to start a new life on the other side of the world wasn't easy.

Fortunately, she had Olivia and Addison, who Kristen had also quickly made friends with.

Kristen knew Harper would be fine.

Choosing to stay in Manhattan for a few more days after the two had left for their honeymoon had been strategic. She wanted to spend all the time she could with Harper doing wedding and best friend's stuff. Not walking up the Empire State Building and going to Times Square.

The bus tour she'd done today had been interesting. It picked her up near Daniel and Harper's building, and the further they traveled, the more Kristen realized how insular her holiday had been.

Manhattan was a dynamic place, but now she wasn't hanging with billionaires, she was seeing another side of the Big Apple.

Kristen had a number of places on her must-see list. One of them had been The Plaza. She was a big fan of high tea and was hoping to spend one afternoon lazily sipping something delicious and nibbling on a cucumber sandwich. Then wandering around Central Park. Dinner was for those with bank accounts much bigger than hers. It was booked months in advance.

So, when Jackson surprised her outside Macy's and couldn't even say a simple *sorry,* she'd set him an impossible task. Smug was the best way to describe her attitude, up until twenty minutes ago.

She had been feet-up, watching Netflix and flicking through Uber Eats, when Jackson had texted.

I like your blue dress, but you choose. See you in thirty minutes, gorgeous. J x

Her feet had landed on the ground faster than the speed of sound.

He'd gotten them a table at The Plaza?

How the hell had he pulled that off?

Kristen had flown down to her room and into the shower like her life depended on it. She wasn't going to The Plaza with dirty hair.

Now, with her hair twisted over one shoulder and make-up done, she just had to choose something to wear.

Clearly *not* the blue dress.

Hands clammy with nerves, she pulled out a mid-thigh-length rich burgundy dress. The V-neck dipped low in the front, and it had chiffon sleeves, which billowed to the wrist.

Then she pulled on a pair of black heels and adorned her outfit with simple silver jewelry—a silver bangle and diamond studs Harper had given her as a gift for being her bridesmaid. They were two carat in total, so sparkled brilliantly.

Then she added a spot of Estee Lauder *Beautiful* perfume on her wrists and stared in the mirror.

What was she doing?

This would be the fourth date she'd been on with Jackson, if she counted the last disaster. It would be their last. It had to be.

The man elicited far too much reaction from her to be safe. If he happened to kiss her, she'd let him. God knows they both needed to get it out of their system.

Kristen would hear his apology, enjoy dinner, a goodbye kiss, then stay away from him.

Dufort genes were too intoxicating.

JACKSON stepped out of the car, tugging on the sleeves of his Armani suit as he stared up at the building Kristen was staying in.

Daniel's building.

His brother. The same one he'd had to ring to ask about getting a table at The Plaza tonight.

His father had been unsuccessful, which had surprised Jackson and forced him to ring the one man he did not want to ring. But Johnathan had said he would be the only one able to pull those powerful strings.

So then, because he wasn't suicidal, he'd tried Fletcher, who hadn't answered his phone. He didn't bother ringing Hunter.

His finger had hovered over Daniel's name for a good five fucking minutes before he finally pushed call. What bothered him more than having to swallow his pride and ask for the guy's help was that he was doing it for a girl.

A girl he'd never see again after this week. Less than a week. Four days, as she'd pointed out.

Why?

Those late-night phone calls when she had been in the Hamptons had changed something between them. Plus, he had no doubt she would taste like the goddess she was, but interrupting Daniel on his honeymoon was a mad man's move.

"That's a huge favor you're asking," Daniel had said. Well, he'd actually growled, rather than spoken, each word slowly. After first asking him if he'd lost his goddamn mind.

Throw in a few more F words, and it was word for word.

"Daniel! Get off that phone, or I will divorce you," Harper had cried in the background.

"Explain. Fast," Daniel had growled again.

"Kristen—"

"No."

Jackson had rolled his eyes.

"Wait. I wanted to apologize for hurting her. She said her dream was to go to The Plaza for dinner. I promised her."

So, yes, fine, he'd stretched the truth a little. More than a little, but the silence that followed told him it had worked.

"Interrupt me again on my honeymoon, and I will end you," Daniel growled.

"Nice chat, bro," Jackson had replied, but the call had already ended.

Jackson stood on Broadway, staring at his phone for a good ten minutes, wondering whether that meant Daniel was going to get him a booking or not.

Ten *long* minutes.

He'd been unsure whether to ring his grumpy half-brother back, which would have completely meant he was insane. Or try someone else?

After pacing back and forth in front of his waiting car, his phone had finally beeped.

Daniel: Table booked for eight o'clock. I'm not your fucking secretary.

Jackson had let out a *whoop* and climbed into his car.

Now, he stood on the sidewalk once more, waiting for Kristen to come down. Jackson didn't have access to the penthouse and wasn't about to ask. Not the doorman, not Kristen, and definitely not Daniel.

He took a few steps and dug his hands into his tailored designer pants, staring out at the city.

Jackson let out a sigh.

What was he doing here? He could have just told Kristen he was sorry outside Macy's and left her to her holiday. Daniel and Harper would've been pissed with him for a while, then everyone would have gotten over it. It would be known as that time he dated her friend to get inside the Dufort family.

Thing was, it wasn't necessarily true.

Jackson had seized an opportunity, but that didn't take away from the fact he thought Kristen was fucking gorgeous and had bewitched him with those emerald, green eyes and her sexy curves. More, he'd found himself enchanted, listening to her accent as she told him about her life and family back home.

He was a red-blooded man.

They both desired one another, and he hadn't forced her into bed. He'd been quite the gentleman.

The truth was, Jackson liked her.

She'd been holding back, and if she'd been any other woman, he might have let loose his natural dominant nature and strongly encouraged her back to his hotel and bed, but she was Harper's best friend. That was the extent to which he'd acted differently because of the Dufort family. Yes, she had given him access to Daniel. But he already had connections with them via Appopolis.

He'd had a plan.

It hadn't included meeting a gorgeous blonde who had distracted him.

Now the cat was out of the bag.

Now he had no reason to hold back.

Now, when he fucked her, he would claim her submission as she knelt before him and took his thick cock down her throat.

"This better be the real Plaza. If it's a food court inside some plaza, you'll live to regret it," Kristen said from behind him.

Jackson grinned, turned, and then his smile vanished.

Jesus.

She was dressed to kill.

CHAPTER EIGHT

"**I** know, I look sexy. Blah, blah. Let's go," Kristen said, waving her purse in the air as she continued past him.

Jackson reached out and grabbed her arm. "Stop."

Her head turned.

Ignoring her sassy gaze, he walked around her, stopping as he cast his eyes over the length of her body.

"You're fucking gorgeous. Look at you," Jackson said, shaking his head.

"Thank you." Her eyes darted away.

She was hurt.

More than he'd realized.

Holding her eyes for a moment once they finally met his, he nodded, then walked her to the car. James, his driver, opened the door, and they climbed inside.

"Thank you for coming," he said, as the vehicle moved into traffic.

"Are we really going to The Plaza?" Kristen asked, arranging her dress.

Jackson nodded, his hand itching to touch her.

She dropped her purse onto her lap, her hands landing on top of it, and the fabric of her dress rode up an inch. The already short skirt exposed her tanned upper thigh, teasing him.

Jackson pressed his lips together and swallowed a groan.

"None of this was necessary. You could've texted or phoned, Jackson." She turned to face him. "You know that, right?"

Flickers of green flames swirled in her eyes as they held his.

"Absolutely not," he said, turning from her.

It was that or kiss her without permission.

Tempting, but he wouldn't.

Not yet.

By the end of the night, Kristen would know he planned to claim her body. And he'd know if the fire he saw in her eyes turned the kitten act she played so well into a wild tiger.

THE driver pulled up outside The Plaza. The hotel was an icon in NYC and had been frequented by celebrities, world leaders, royals, Hollywood legends, and high society for more than 100 years.

It was no wonder Daniel had been able to pull strings, given he was in the same industry.

A doorman in tails opened his door.

Jackson hopped out and reached for Kristen's hand. When she blinked and slipped her hand into his, the warmth of her skin calmed him.

Interesting.

Jackson mentally shook his head, then watched her step out and take in the famous landmark. He'd put money on the fact Kristen had no idea she'd stepped closer and leaned into him, as if she felt safe with him.

Was chest-beating appropriate before dinner?

Because Jackson had the sudden desire to do it.

"It's stunning." She sighed as they made their way inside the hotel.

No, it's a hotel. You are stunning, little kitten.

He kept his thoughts to himself and smiled as they continued walking through the lobby.

"Welcome to The Plaza. This way, please," the waiter said in greeting and waved them inside.

Kristen shot him a grin. "Just like on the movies."

Jackson placed a hand in the small of her back to keep her upright as she swiveled to take in the huge golden dome above them.

"Oh my gosh." She giggled, nearly tripping.

God, it sounded delightful.

He steadied her.

Did I just use the word "delightful"?

Their seats were pulled out, and they sat down, then their napkins shaken out and elegantly placed on their laps.

Glittering eyes met his across the table. Jackson had a strong feeling he might be forgiven.

"A drink, madam?"

She took the menu, and before she'd had a second to read it, he ordered.

"Two Monte Carlos."

"Yes, sir."

As the man disappeared to get their drinks, Kristen lowered her menu. "You can't just order for me."

"You can't come to The Plaza and not have a Monte Carlo. I've already intervened and stopped you being arrested once in this town, young lady. I'll not do it a second time." He shook his head, all mock serious.

Kristen forced back her smile, but he'd seen it.

"Plus, I know you love whisky." He shrugged.

"Arrogant and charming. A lethal combination, Mr. Wiles." Kristen shook her head, but she was melting, and they both knew it.

He smiled, failing to hide his happiness. Correction. He wasn't trying to hide it. She was a beautiful, smart woman, and he knew how lucky he was she'd agreed to go out with him again.

Jackson wasn't about to fuck this up.

He'd taken his suit jacket off before sitting. Now, he rolled his sleeves a little higher, mid-way up his forearms, and fiddled with his silverware. When he lifted his eyes, she was watching him.

"Why am I here, Jackson? I'm no use to you now." Kristen lifted her glass of water to her lips.

Jackson studied her face. "I appreciate you would think that. First, I owe you an apology—"

"Wait, wait." Kristen held up her hand. "Before you say anything else, please know that while I was upset, I was thinking about you meeting your dad for the first time. It must have been difficult. I know it wasn't all about me, but—"

"Woman, let me apologize," Jackson said cutting her off.

She swallowed and nodded.

"I'm sorry," he said, then shook his head. "That's a lie. I'm not sorry."

Her brows raised slowly.

"The night I met you, when our eyes met…I crossed the room to meet you, Kristen. You and you alone. I'd already met Hunter and Fletcher. I didn't need an introduction."

"Dating me helped," she said, glancing up as their drinks arrived, the glasses embossed with the double *P* brand infamous of The Plaza.

They waited for the server to leave, then he lifted his glass.

"Yes. But. I could've dated any number of women in Manhattan who are acquainted with them. One with far less consequences. You are, after all, Harpers best friend."

"I told you that the night we met," she said quietly.

He nodded slowly. "Yes. Exactly"

They stared at each other, the noise of the restaurant buzzing around them.

"I've asked myself a dozen times in the past twenty-four hours why I kept seeing you, Kristen. It comes back to this. I find myself incapable of staying away."

"Jackson," she whispered.

"I was hoping I wasn't alone." He knew he wasn't but was unsure if she would own the desire pulsing in her eyes.

Her mouth softly parted as his heart thumped.

This entire speech of his was unrehearsed. The words just fell out, and he could tell he was overwhelming her.

But they didn't have time.

He needed her trust if he was going to have her fully.

If only temporarily.

"When you were in the Hamptons, I couldn't wait for you to return. I told myself I had alternative motivations to do with the Dufort's, but it wasn't them I was dying to see."

Kristen chewed her bottom lip.

"It was you," he admitted.

"Oh." Kristen looked far more surprised than he had expected. Then she took a long sip of her drink, and her eyes flew open. "Oh my god, this is good."

"Ye of little faith." He winked, lifting his own glass and taking another sip.

Kristen placed her glass on the table and let out a sigh. "Look, you don't need to sugarcoat this. I get it. You wanted to know your family. We didn't sleep together, which is good, as I'd probably be ten times more upset. And anyway, I am heading home in a few days."

Jackson shook his head. "Tell me this chemistry between us is one-sided. Tell me I'm imagining it, Kristen. And don't lie to me."

She stilled, then swallowed slowly.

"I—"

"No lies," he said firmly, holding her gaze across the table, giving her a taste of the dominance she could expect from him if she said yes.

"I live in New Zealand," she whispered, her voice small.

"Not tonight, you don't."
Kristen's eyes dropped to the table.
Good girl.

CHAPTER NINE

Kristen could barely breathe. Every cell in her body felt like it was trembling under his powerful sexual gaze. She knew exactly what Jackson wanted. What he was asking.

For the hundredth time, she wondered what she was doing here. What was a middle-class kiwi girl doing having dinner with a multi-millionaire tech genius who was now part of the Dufort dynasty?

A billion-dollar empire.

A man who had graced the cover of *Forbes* magazine.

Not that she'd seen it, but a quick Google search had brought up dozens of results along with many others, his handsome face smiling back at her.

Taking another healthy gulp of her delicious Monte Carlo, Kristen glanced around at the people dining.

The room dripped wealth and luxury. Women in beautiful designer dresses and large diamond rings. Men in smart tailored suits with large timepieces hanging on their wrists. Cocktails being sipped and champagne poured. Candles flickered, and silverware dinged delicately.

People laughed, and Kristen thought she'd be that happy if her mortgage was paid too. Her eyes flew open wider when she saw Blake and Ryan dining in the back with a table full of friends.

Celebrities.

She was dining with famous people. Well, not at the same table, but still.

As she turned back to Jackson, Kristen swallowed again. She'd been looking for a distraction. His dominant sexuality was incredibly intoxicating.

And a little scary.

Men like him didn't take no for an answer. She didn't mean in a non-consensual way. If she said yes, he'd take all of her.

How she knew this, she wasn't sure. It was a sense.

All her past lovers had been good, not great. Kristen had never complained, but a part of her wished one of them had more of what Jackson was showing her.

Offering her.

A masculine rawness that had her thighs clenching and heart pounding.

"How did you get a booking?" she asked, and he smiled, leaning back in his chair and, for some reason, letting her get away with not answering his question.

Kristen wanted to say yes, but she knew she shouldn't.

It was hard to know if he was telling the truth about wanting her and not using her to get to the Dufort's. She had to admit, the chemistry and pull toward one another was real.

Which was why she had been so upset. To hear him say he'd felt it too was nice, and a relief.

Still, she wasn't about to lay down and spread her legs. Even if her body was quite keen on the idea.

Damn hormones.

"I sold my soul," Jackson said, sliding his glass a few inches from his fingers, then dragging it back. He lifted his eyes to hers, then let out a laugh. "I'm not joking."

Kristen couldn't help but smirk. "You rang Daniel."

He nodded, and they both laughed.

"Oh boy," she said, taking another sip.

"We should order." Jackson opened the menu. "That is, if I'm forgiven."

"I shouldn't, but yes, you're forgiven." She opened her menu and then lowered it again. "For the record, yes, I wanted to see you again."

Jackson smiled, and damn, it lit up the whole room.

Men should not be allowed to be this good-looking and charming. It was a danger to the population control on the planet.

"Stop. Don't get excited," she said, then laughed because he was now leaning back, looking like the cat who'd gotten the cream.

"Not excited. Not at all." Those dimples of his made an appearance.

She groaned inwardly.

How was she going to resist this man?

Kristen liked him too much. She had this bad habit of opening her heart way too quickly to men and falling. Always for the wrong ones.

And Jackson Wiles was most definitely the wrong one.

She lowered her voice. "I know what you want, and yes, it would be nice—"

"Nice? No, sweetheart, *nice* isn't what I have planned for you," he purred.

God, her ovaries had just started doing the tango.

She had to fight this.

Kristen had to get home and pull out her vibrator to relieve the ache between her legs and even her nipples.

"Okay, but I'm not…"

Capable of having a one-night stand without falling love with you, so you should run far, far away.

Jackson leaned forward conspiratorially. "What?"

She gave him that look.

"Help me out here, beautiful? What?"

"Jackson…"

"Not a man?" he asked.

"Really?" she arched a brow.

"Good. Not a man," he said, glancing at his menu. "Vegan? You know I'm from L.A., right? Vegan is fine with me."

"Idiot." She tried not to laugh.

"Liberal?" he asked. "Actually, don't answer that. I don't want to go near politics."

"Stop being silly. Also, I don't understand American politics."

"God, you're the perfect woman," Jackson moaned, shaking his head.

No, she wasn't perfect. Not at all.

"Except when you consider what I was really trying to say." Kristen glanced at the menu, focusing on what she was going to order. She felt his eyes on her and looked up. "I mean it."

"I don't think you do," Jackson replied.

Snapping her mouth shut—which had gaped open in response—when the server turned up, Kristen ordered the steak and let his comment hang.

Because she wasn't sure.

Ignoring her attraction to Jackson was stupid and impossible. Masculine energy poured off him. Coupled with his sizzling gaze, the fit of his dark navy shirt across his muscular chest, and those bare sexy forearms, she was surprised she wasn't pregnant just by looking at him.

Even the heavy, no doubt pricy, timepiece on his wrist looked sexy.

He was a Dufort, all right.

Tonight, Jackson was being far more dominant than he'd been previously. As if everything he'd been holding back was now let loose. He was playing all his cards. It was both exhilarating and terrifying.

Her nipples hardened under her dress as she bit her bottom lip. Jackson took a slow sip of his drink, wildfire in his eyes as they roamed over her breasts.

He knew.

Jackson knew exactly how her body was reacting to him. When his glass lowered, the slight tilt of his lips told her he was pleased.

And the terrifying thing was, she wanted to please him.

THE rest of the evening was incredible. Every single mouthful was delicious. The service impeccable. The ambience luxurious and yet relaxed.

Jackson totally charming.

He'd released her from his intoxicating hold when the food had arrived and asked her more about her career. Jackson knew she was a florist, but he wanted to know how she'd chosen that path.

"I've loved nature since I was a little. I always had my hands in the mud. My mother growling I was getting my clothes dirty." She laughed, and he watched her with what looked like delight in his eyes.

Why, she didn't know.

He seemed genuinely interested in her.

Part of her wanted to drop her napkin and say, "Let's just skip to the part where you make me scream because you know I'm a sure thing." The other part of her wanted to kiss him goodnight and lie in bed dreaming that he'd fall in love with her and sweep her off her feet.

See, already going down a dangerous path with yet another man. Jackson is not going to fall in love with you. He wants to fuck you and then wave you off as you fly to the other side of the world, while he pursues other women.

Not that she'd fallen in love with her other boyfriends, per say, but she'd hoped for more commitment from them.

Which was hardly a tall order.

The reality was, Jackson lived in the USA. She lived in New Zealand. If she was going to sleep with him, she had to realize it would be a one-night event.

Kristen still had time to see how she felt by the end of the night; however, she liked him, and she was incredibly attracted to him.

If she managed her expectations, then what could it hurt? Without a doubt in her mind, she knew he would turn the desire they felt for one another and give her a night to remember.

A very pleasurable one.

"I thought I wanted to be a landscaper, but after volunteering as part of a school program, I quickly changed my mind."

"Too much hard work?" he teased.

"No. Well…kind of. The location we were taken to was set up for a TV show. It was exciting, with all the cameras and celebrities doing shots inside, while we worked on the gardens. Then the rain arrived."

She recalled how she'd run inside to shelter but quickly got told to get back out there. The gardeners had to keep working.

"For five hours, the rain poured as we weeded and planted. It was horrible." She laughed, shivering at the memory. "It wasn't summer either."

"They couldn't wait until the rain stopped?" Jackson asked.

"They were filming outside the next day, so we had to keep going. It was one of those home reno shows. Perhaps it was fate. I returned to school the next day complaining, and the teacher joked I should just become a florist. So, I did." She laughed.

It wasn't that straightforward, but it was the funny story she'd told many times. It had worked out because now, ten years later, she was the manager of The Rose Room—the top boutique florist in Auckland's trendy suburb, Ponsonby.

"Perhaps it was fate. If you believe in that sort of thing." He swirled the liquid in his glass and watched her carefully.

Kristen wasn't going to have a philosophical conversation with him right now. Especially as she had a feeling life had brought them back together for a reason.

"Tell me about what happened with Johnathan," she said, switching the focus back on him.

"It was uncomfortable." He shared the conversation he'd had with his dad and half-brothers.

As they continued talking, Kristen noticed he never answered questions about his family in Los Angeles. She got short answers.

"What's your mom like? Your non-dad?" She shrugged.

Jackson let out a laugh at her joke.

"Their life isn't glamorous. Not like the Dufort's. I grew up in an average, middle-class home, and my parents worked all their lives."

He wouldn't say any more.

"Yes, well, not many people live the same luxurious life as Daniel and Harper," Kristen said. "But you do now."

Jackson nodded. "I do."

She sensed a humbleness about him that he rarely showed. Jackson was always confident, not cocky, but he had worked to get where he was. Not to disrespect what the Dufort men had done. Running a billion-dollar empire was not for the faint-hearted. It was just different.

"Did you always know you were clever?" she asked, twirling the stem of the wine glass she was now drinking from on the crisp white tablecloth.

He snorted.

"I don't know how to answer that without sounding like a dick." Jackson smirked, wiping his mouth with his napkin and dropping it on his plate. "Did you always know you were incredibly gorgeous?"

"I never said I was. And stop deflecting," she said.

"Touché."

Kristen let out a small laugh, lining her cutlery on her plate to show she had finished. Jackson did the same, and in seconds, their plates were cleared.

Jackson stilled and studied her.

Their eyes locked for a long moment.

"So, Kristen Holle, how many men in New Zealand are awaiting your arrival?" he asked, his voice darkening. As did his eyes, like he was not happy about the idea.

"Probably less than the amount of women in L.A. in your little black book," she replied. Then, when his eyes narrowed, she let out a sigh. "Jeremy Ogar. My ex."

Jackson's jaw twitched.

"It ended a few months ago, once I realized he was more committed to his…well, everything, more than me."

They'd been on and off for six months, until she finally dumped his useless non-committal, cheating ass. Kristen truly had the worst taste in men. She seemed to attract the type who never wanted anything serious.

Not that they'd admit it upfront. Then, after a few months, when things should naturally progress, they would tell her she was going too fast or she was pushy. Or worse, insecure.

Commonly known as gaslighting now.

Kristen knew she wasn't being unreasonable. Friends around her were getting married and having kids. A year from her thirtieth birthday, she wondered if she would ever meet the one.

Or just someone.

She wanted to settle down, wanted to be a mom.

"Good," Jackson said, and she blanched.

"Gee, thanks," Kristen scoffed, but he leaned forward and took her hand, her skin heating under his touch.

"I'm glad you're not with someone who doesn't appreciate you, and that you're free to explore this fire burning between us while you're in New York."

She was free, but was she brave enough?

CHAPTER TEN

"Come. Let's walk," Jackson said, taking Kristen's hand when they stepped out of The Plaza.

"Home?" she asked.

"No." He laughed, leading her across the road to Central Park.

There was no way he was taking her home yet. Or rather, taking her home to his hotel. He'd seen the desire and need from across the table. Hell, Jackson was pretty sure everyone in the restaurant was aware of the chemistry between them, but there was still a wall up.

One he was going to knock down.

"Isn't it dangerous this late at night?" she asked.

It was only eleven o'clock, so the park was still open, but Jackson was a large man. His driver was also maneuvering to pick them up as planned.

He'd grown up in Los Angeles. Perhaps not the bad part, but Jackson knew how to take care of himself. And the woman on his arm.

"I'll save you from any bad guys." He winked, squeezing her hand.

She snorted.

"I think *you* might be the bad guy."

Smiling to himself, he let go of her hand as they entered the park near Lombard Lamp and tucked her arm into his elbow. Then, they began to walk around The Pond.

The night was mild with a small breeze, perfect for a romantic stroll.

It wasn't romance he was after with Kristen, but he knew this was on her bucket list so was happy to spend the time watching the delight on her face as she took it all in.

"You really are pulling out all the stops, Jackson Wiles," Kristen said.

"I'm a nice guy. Just ask my mom." He smirked, not glancing down.

"Speaking of parents, when are you going to see your dad again?" Kristen asked as they reached the bridge.

Jackson glanced across the water. He hadn't phoned his mother and couldn't. She was too sick to deal with this.

Why was Johnathan so adamant Jenna tell him her story? It wasn't like the two had a relationship. The cat was out of the bag. Jackson knew Trevor wasn't his father, so why not just spill the beans?

Had Johnathan done something so terrible he couldn't admit to it?

Jackson wasn't asking her. Not right now. Not when she was in such a delicate state. Grieving her husband and dealing with non-Hodgkin's lymphoma.

Cancer.

She needed to heal and stay stress free, as her doctor had said, to recover from her treatment and possibly live for a few more years. Or she could go down fast. They didn't know at this stage.

So yeah, he was being really fucking protective of her. His own selfish needs could wait.

If it meant he had to return to L.A. without answers, then he would, but that didn't mean he was giving up on his father yet.

Kristen stopped halfway across the bridge and turned to glance back the way they'd come. The high-rises sparkled against the black stary sky.

"Manhattan really is an amazing city," she said, leaning against the railing and letting out a sigh.

"It is," he agreed. "Magical." Jackson closed the gap, stepping up behind her, and laid his hands on her arms.

She stilled.

"Tell me to stop and I will," he said gruffly. "But I'm about to lose my mind if I don't touch you."

Kristen turned slowly.

"If I don't kiss you…" His fingers drew a line down her cheek."

She shivered under his touch.

"Again," he added, and her eyes widened. He smiled. "You remember, I know you do."

She opened her mouth and then shut it, which just allowed his thumb to slide over her bottom lip.

"It was…"

"Hot. Great. Fucking amazing," Jackson said, inching closer, his body pressing against hers. "You're going to have to tell me to stop, sweetheart, because in another second, I won't be able to keep my mouth off you."

The shudder he felt run through her hit him right in the cock.

Fuck. He needed to be inside this woman.

Kristen's mouth parted, and before she'd finished saying *kiss me,* he slammed his lips down on hers.

The world spun.

She opened fully to him as fireworks exploded inside his body. Was it the Fourth of July? It fucking felt like it.

His arms wrapped around her, pulling her hard against his body as her fingers dug into his pecs.

God, yes.

His tongue lapped hers, tasting her, owning her, claiming her, as little mewls sounded in the back of her throat.

That's it, little kitten, this is just the beginning.

Now to unleash the tiger within and get that mouth of hers on his cock.

TWENTY minutes later, Jackson slammed open the door to his hotel room and pulled Kristen inside. His mouth landed back on hers, silencing her *I shouldn't be doing this.*

His lips sucking hers, he pulled off his jacket and began undoing his shirt buttons.

They pulled apart, panting.

"Oh God," she moaned as he ripped his shirt clean off.

He knew she was impressed by his ripped abs and the dusting of hair leading down to his cock—her eyes were locked there.

Jackson took in her dress, nudging the straps off her shoulders. "You have ten seconds to tell me how to get this dress off you, or I'm ripping it straight down the middle," he growled.

She gasped.

Kristen spun and showed him the hidden zipper. "What are we doing?"

"Want me to explain it, sweetheart, or show you?" Jackson pulled the dress over her head.

Fucking hell. It was his turn for his mind to freeze. Jesus, she was sexy as fuck.

Kristen's hands went to her body, but he grabbed them.

"Don't. Let me look at you," he demanded. "Jesus, how are you so goddamn beautiful?"

"Are you insane? These are control panties." She tugged at the skin-colored briefs. "My grandma wears sexier undies."

His eyes shot to hers.

"Okay, ignore that. Weird. I don't know why I am talking. Please stop me," she said.

Jackson smiled.

The bottoms might have been less sexy than they could have been, but her bra was black lace, and he could see her pert nipples as clear as day through it.

He swallowed.

"I need to get these off, but it won't be sexy. Can you turn or something?"

"No," he growled.

"God, why are you all such cave men?" Kristen signed.

He frowned. "Who?"

"All you Dufort men," she answered as she tugged at the briefs.

"Wait. All of us? First, I'm not a Dufort. Technically. And who else have you slept with?" Jackson asked, his chest tightening. "It better not be fucking Hunter. If you have, I'll kill him."

She pushed at his chest. "I have *not* slept with Hunter. He's with Addison."

Jackson grabbed her wrists and tugged her to him, claiming her mouth once more. Then he lifted her and carried her to the bed. Lowering her, he lay over her, his palm flat on the sheet.

"You drive me crazy, little kitten," he growled. "I am going to fuck you so hard you will never want another man."

"Well, you better help me get these undies off, or neither of us are fucking anyone."

CHAPTER ELEVEN

Kristen blinked awake, trying to get her bearings. Sun poured into the room, and she pressed her eyes closed again.

Then they flew open.

On the TV across from her hung her dress. Beside her lay one very muscular naked body.

Jackson.

Holy hell.

She'd had sex with Jackson Wiles.

Could she call it sex? It had been more like a sexual awakening. Or a spiritual experience of the body.

After finally pulling those damn Kardashian control whatever's off her ass, Jackson had spread her legs open and shoved his face between them. While she was gasping in surprise, he was already sucking on her clitoris.

She'd cried out and jolted when he bit it.

His reaction? Jackson had slapped his palm on her tummy and pressed her back down, the dominance sending ripples of pleasure through her body.

Kristen had secretly dreamed of a lover like this but had never known they really existed outside of a fantasy or sex club.

As she arched and moaned, Jackson had pinched her nipple and told her, "I own your pleasure tonight, sweetheart. I won't be gentle, but I will make you scream."

He licked her pussy in one long sweep, then added, "If you tell me to stop, I will, but then this will be over. That's how I work."

He'd climbed up her body and cupped her face.

"Tell me you understand, sweetheart."

Her eyes had searched his and found a primal truth. Jackson was in control. Unless she opted out, she was submitting her body to him for absolute pleasure.

Trembling, she'd nodded.

"Good girl," he'd said, and her pussy had pulsed. "Grab the headboard and don't let go."

Kristen hooked her fingers around the bars over her head. Jackson reached for a tie lying on his bedside table and wrapped it around her wrists.

She had a moment of panic. Sure, she had known this man, and technically, he was related to Harper's husband, but this could end badly for her.

She'd seen the tv shows.

It must have shown in her expression because he ran his fingers over her face. "The only pain you'll feel tonight is pleasure. Remember, you can stop me at any point."

Kristen had nodded, then he'd slid back down her body, holding her stare as he pressed two fingers inside her.

She'd arched and cried out.

It felt like her pussy was weeping under his mouth. Or maybe she had already been orgasming.

It had been six months since she'd had sex, and Jackson was the hottest guy she'd ever slept with. And the most talented.

What he could do with his mouth should be illegal. Nipping at her flesh, he sucked, licked, and swirled with such skill, all she could do was moan and arch against the strong grip he had on her hips.

"Wider," he'd said, spreading her so he could lick her further. His fingers sliding in and out of her as he stimulated her clit, setting off yet another spasm of utter pleasure.

"I want to taste every inch of you." Jackson had climbed her body after she'd come once more. He'd sucked in a nipple and let it pop, before standing to pull off his jeans.

That's when she'd truly gasped.

His smirk said it all, but damn, he deserved to be as arrogant as he wanted.

Hard against his stomach was the most gorgeous cock she'd ever seen. It was swollen and thick, with a dark purple head. Then, when Jackson stroked it, her body completely took control.

"We're only just getting started, sweetheart. You're going to take me down your throat and swallow."

Oh God.

She hadn't swallowed before.

Blow jobs she'd done, but swallowing? Nope.

He stepped closer to her, his hand skillfully sliding up and down his shaft, and she had opened her mouth.

"That's it, good girl," Jackson had said as she'd wrapped her lips around his large head. "God, your mouth is so hot. Fuck me with it, Kris."

One of his hands had cupped the back of her head, the other reaching to pleasure her body more. He thumbed her nipple, then moved down to her clit.

Kristen moved up and over his member, sucking and lapping, wondering how he even fit inside her mouth. Jackson was thick. Long, not unusually long, but thick. She couldn't wait to feel him inside her and had no concerns this was a man who knew what to do with it.

"Holy shit, look at you sucking my dick," Jackson moaned, grabbing her face. "So damn sexy."

She'd felt him swell, his eyes locked with hers.

"Fuck, I'm going to come. Relax your throat," he'd ordered. With a moan and half nod, she'd let him take control. Two hands on the side of her head, he'd fucked her mouth.

No, he'd fucked her throat.

She hadn't been able to breath.

"Relax, Kris. Fuck, relax more. Breathe through your nose," he'd said, his teeth clenched. Then, "Oh shiiiit."

He'd climaxed, the hot salty liquid pouring down her throat.

She gagged. He'd pulled out of her mouth and let her catch her breath, then kissed her.

"That was the single most fucking sexy thing I've ever seen. You're incredible," he growled.

Well, that was good because she'd nearly died of suffocation by his cock, but despite the lack of oxygen, her pussy was craving to be filled.

Then, with her lying on her back, Jackson climbed onto the bed, and they'd kissed and stroked one another until he put a condom on.

"I feel like I've waited an eternity to be inside you."

"I'm nervous," she'd said honestly.

It seemed like a strange thing to say, given what they had already done, but there was a whole other level of intimacy when a man entered you.

"I know," he'd replied, kissing her as the rubber slid over his still-hard cock.

Jackson never asked her why, but there was a look in his eyes she was unfamiliar with. Dominance, yes. But something else. It was like he cared but more powerful.

Protective.

Suddenly, she had known he wouldn't hurt her. Not just physically. He was cherishing her. Every touch was accompanied with heated glances, compliments, moans of appreciation.

"On your knees, sweetheart," Jackson said, untying her wrists. "I want this sexy ass in the air so I can slam into you, deep and hard."

As her arms flopped, he'd rubbed them, then all but flipped her over. Kristen had grabbed a pillow, clenching the linen as his fingers slid through her wet pussy.

Jackson rubbed his cock around the moisture before thrusting inside her. "Holy fuck."

As he filled her, Kristen's head arched, and her heart cracked open. He felt incredible. Perfect. She would never regret giving Jackson her forgiveness and having this incredible sexual experience.

"Yes, more. Harder," she cried.

His fingers dug into her hips. "Thumb on your clit, baby. Now."

Kristen reached between her legs and began to circle madly as he slammed against her thighs. Then, when his thumb teased her ass, she lost it.

"Oh God. Shit," she cried into the pillow.

"Not yet," he ordered her, and she knew he meant her orgasm.

Jackson had pulled out, fallen on the bed, and pulled her on top of him. Her nipples raw against his broad chest, her pussy swollen as he lifted her to slide inside.

She sat up and began to move, their eyes connecting at the incredible feel of this angle.

"Holy mother of God, woman," Jackson said, his eyes wide. "Ride me. Fuck me. I want you coming on my cock."

It hadn't taken much.

Jackson had done much of the work. The orgasm shuddered through her body, pressing her down harder on him and moving her until he released in a cry.

"Fuck." His head flung back.

Eventually, they'd collapsed from exhaustion, but sometime during the night, she'd woken to him slipping inside her again.

"Let me just play," he'd said. "I'm not sheathed."

Jackson had lazily slid inside her, his fingers circling her clit.

She'd never come so much in her life.

"Oh God," Kristen cried. "Jackson, it's all too much. I feel like I'm going to die from pleasure."

"Remember, your body is mine tonight. Pinch your nipples," he'd instructed.

She could barely remember if she'd come again, or they'd just slipped into sleep. It was all a blur.

An arm reached out for her, and she turned to face him. "Morning," she said croakily.

Jackson pulled her flush against him. "Good morning, sexy girl."

They lay staring at each other.

No expression, just that still moment between two people who had been intimate, where nothing mattered. Where the outside world and all of reality didn't exist, just the two of them, their bodies, and their night together.

Then he blinked.

"You were amazing," Jackson said, brushing a finger over her forehead. "You submitted to me. Have you done that before?"

"No. Not like that."

"Good. That makes me happy."

"You like control."

"I need control. It's different. But I have my kink limits." He slid his hand down and squeezed her ass.

Kristen flinched.

His head lifted from the pillow. "I hurt you?"

Jesus, was he insane?

"I'm sore. It's nice sore, but sorry, buddy, you're not pounding me this morning."

"Would we call it pounding?" he asked, quirking a brow.

She let out a laugh and closed her eyes. "Fine, artfully thrusting."

"Better," Jackson said, leaning over her. "Now, what are we doing today?"

What?

Her eyes opened. "We?" She hadn't been expecting that.

Jackson kissed her fast on the lips and nodded. "Yes. Until your plane takes off, you're mine."

"It's rude to assume. Perhaps you might like to ask."

He kissed the side of her neck.

"I think we established last night that I am in control," the arrogant man said, still kissing her.

When she didn't reply, he lifted his head.

"Are you going to say no? Because I really don't want you to do that," he said thickly, his voice low."

She bit her lip. "I just thought it would be one night."

"Is that what you want?" he asked, his eyes drilled into hers.

Was it?

Kristen had expected to awkwardly say goodbye, then spend the next three days wishing she had more time with him.

Could she do this?

Sex was one thing, but a holiday romance, even if a short one, with this incredible man would surely see her go home with: a) a really sore pussy, and b) an unfulfilled crush at best.

And maybe a broken heart.

Because Jackson Wiles was everything she had never wished for. Never believed was possible.

And he would forget her before her plane landed back in New Zealand.

"No. But let's negotiate. I'll go do my touristy things, and then we can do more of this in the evenings."

"Things like licking your pussy and fucking your brains out?"

A blush hit her cheeks, and he laughed.

"You are adorable. Also, no deal. It's all or nothing."

She pouted.

His mouth landed gently on her nipple. "So, then its settled. I'm taking you out today, then tonight we'll do the *pounding*."

Kristen couldn't hold back her laugh.

"Why would you want to do boring tours with me?" she asked, and he lifted his head.

"What part of *you are mine*, do you not understand?" he asked, his eyes serious. "In fact, I want you to move in here. Let's get your bag, and it will save time, given it's only a few days."

Her mouth parted in surprise. Was he joking? No, she could see he wasn't joking.

His hotel was not some small box. It was the penthouse suite and had multiple rooms, a large living area, and from memory, she'd seen a kitchen as he'd carried her through the apartment.

Still, he was out of his mind.

When she didn't answer, he leaned right over her, his eyes locking with hers.

"Tell me last night wasn't incredible," Jackson said.

"It was," she whispered.

"Then why spend a minute apart? We have three days, Kris."

She nodded because he was right.

The thought of walking out the door, or him leaving, felt wrong. She did want to spend as much time as she could with him while in NYC.

"Okay," she said, as Jackson claimed her mouth once more.

Still, as right as it felt, a thread of fear snaked down her spine.

It was as if she knew it wasn't going to end well.

CHAPTER TWELVE

Jackson handed Kristen the ice cream and grinned as he watched her lick it.

"Stop," she said, blushing.

"Why, when seeing your cheeks deepen like that makes me so damn hard."

"Can you stop thinking about sex?" She frowned. "Let me believe, just for five minutes, that you like me for my intelligent conversation. Or hilarious sense of humor."

Jackson frowned as well. "Is that what you think?" he said, as they sat down on a park bench. "If that was the case, I would have just stayed in the hotel with you all day."

Kristen crossed her legs. "I guess."

The honest truth was, he should be doing a hell of a lot of other things than playing tourist with this sexy kiwi woman. Like working.

He traveled often for business, letting his amazing CEO, Kevin, take care of the day-to-day management of Appopolis.

But that didn't mean he could disappear.

Or ignore the hundreds of emails he knew were piling up in his inbox.

In fact, there was an important contract they were working on right now with the U.S. government. His company provided a range of high-tech capabilities to organizations around the country, and now some internationally. This specific technology would move the U.S. military into the future with what he called tech-wear: smart glasses, exoskeleton suits, and other tech-controlled creations that would assist them in modern warfare.

Speaking to the right people so they didn't appear like a bunch of mid-twenties selling sci-fi video game equipment was key.

Those who knew just knew. The future of the battlefield looked way different.

Jackson had dreamed of this since college. His company had what it took to work with the U.S. government, and after months of discussions, it looked like a meeting with officials was on the cards.

He was trying not to get excited, as these things were a long game, but if Appopolis was successful in their bid, it would be a one-point-two-billion-dollar project over five years.

So no, he didn't need daddy Dufort's money.

He also didn't have the signed contract yet.

Kevin had texted him this morning to say the meeting was being set up, and he'd let him know the day and time soon.

They would want to meet in person.

Jackson nudged his arm against hers. "You're just very beautiful, and I'm very attracted to you. In case that wasn't obvious."

Those beautiful green eyes lifted to his. "Clear as day."

He swapped his ice cream to the other hand and slid his arm behind her on the bench. She leaned into him, her denim shorts showing off her long tanned legs. His thumb lazily pushed the spaghetti strap of her top when it threatened to slip.

Around them, kids played while moms and nannies sat talking. The birds sang happily in the trees.

This was nice.

Jackson didn't want Kristen to think all he was after was sex, but in less than a week, what more could it be?

If…

No, he wasn't going there. He had too much happening in his family life right now to even think about what might be possible. Especially with someone who lived on the other side of the planet.

Way too complicated.

But damn, the way it had felt being inside her last night. Waking up with her. He'd never felt this way.

Perhaps it was because it was temporary, and he'd let himself be freer. Or the way she had submitted so beautifully to him. Was there anything sexier?

The things he wanted to do with Kristen, if only they had time and were back at his house in L.A. He had toys. Gadgets that would make her weep with pleasure.

"Do you date?" she suddenly asked, as if reading his mind.

His brows shot up. "Ah, sometimes."

Mostly, he didn't. He slept with women, but he didn't have relationships. Since that *Forbes* article had come out a few years ago, his sex life had improved. Funny how life worked like that.

"Have you been in love?" she asked next, glancing up at him with those big green eyes of hers.

"Are those lashes of yours real?" he asked.

"Don't deflect. Have you or haven't you?" Kristen pressed.

Jackson drew in a long breath.

"No," he finally answered. "I date but, like, mostly only for—"

"Let me guess. One night." She laughed.

Correct.

He hated that she knew that and that he was forced to admit it. Why? There wasn't anything wrong with it, was there? He was a young twenty-four-year-old virile man.

The idea of settling down was unappealing at this point in his life. His focus was on his business and making sure his mom got through this cancer treatment so she could live for a few more years.

And now, getting to know his real father and brothers.

"Why is that funny?"

"I guess it's in the Dufort genes," Kristen replied. "Playboys, all of you. One day, you'll fall in love with someone, and it will hit you like a ton of bricks."

She meant like Daniel, Fletcher, and Hunter seemed to have.

Was she hoping it was with her?

"What about you?" Jackson asked.

"Me?"

"Yeah. Are you going to fall in love and settle down?" Jackson asked, hating the feeling in his chest as he imagined some random guy walking up right now and pulling Kristen in for a kiss. Taking her away from him.

Fuck that.

"I hope so. I want to be a mom," she said, crunching on her ice cream cone. "I should get serious about it when I get home."

Wrong answer.

Shit, what was wrong with him?

"I'm going to be thirty in a year. My father thinks I'm going to be left on the shelf, or some archaic thing like that, but he's right," Kristen continued.

"No, he's not," Jackson growled. "Thirty isn't old."

"It's older than you." She smirked.

"By four years and nine months," he answered and then realized his mistake.

Shit.

Kristen turned her head and stared at him. "How did you know that?"

Jackson saw the moment she worked it out.

"You hacked into my account?"

"Not yours. I wouldn't do that. I took a peek…elsewhere."

Jackson wasn't going to say where. He never talked about his skills and ability to get into basically any system on Earth. With enough time.

And yeah, the FBI was aware of him. He was aware they were aware. Occasionally, they dropped by to say hello and remind him he was on their radar.

Fun.

"Don't ask me where," Jackson said darkly.

"What did you find out?" Kristen swallowed, still staring at him, her ice cream dripping down her fingers.

Jackson leaned down and kissed her lips. "Don't ask me those questions. But, good news, you're getting a nice tax refund this year."

Her green eyes flew open. "Really?"

He laughed and nodded. "Ice cream."

"Oh, crap," she said, licking her hand and mopping it up with a napkin. "You should be careful. What if you got caught?"

"No one is going to catch me, sweetheart, but thank you for your concern." Jackson rubbed her shoulder.

His phone rang.

Johnathan Dufort.

"Take it," Kristen said, leaning and spotting the name pop up on his screen. "I'll be right here, freaking out about what else you learned about me."

He stood, laughing, and walked a few feet away. "Jackson Wiles."

"Jackson, it's your father."

Wow. He'd taken no time in diving right into the parental role.

"Hi, Johnathan…I'm not sure I'm ready or will ever call you Dad, but I appreciate you accepting me so fast."

There was a moment of silence.

"The boys call me Johnathan. A side effect of working in business together. But I *am* your father, as I said the other night. Now, listen. I appreciate you coming to New York to meet me. It would have been inappropriate of me to take the first step."

"Why?"

"That's why I'm ringing. Have you spoken to your mother?"

Jackson sighed.

"No. I can't. Don't ask me to explain. I just can't. But I don't want to leave without some answers. Can you at least give me that?" Jackson asked, rubbing the back of his head.

"I've had time to think about it. Join me for breakfast at my apartment. We'll talk," Johnathan said.

Jackson turned and watched as Kristen stretched out her legs, lifting her face to the sun.

An emotion flashed through him. The need to know where he'd come from was powerful, but he had limited time with the gorgeous sexy woman before him.

Was he choosing her?

God, he'd even ignored a few work calls today. His inbox pinging away, but they could wait.

"I'll be there at seven thirty," Jackson said, knowing she would sleep while he was away.

"Good. I assume you are a coffee drinker."

Jackson laughed. "Actually, no. Water is fine, but I'll have all the eggs on offer."

His father let out an amused sound. "See you tomorrow."

Jackson pocketed his phone and walked back over to the beautiful blonde who tasted like cinnamon and honey. He sat and lay his arm behind her, smiling down at her expectant face.

"Okay?" Kristen asked, and he smiled at her thoughtfulness.

"I'm meeting him for breakfast first thing. It won't take long, then I'll be home."

Home. As if being with her was just that.

Strangely, it felt right.

"Take the day if you need. It's important," Kristen said.

It was.

But damn you, you sexy little thing. You're only here for a few days. I have the rest of my life to get to know my father. And get answers.

Time he couldn't bend.

Unfortunately.

"No. I'll be back by ten at the latest," he said firmly.

Kristen wasn't getting away from him.

"Okay. Today was fun. Thank you," she said, giving him a shy smile.

He'd taken her to the Shakespeare Gardens, just below Belvedere Castle, in Central Park. Being a florist, he figured she'd love the tourist spot, which had four-acres of flowers and plants resembling an English countryside from Shakespeare's works.

She'd seen a lot of the luxurious side of Manhattan while Harper and Daniel were in the city, so when he asked if it was something she'd like to do, Kristen had lit up like a Christmas tree.

"Yes! I've heard of it."

Jackson had felt like he'd been on a private garden tour. She'd pointed out all the flowers, telling him their names and history. Oohing and ahhing over plants they didn't have back home.

Then they'd walked around the area until they came to a large granite bench. It was curved.

"Go sit over there," she told him, pointing to the other end.

"Ah, why?" he'd asked. "Is this like school? I promise I will keep my hands to myself."

A lie

"No." She laughed. "This is the whispering seat. Or something. Just do it."

So he had. Then she'd turned her back to him and whispered, "You are forgiven. Officially."

Jackson grinned.

"And you are adorable. Get your lips over here."

Jackson spotted the engraving in the middle of the bench as she made her way over. The monument was dedicated to Charles B. Stover, the Parks Commissioner who had apparently been in the role in the early nineteen hundreds and vastly contributed to improving the parks in New York City.

"You're welcome," Jackson replied, coming back to the present.

"So what did Johnathan say on the phone?" Kristen asked. "You don't have to tell me. I guess I'm just curious."

God, she amazed him. He could tell she wasn't just being nosy. There was a genuine hint of caring about her enquiry, a vulnerable glint in her eyes and pink on her cheeks.

Despite the temporary nature of their relationship, or perhaps because of it, he found himself wanting to open up, to share what was going on.

Jackson had friends back home, but right now, he wanted to keep the fact that Johnathan Dufort was his father to himself. In truth, he wasn't that close to any of his friends. Not close enough he'd trust them with this information.

Both he and his father were public figures, so when the information got out—and it would—some media outlet would make a big deal about it.

Jackson had to protect his mother.

Kristen knew. So, who better to open up to than someone who already had all the facts and no agenda in outing him, if she even thought about the idea.

He knew already she wouldn't. It wasn't in her nature.

Jackson trusted her, so he began to talk.

"He wanted me to speak to Mom before telling me anything more after the other night. I don't know why," Jackson said. "I sense the two of them have secrets."

"What kind of secrets?"

"I'm not sure." He glanced at her, then added, "My mother was a singer—a famous one. At least for a short time."

"Really? What was her name? Wait, Wiles…I don't know an artist with that name," Kristen said, tilting her head, and she looked adorable.

Kissable.

That could wait. He was enjoying opening up to someone and sharing his story.

"Her stage name was Jenna Stone. She sang rock ballads as a solo artist." None of this was confidential—she could Google it if she'd been curious. "Hit the top of the charts in the mid-nineties with two songs, then she got pregnant. With me, obviously."

Kristen spun to face him, straight on.

"Holy shit, my sister loved her! Karen's, like, fifteen years older than me. Jenna Stone is your mom. Wow." Then she tapped her finger in the air. "Lay on me. Layyyy, lay on me," she sang.

"That's the one." He laughed.

Though he knew the song, it hadn't filled the rooms in his house like he imagined other kids with famous musical parents. It was as if she wanted to forget about her music career.

"Is that why she stopped singing? Because she had a baby? Had you?"

That was what he wanted to find out. Jackson was starting to think it was, but even in the nineties, industries were more accepting of working moms. It didn't make sense.

Unless Trevor had forced her to stop working. It was a possibility. So why did she stay with him? She had money.

Jackson mentally shook his head. Around and around in circles he'd go with all the guessing.

Tomorrow, his real father would hopefully answer them.

"I have no idea. She won't talk about it. I found the album in a box in the garage when I was about ten years old. Before that, I had no idea she could even sing."

"That's weird."

It was, when he looked back now. Then, he'd just accepted it, as kids did.

"I figured her career had collapsed and she was upset about it, when I gave it much thought as I was growing up. Like it wasn't really a big deal," Jackson said, lifting a shoulder. "Now, it has to be connected."

"Do you think Johnathan had something to do with it?" Kristen asked.

He tilted his head as he stared out across the park.

"At this point, I have to think he did. But why? I did a search, and there is no controversy around her career. She simply just stopped. In fact, there was no media around her being pregnant either. She just faded to black."

If he wanted to, he could hack Johnathan's computers, but it was unlikely to be a document labelled: *here's what happened.*

Plus, now he had agreed to meet with him and share more information. Jackson was hoping, by tomorrow morning, the mystery would be solved.

There was always two sides, but for now, he was happy to hear his father's story.

Then, if his mother's recovery continued to go well, he could talk to her about it. Not before then.

"Why don't you ask her? You deserve to know, Jackson," Kristen said softy.

"It's not that simple." He sighed, then smiled, tossing his napkin in the trash can. Jackson had to be careful. She was Harper's best friend, and that was just a few degrees too close to his father. "Families, huh? Complicated."

"Not really. Unless she'd dead, you *can* ask her," Kristen said, making him choke.

"She's not dead," Jackson said, coughing.

Kristen wasn't to be swayed, even as she patted him on the back.

"Then ask her. Some people don't have the choice. You do," she pressed.

Jackson couldn't argue with that logic. Especially given Trevor had just dropped dead six months ago.

But she was ill. She'd just finished chemotherapy and was awaiting radiation treatment. Now was not the time. They said if she got through this part, she might have another ten or more years left.

Or not.

When Jackson had pushed, they shared that, if she went into remission, when it eventually returned—and it would—the end would be swift.

So, they were living in limbo, waiting. Trevor dead, and his mother fighting for her life.

"For now," he said, and his eyes met Kristen's.

Why was he telling her this much? Perhaps because he knew her parents had been through cancer treatment, and she would understand.

"She's ill."

"Oh my god. I'm so sorry." Her hand flew to his thigh, and she dug her fingers in. "I'm such an idiot. Jesus. *She's not dead.* Someone shut me up."

He let out a small laugh.

"It's okay. You've been through it."

"Cancer?" she asked, and he nodded.

"Non-Hodgkins."

Kristen turned to glance over the park. "God, I hate that fucking disease."

Yeah. So did he.

And if his mother took her secrets with her, Jackson would be pissed. It might be her life, but he deserved to know about how his parents met and why they weren't together.

The real story.

He wasn't naive enough to think they had some great affair, he their love child, but Jackson was a man who dealt with facts. Building a relationship with his father if he'd fucked his mother over wasn't going to happen.

If she'd tossed the billionaire away, Jackson also wanted to know.

What decisions were made by his birth parents that left him without his real father? Not to appoint blame, but so he knew his history. Everyone deserved that. Especially as the truth had been kept from him for twenty-four years.

"Are your parents in love?" he heard himself ask.

Kristen glanced up and pressed her lips together in thought. "Love? I guess they are. They're pretty old, but I've seen them holding hands and giving each other little hugs from time to time."

He twisted and tucked her blonde hair behind her ear. "That's beautiful. I've never seen my parents do that. Never."

"Everyone is different in how they show love, I suppose." She shrugged, then twisted her body to face him. "You say your parents aren't affectionate, but you're always touching me. Daniel can't keep his hands off Harper. Nature or nurture? Interesting, huh?"

"Maybe it's the Dufort genes." He laughed, then went quiet.

Was he affectionate with her? Jackson took note of the way his body was wrapped around hers protectively.

They looked like lovers.

Like a couple.

Jackson had been exaggerating earlier. He *did* date women. Only a few days here or there, never anything serious. But he'd never held hands with them as he'd done all day with Kristen. He'd never sat eating an ice cream with his arm wrapped around any of them.

Why was he doing it now?

The need to be in constant physical contact with her felt almost natural.

He slowly leaned back and shifted on the seat.

"And now he pulls away," Kristen said, rolling her eyes. "It doesn't mean anything. Just an observation."

It did mean something. He just wasn't sure what.

"Another observation, little kitten, is the time. If you want to get to the show on time, we must get going now."

"Shit," Kristen said, jumping up.

This time, he was aware when he put his arm around her and walked across the park to his waiting car. He had no desire to remove it.

When she smirked at him, he dropped his mouth to hers.

"Not a word," he growled against her lips.

Kristen giggled, and he straightened, smiling privately to himself.

Damn, he was a bit smitten with his kitten.

CHAPTER THIRTEEN

Jackson had dropped her at Daniel's penthouse to pack, while he took care of some business. An hour later, when she climbed into the back of his car to head back to his hotel, Kristen learned exactly what that business had been.

On the seat was a white box with a white ribbon and a gold embossed DIOR.

"For you," he said, lifting it and putting it on her lap.

"Jackson!" she gasped.

"Open it."

"What is it?" She pulled the ribbon and lifted the lid. "Oh my goodness."

Kristen pulled out the black sequined DIOR dress, which felt as expensive as she imagined it probably was.

From what she could see, it was an off-the-shoulder-style that would fit snugly to the knee, with a generous split up the front.

"This is way too fancy."

"We've been upgraded. You're wearing it," Jackson said, with a hint of the dominance he'd shown in the bedroom the night before.

There was something new in his eyes. An intensity that pulled her in.

"Upgraded?"

Kristen had purchased tickets, and when he'd said he would join her, he had mentioned he would ensure they could sit together.

She hadn't expected anything fancy tonight, but she was beginning to realize underestimating this man was a mistake.

"To box seats. Unless you want to sit in the Orchestra. But...I'd rather have the privacy."

Privacy?

"Wear the dress and leave your panties at home," Jackson said, and her body flushed as he leaned down and kissed her neck.

Ten seconds with the man and her panties were already wet. He was incorrigible.

"Do you buy dresses for all your dates? Wait, how did you know my size? And how did you get this so fast?" Kristen asked, wondering where one got a DIOR gown in an hour.

Resting back in the seat, Jackson simply winked at her. "Money is powerful, sweetheart. You'd be surprised what you can make happen when your net worth is all over the internet."

Indeed.

"Also, no. I've never bought a dress for a woman before. Not even my mother." He smirked. "As for your size, I had my hands all over your body, my cock deep inside you last night. You don't think I know your body?"

Damn him.

She wriggled in her seat, clenching her core. The way he talked would have her jumping his bones if he didn't stop.

"And what I don't know, I'll be investigating further tonight. When you're less sore." He grinned and took her hand, kissing it.

Kristen let out a moan.

When the car pulled up to the Waldorf-Astoria, Jackson organized a porter to take her bags up to their room. He'd quickly had a shower, kissed her softly, then left her to get ready while he checked a few emails.

"If I stay in this room a minute longer, I'm going to lift you onto that bench and make you forget about the theater and any other plans you have in New York," he'd said as she'd moaned.

God, what he did to her.

It didn't help he was so damn handsome.

The way he looked at her, touched her, desired her, was like a fantasy.

As she showered, Kristen took a moment to catch her breath. How was she staying in the Waldorf-Astoria hotel with Jackson Wiles?

In his hotel room.

This was insane.

The past two days had been crazy. Dinner at The Plaza, the most incredible sex of her life, a romantic day in Manhattan walking around Central Park. And now, going to Times Square, wearing a DIOR dress worth more than her mortgage payment this month.

At a guess.

Probably two months.

More than that, she just couldn't even comprehend.

When she toweled off, Kristen did her hair up in a French twist, added a little more makeup than usual, then slid the dress on.

She'd been right about the style. The black sleeves sat off her shoulder, and the neckline draped elegantly across her breasts, the rest hugging her curves to just above her knees. The split sexy but just provocative enough to still be classy.

Because DIOR.

It was absolutely stunning. Kristen barely recognized the woman staring back at her in the mirror.

She looked so…wealthy. As anyone would in this dress. But there was more—she was glowing. Clearly, orgasms were the best skincare on the planet.

After all that sex talk and tension in the car, she wasn't opposed to another one. Then she remembered Jackson had told her to keep her panties off. She quickly tugged them down her legs and threw them around the corner into her open suitcase, just before he stepped into the doorway.

Dark swirling eyes slid over her body, finally landing on hers.

"No panties?"

Kristen shook her head, too stunned to speak.

She was too busy trying to take stock of the most gorgeous man she'd ever seen in her life, standing right in front of her.

Jackson wore a black, clearly custom-made suit, a white shirt, and black bow tie. With day-old scruff on his face and his slightly dark, curly hair licking the top of his collar, he looked like a damn fashion model.

Why the hell is he interested in me?

No point overthinking that, but it wasn't the first time she'd wondered.

"We better get out of this hotel, or I am going to fuck you against that counter right goddamn now, kitten," Jackson said, his voice thick.

She let out a little mew when he dropped a kiss on her shoulder.

Kristen continued to stare at him as Jackson slapped some aftershave on his face, then moved behind her, placing his hands on her hips.

"We're quite the couple," he said, catching her eyes in the mirror.

She couldn't argue.

Despite just a few weeks ago being the girl who had flown in from Auckland wearing a pair of leggings and a sweatshirt from Calvin Klein—which she'd thought was fancy—now stood a woman who had been thoroughly fucked and lived like a billionaire for weeks.

Except, that wasn't what she was focused on.

It was the way Jackson was staring at her. The way the butterflies in her stomach were swirling like maniacs, the way her nipples hardened, eager for his touch, and her pussy moistened whenever he tempted her.

How her chest was tight with feeling for this man. How she could imagine standing beside him in their bathroom for the next fifty or so years, watching him gaze at her like that.

Did he know there was more than desire in his eyes?

Was she imagining it?

Was she insane, wishing this man wanted her and would give her the greatest gift of her life? Him and their child.

Totally insane.

She'd slept with him once. This was a four-day fling. Affair. Four-night stand.

Call it what you like.

It wasn't a relationship.

Perhaps it was her ovaries calling. Harper had asked her once, when they were younger, if she wanted kids, and her reaction had been, "Yes. One hundred percent. With the right man, though. I want to be married, not end up a single mom and living on the benefit." The government unemployment support in New Zealand.

And she'd meant it.

Yet here she was, bumping up against thirty, and she still hadn't met Mr. Right.

So why did Jackson feel like he was that guy? Perhaps it was the lifestyle and the fact it felt like they were on a four-day date. He was clearly being on his best behavior. In normal life, when he was home, he might be a total ass.

But the way he was looking at her right now, she couldn't be wrong. Jackson's eyes were like molten fire.

"What's going on in that mind of yours?" he asked.

Hard no. She was not sharing a single one of those irrational thoughts.

Oh hey, just wondering, would you like to impregnant me and spend the rest of your life with me, handsome? Yes? Oh great. Thanks.

Certifiably. Insane.

Jackson spun her around, cupping her face, and with a light growl said, "Tell me, little kitten."

"Just that I'm looking forward to not having panties on at the theater," she said, leaning into his chest.

His big muscular chest.

So damn perfect.

He grunted. "Hmm, little liar. I will get it out of you, lick by lick, when we get home."

Then he gave her a hint of what was to come when his tongue ran along her bottom lip. She moaned as he slapped her ass and hurried her out the door.

WHEN they arrived in Times Square, there was no waiting in queue, unlike the other million people lined up. Jackson led her straight to the door and gave his name, and they were led inside to their box seats. The view was great, not excellent; however, they did have privacy.

And champagne.

Kristen had been dying to see *Chicago*, the musical, for years. Very few shows came to New Zealand, and timing was everything. Seeing it on Broadway was a dream come true.

Now, here she was, with the sexiest man in Manhattan. She was sure of it. Kristen shot him a smile, and he winked at her.

Below them, the theater began to fill.

Jackson wrapped his arm along the back of her seat as the theater went dark and silent.

"Here's what's going to happen," his voice quietly rich as his other hand slid up her thigh. "You're going to watch the show, and at some point, I'm going to make you come."

Her breath hitched.

"Don't take your eyes off the show. Understand?" Jackson ordered gruffly.

Kristen nodded, suppressing a moan as her heart thundered. Then, to give her a small taste, apparently, he nudged her legs apart, and his fingers brushed over her pussy.

A little gasp escaped her.

Then he sat back.

Kristen turned, her mouth gaping.

"Eyes on the show," he ordered. "I'm in charge with how this happens."

Oh my god. A shudder ran through her as her pussy throbbed. She was already wet, her nipples hard as damn rocks. Kristen needed his touch, wriggling as she clenched her core.

Jackson ran his fingers along the bare skin on her shoulders.

Goddamn him.

Then the lights burst on, and the music started. Within minutes, her body had calmed, and she was able to focus on the show. The performers were amazing.

Dancing, singing, flying all over the stage.

The colors out of this world.

It must have been over thirty minutes before she felt his hand on her thigh again.

She flinched and heard his soft, *"Ssshhhh."*

Kristen's legs had naturally closed, so Jackson nudged them open again, her dress slipping easily up her thighs.

Under his touch, Kristen felt how wet she still was. When he slid between her flesh, she caught her breath and forced her eyes to stay on the show, her breasts heaving.

My God. She never did things like this in public.

What if there were cameras?

Or if someone from across, in another box, noticed her expression?

Circling around her juices, Jackson tapped her pussy, and she jumped.

"Easy baby," he growled low, then slid to the floor in front of her.

Holy shit.

"Jackson," she gasped.

"Watch the show, or I'll stop." Then his mouth was on her again, surrounding her entire pussy in one smooth, dominant move.

Kristen gripped the edges of her seat, pleasure plowing through her. Her nipples aching to be touched, her face on fire.

How was this her life?

Chicago continued to play out in front of her as Jackson slid two fingers inside, fucking her while she watched three women in black costumes sing and dance, swirling each other around.

Kristen wasn't sure she could hold on for much longer.

When she got close, he would stop.

And again.

His tongue kissing her open thighs, then back on her pussy.

Finally, holding her thighs open as his tongue did magical things, with two fingers pressed inside her, Jackson's thumb strummed her clit. It was all she could take. Wildfire rushed through her, and she began to tremble.

"Come for me baby, come on my face," Jackson ordered in a low growl.

Kristen threw a hand over her mouth—and how the hell he'd timed it, she didn't know—but the crowd burst into applause.

Just as her orgasm exploded.

JACKSON slid back into his seat as the lights brightened. He licked his lips.

A panting Kristen turned to him, flushed and looking so damn gorgeous, he was tempted to throw her to the ground and slam his cock inside her.

Instead, he leaned over and kissed her, knowing she'd taste herself on his lips.

Kristen groaned and pressed her body against his.

The willpower it took not to take her…

Jackson grinned, stood, and held out his hand. "Shall we head down to intermission?"

"You're going to kill me," she said, and he felt her hand trembling, the pleasure he'd just given her still cascading through her body.

Talk about making a man feel like a giant.

Kristen was a goddess, but she had no idea.

Jackson wrapped an arm around her shoulders and leaned down, his voice thick and low. "Not a bad way to go, though, is it?"

She let out a wobbly moan, and he laughed.

The truth was, she might be the death of him.

He liked this woman far too damn much. And in two days, she was fucking leaving.

CHAPTER FOURTEEN

Despite the theater orgasm, or maybe because of it, Kristen launched at him the moment the hotel door closed behind them.

"Hey, kitten, slow down."

"No. I need you inside me. Pronto," she said, pressing her mouth against his.

"Which I also want, but remember who is in charge here," he said darkly.

Her body softened in his arms and green eyes met his.

"Good girl. Now, get onto your knees and pull those titties out. I want to play with them while you suck my cock."

Despite her mouth falling open, Kristen did as she was told. "Okay."

If she called him "sir," he was going to come all over her face. But he'd held back on instructing her to do that, unsure how much she could handle at once, especially given their short time together.

Unzipping, Jackson pulled his cock out and began to stroke it as Kristen tugged her dress down. As her breasts popped out, her eyes met his.

"Such a sexy girl," he said, cupping the back of her head. "Open for me, Kristen, and fuck my cock with your hot mouth."

Her groan was muffled as he slid inside.

Jackson knew he was thick, but she took him perfectly. Her head bobbed, her suction perfect, and he reached and pinched her nipple.

"I'd love to see clamps on these gorgeous pink buds," he said, pinching hard. "Would you like that?"

Big eyes held his as she continued sliding him in and out of her mouth.

"Silver studs pinching these so you are always wet and needing my dick," he said, his balls tightening. "Oh, fuck, yes."

He gripped her hair with his fist and pumped harder.

Kristen pressed her fingers into his thighs, hard.

"I'm going to come on your tits," he growled, thrusting more, then pulling out and fucking his hand until his cream burst out onto her soft tanned skin.

"Ohh!" she cried as she rubbed it into her skin.

Like a fucking sex kitten.

His sex kitten.

"Turn around," he ordered, unzipping her dress and removing the bra that was already tugged down.

As Kristen licked her lips, dazed, Jackson removed his clothes, then lifted her, wrapping her legs around his waist, his cock nudging at her wet entrance. He walked to the sofa and settled her on the back of it. Jackson inched away, slipping his fingers through her pussy, then slid them into his mouth.

"You have the most intoxicating taste, sweetheart." He replaced his fingers and leaned to kiss her.

"Jackson, my God, I need you in me."

"You want my cock in your pussy and your mouth, greedy girl?"

She nodded and mumbled something he couldn't understand. But he did know those green eyes pleading him were saying yes.

Then something snapped in him. Jackson needed more. He needed her total submission.

"Beg me. And from now on, when I'm fucking you, I want you to call me 'sir'."

Kristen's eyes widened. "I can't—"

His fingers pressed inside her. The other hand pinched her nipple.

"Are you saying no? Shall I stop?" Jackson asked, stilling.

"No! No!" she cried. "Please, no. I…God, Jackson."

His hand moved from her breast and gripped her jaw. "Plead for my cock, and I will pleasure you, kitten. I will give you all you need."

A whimper escaped, and he licked her lip.

She blinked.

Giving a little, he moved his fingers inside her some more, then pulled out, showing her he was serious.

Her body pressed into his hand.

Jackson moved away a few inches, then slapped her pussy.

"Bad girl," he growled. "Do I need to punish you for a few hours, or will you do as you're told?"

Kristen's eyes were glistening with need, her chest heaving. "Goddamn it. Please, sir."

He smiled.

Thank fucking God. He might have just come, but his cock wanted inside this woman so bad.

He tilted her chin as he thrust inside her.

Then again.

Hard.

Sharp.

Deep.

"Ohgod, ohgod, fuck!" she cried.

"Good. Girl," Jackson growled, slamming in one hard thrust after another, his cock tight inside her needy pussy.

Tears threatened to leak from one of her eyes, but he swept it away with his thumb.

"You are the single most sexy thing I've seen in my goddamn life."

His fingers found her clit, and he pinched.

"Come for me, Kris, now."

He released her face as she cried out his name.

That's right, baby. Remember this. Remember me. Because I sure as fucking hell will never forget you.

As she slumped against him and he carried her into the bedroom, Jackson had this powerful need to both keep her and run.

Falling for Kristen Holle was never part of the plan.

WAKING up with Kristen draped over his chest, her fingers resting on his bicep, had filled him with a whole bunch of stupid joy.

He'd worn her out, pleasured her into a near coma.

What man wouldn't be proud?

He was fighting the desire to claim this woman when he knew he had far greater priorities in his life.

Yet when Kevin, his CEO, had messaged overnight that the government executives wanted to meet the next day to discuss the tech contract, Jackson had replied, asking if it could be put off another day.

Was he insane?

Yes was the damn answer.

Kristen flew home tomorrow night, and he wanted to spend every second with her. He just couldn't bring himself to leave her early and fly to Washington.

Hello, one point two billion dollars!

However, it was damn short notice, and he wanted to wrap up things with his birth father. After spending the last day with Kristen, Appopolis would have all his attention once more.

His business had dominated his life since he created it a few years ago. It was a risk to ask for a different meeting date—a potentially expensive risk—but he was confident he had the best tech and they would wait for him.

Or he really was cock-struck by this woman and would live to regret it.

Jackson shook his head. He'd left her a note, just in case she woke and forgot where he was.

On the way to his father's, his phone received a text.

Fletcher.

Well, shit.

New bar opening tonight in Soho if you'd like to join us. Details in attached image.

An olive branch.

Jackson wasn't surprised it came from Fletcher.

Daniel would rather punch him in the face, and Hunter was probably still digging through his father's dishes, looking for DNA on the whisky glass Jackson had drunk from.

He let out a quiet snort, then made the decision to go. But he wasn't going alone. He knew Kristen had a New York harbor cruise booked tonight, but he'd already decided to sabotage it.

In a good way.

An idea came to mind.

Thanks, I'll be there. Also, know anyone with a boat? You can drive there…

He let out another silent snort. Fucking smartass.

No shit, sherlock. Do you, or not?

Yes. Me.

Of course. What was he thinking? His brother was a billionaire. Of course, he had all the toys.

Jackson pressed the green button and rang Fletcher.

"What do you need a boat for?" Fletcher said instead of a greeting. "And am I going to regret this?"

Jackson laughed. "So that's a yes, then?"

"Technically, its owned by the company, so yes, but whether the captain is available and willing to get out of bed at the last minute on a Saturday morning is another thing."

Fair enough, but he wasn't giving up.

"I'm taking Kristen out for the day," Jackson said, to alleviate his brother's concerns.

"Dude. Daniel will lose his shit—"

Fuck that.

Nobody told him what he could and couldn't do.

"Who I date is none of Daniel's concerns. Kristen has forgiven me. Plus, he got us a table at The Plaza."

Fletcher cursed again. "Seriously? That's pulling some big strings."

Yeah, Jackson could only imagine what it might cost him down the line. Daniel was a man who dealt in deals. So was he.

A price he would happily pay for the pleasure his kitten brought him.

And her.

His cock twitched to be back with her.

"She's here for two more days. I don't want her going on those group cruises with random strangers. She deserves better," Jackson said, as if that was some solid reasoning.

In his head, it was.

"I agree. But can we pause for a moment. You like her." Fletcher whistled.

More than liked, but Jackson couldn't overthink it.

Her leaving was something he wasn't willing to process, even if it was happening tomorrow.

Fuck.

"I'm bringing her tonight," Jackson noted, ignoring his comment.

Fletcher was quiet for a moment. "Olivia will be happy to see her."

They let that hang for a moment before Jackson spoke.

"Appreciate the invite."

There was more silence, then Fletcher said, "I'm a stepdad."

"Um, congratulations," Jackson replied, unsure where this was going.

He heard the scoff.

"Sammy's father is locked up. He's an asshole. Long story. Anyway, she's young and will barely remember him if he ever gets out," Fletcher said. "Which we hope he won't."

Jackson watched a yellow cab cut them off and his driver curse. New York traffic was an interesting experience. But it wasn't the traffic he was focused on. He was waiting for Fletcher to explain the reason for his little story.

"My point is, not knowing who your birth parents are is a big deal. You were lied to. I get you want answers," Fletcher added. "And you probably want to know us. As your brothers."

Jackson let out a sigh.

"Yeah. I get how fucked up this is, though." Jackson was feeling overwhelmed and grateful for the chance to talk to Fletcher like this.

In his head, he gave Fletcher the sensitive-brother label. Whether he truly was or not was another thing. Accepting another man's kid was a good indication, he figured.

"Daniel and Hunter will come around. Give them time. I have my own child on the way, so I guess my mindset is in a different place from theirs."

"That's exciting, man," Jackson replied. "And congratulations."

"Thanks. Yeah. It is." There was a wistfulness in Fletcher's voice. "Anyway, I'll ring Captain Brinks and see if he's available. Wait for my text."

"Thanks, Fletcher."

"No problem. Oh, and whatever you do, don't break it. It's Hunters favorite toy. Well, except for Addison now."

Jackson snorted.

How the hell did one break a super yacht?

He glanced down at his phone several minutes later, just as he arrived at his father's building. The captain and crew were willing to work at short notice and were on their way to set up the Dufort yacht now.

Excellent.

Jackson smiled.

He couldn't wait to surprise Kristen.

Fletcher had given him a recommendation on tipping Captain Brinks, which made him gulp. But it was totally worth it to see those green eyes light up.

Jackson shot Kristen a text, which she'd get when she woke up.

I have a surprise for you. Be home at ten.

JACKSON stepped into his father's apartment and was hit with delicious smells of breakfast. Coffee, eggs, toast, bacon.

"Hungry?" Johnathan said, as he walked over to the table. It was covered in dishes, jugs of juice, plates, and silverware.

"This looks amazing. I take it you have a chef?" Jackson grinned and took a seat.

"For the past twenty years." Johnathan nodded. "As the owner of a huge dynasty, there's no time to spend on domestic chores. Plus, cooking is someone else's passion, and I'm providing employment opportunities for them."

"Not everyone can be a billionaire," Jackson said. "I'm sure you pay well." He poured himself a glass of juice.

"The same woman has worked for me for over eight years now, so she seems happy," his father said.

From what he knew of Johnathan Dufort, that surprised Jackson. He had a reputation of sleeping with women who worked for him and going through workers. Perhaps the rumors and media weren't entirely accurate?

Jackson added some poached eggs to his plate, along with toast, grilled tomatoes, and some sliced avocado.

Johnathan lifted his coffee and sipped, watching Jackson eat, then finally asked. "So, where do we start?"

Don't dig up ghosts, Jackson, I beg you.

"From the beginning, I suppose," Jackson said, crunching on his toast.

Johnathan dropped the coffee cup into the saucer. "Actually, I think it's wiser if I start at the end and work backward. I fell in love with your mother."

Jackson's fork froze halfway to his mouth.

What?

He had not been expecting that. If he had loved her, then why weren't they together? Johnathan Dufort was a powerful man.

It left only one thing—Johnathan had chosen his family over Jackson and his mother, and that stung.

"You loved her?" he asked, his fork clanging as it dropped on the plate.

Johnathan nodded.

"Which was quite an inconvenience, honestly," he said, shaking his head. "Not what you want to hear, but I'm going to tell you the truth."

Jackson sat watching as Johnathan continued talking.

"She turned up at the event I told you about. All glimmer and fame. Jenna was gorgeous. I couldn't keep my eyes off her. Then we were introduced. She was smart, beautiful, and funny."

My mother is funny?

Jackson loved his mother, but funny wasn't something he ever associated her with. In a way, she had always seemed...angry at life.

Perhaps he was about to find out why.

"The party began to thin, and there we were, still talking. Both married. So, I asked her if she wanted to have a nightcap in a more private bar." He lifted his eyes to Jackson.

"Withhold judgement, if you will. I realized then exactly what I was doing but…well, she's your mother, so I'll give you the PG version."

"Thanks," Jackson said flatly.

"We spent the night together, and I told her I wanted to see her again. It wasn't just sex. We talked and shared how we felt about our lives. My marriage was unhappy. So was hers. I had the three boys by then, as I mentioned the other night. They were little."

Jackson decided to keep eating.

"I wanted her, even though I felt a lot of guilt. Your mother shared, one night, that she was having trouble conceiving children with Trevor."

"Really?" Jackson said, frowning. Then he nodded because it made sense. They'd never had any other children besides him.

Johnathan nodded.

"She was desperate to have children. Hoping it would improve the marriage. We all know it doesn't work that way, but who was I to tell her. Our time together was about supporting one another and… pleasure."

Jackson drank his juice, thinking he could relate, but winced at the word being used in relation to his mother.

"Fast forward," Jackson said.

Johnathan let out a laugh. "Well, you know this part. She got pregnant."

"She told you then?"

Johnathan nodded.

"And you kicked her to the curb," Jackson said, but they both knew it was a question.

"No," Johnathan replied sharply.

"Then what the hell happened? Because I have to be honest with you, Trevor was…*is*…an asshole. Why would she choose a man like him over you?"

"Was?" Johnathan demanded, his eyes darkening.
Goddamn it.

The tension in the room shot up as their eyes locked and remained locked.

"Jackson…is your father—Trevor—dead?"

Shit.

Jackson pushed his chair back. "I'm doing the asking here."

Johnathan threw his napkin down on his plate.

Fuck.

"Yes. Fucking hell. Yes, he is," Jackson snapped. "He died six months ago."

Johnathan cursed, then stood and began pacing around the room, his hand running through his short hair.

Jackson watched him. This was quite the reaction to a woman he had loved twenty-four years ago. And nine months. When he finally stopped pacing, Johnathan turned, and their eyes met once more.

Panic laced through Jackson. He jumped up.

"No. No fucking way. You are not contacting her," he shouted.

"Don't tell me what to do, son. I want to speak to her. I *have* to speak to her."

Jesus.

Coming here had been a mistake.

If he caused his mother any goddamn stress over this selfish venture, Jackson would regret it for the rest of his life.

He could have waited.

What did another ten or so years matter?

"Please. Don't. Let me speak to her first. Mom said I wasn't to dig up ghosts. What did she mean by that?" Jackson said. "Tell me everything."

Johnathan shook his head as he stared at his shoes, then slid his hand into his pockets. He let out a sigh.

"I returned from Australia after some business and stopped in L.A. on the way home. To see Jenna. Your mom." He turned to stare out the window at the New York skyline. "We were going to spend the night together in our usual suite. When I got there, she was sitting on the end of the bed, looking upset."

Jackson sat back down.

"Her eyes were swollen. She'd been crying."

Johnathan walked over to the windows and was silent. Jackson gave him the space with his memories and waited.

When Johnathan turned, he had a sad smile. "She was pregnant. With you."

"Not happy about it?" Jackson asked, his chest tightening.

No child wanted to hear that.

"The opposite. She was very happy," Johnathan said, his eyes glistening. "She told me she was in love with me and glad it was my child."

This wasn't where Jackson thought it was going.

"So, what happened?"

Johnathan let out a short laugh. "I made love to her, is what happened. But I promised the PG version, so I'll skip that part."

Jackson snorted. "In a sick way, that's nice to hear."

Johnathan pressed his lips together. "I loved her. I do love her, even to this day."

Jackson's eyes widened.

Did his mother still love this man?

Jesus.

Ghosts…He was starting to get it now.

"Well, why aren't you together? Shit. Just tell me."

"Afterwards, as we lay there, she told me she didn't expect anything of me," Johnathan said. "But we knew the road ahead would be tough if we decided to be together. I had several hotels, and the Dufort brand was well known. Your mom was a music star. The media had already picked up a story of us together, so we had to decide carefully how we proceeded.

"So, I returned to New York for a few weeks while we came to terms with what was happening. I knew then I loved

Jenna enough to leave my wife. I wasn't in love with her anymore and was determined to remain a big part of my boys' life."

An image of what could've been his life flashed before Jackon's eyes.

Jackson and his mother living in this penthouse. Daniel, Fletcher, and Hunter visiting weekends. It was a strange thought.

His eyes narrowed. "Yet her career ended abruptly, and you never spoke again."

"Not until she sent me the baby photo and then asked for your college fund," Johnathan confirmed. "Not because I didn't try. She closed the door, and I do not know why."

"What happened to her music career?"

"You will need to ask her," Johnathan replied darkly. "I have waited just as long for those answers."

Jackson chewed a piece of bacon and shook his heads.

Ghosts.

"I would have married her in a second, Jackson. I mean it when I say I still love your mother. I believe she feels the same way."

"So, she just cut you off?" Jackson asked.

"More or less. After making the decision, the day I was flying to L.A. to meet her again, I woke to a message saying she loved Trevor and was staying with him to make it work. She asked me not to contact her again."

And?

Johnathan didn't fight? Just accepted it and let his mom give birth and never cared to know him?

"So, you just carried on with your life? That doesn't sound like you. It certainly doesn't sound like a man in love," Jackson challenged.

Johnathan's dark eyes lifted to his. "You've never been in love, son. Wait. Just you wait."

Jackson shook his head.

"Bullshit. You had a child on the way," he replied.

There was no way Jackson would sit back and let some woman have his child and not be a part of its life. Not after growing up with a father who wasn't his and being treated like he was useless.

"Trust me, I did try. Your mother was a wealthy woman then, with people protecting her. I wasn't a billionaire twenty-four years ago. I had influence, but not the same as I do now."

God.

So, she ghosted him.

"The media followed her around, getting photo after photo of her as her belly grew. It was the days of the paparazzi, when they were out of control."

The only context Jackson had to that was the death of Princess Diana. Everyone knew the story of her death in the tunnels in Paris after being chased by international media.

After a life of it.

He could only imagine how terrifying it would be.

Jackson nodded. "That's shit. Poor Mom."

Johnathan let out a long sigh.

"But the big news was, she had been dropped by her record company. They all said it was because of the pregnancy. Eventually, it faded away, as she'd not been famous for long."

Why?

That was the great mystery now. Why had they dropped her?

"Do you think that's why they dropped her?"

"Honestly, no. She was a huge hit and not the only pregnant musician," Johnathan said. "I tried to find out but hit wall after all."

Jackson bunched his brows together. "Well, whatever happened, she had no right to keep us apart."

"No. But I'm not innocent here either," Johnathan said. "I was angry. Hurting. Rejected. I had been willing to break up my family for her. I loved her."

Jesus.

"Do the boys know?"

Johnathan shook his head. "And they won't. This is between us."

Jackson nodded. "Of course."

"So, you see. We both made this decision in our own way. I believed, or let myself believe, Trevor thought you were his and their marriage had improved when you were born."

Jackson sat shaking his head.

"She didn't love Trevor. I know it. Something fucking happened."

Johnathan stood with his hands in his pockets, staring at him. "Now he's dead."

"I know what you're thinking, but please, give me time to process this and speak to her," Jackson pleaded.

He wasn't going to tell his father she was ill. Jackson could see in his eyes that Johnathan would jump on his jet and be in L.A. by nightfall.

What that would do to his mother and her fucking *ghosts,* Jackson had no idea.

Until he did, Johnathan would have to wait.

"She's not the woman you once loved. I don't think I've ever seen her happy, if I'm being honest. Now…"

Stop talking.

"Now?" Johnathan asked.

"Now I guess I need to speak to her. I'm returning to L.A. next week. I'll ring you once I have told her we've met. Just give me a few days."

When Johnathan nodded his agreement, they sat in the thick silence for a long while.

"I'm glad you're here," his father said.

Shit.

Emotion built as Jackson's chest tightened.

"I wondered many times what you looked like. What you were like. If you were like me, or Daniel, or any of the boys.

Maybe even my father," Johnathan said. "Or if you looked like your mother. And you do."

Tears prickled, and Jackson clenched his fists so tightly his nails dug into his hands.

Focus on the pain. Do not fucking cry.

"You're a part of this family now. However you want to do that, the doors are open," Johnathan said. "I'll arrange for you to be added to the trust and my will."

"No. That's not necessary."

"The fuck it is. I know you don't want it, but you are my son. So just get over that."

Jackson shook his head. "It will impact my ability to connect with the others."

Meaning his brothers.

"Leave them to me. I built that business, and occasionally, I need to remind them of that. It's your birthright."

Jackson wasn't sure it was a good idea, but it was clear by the stiffness in the man's jaw he wasn't going to discuss it.

"Fletcher invited us out tonight," Jackson said. "A nice step in the right direction of getting to know them."

His father nodded, smiling.

"Well, that's good because I have another family event for you before you go," Johnathan said, his smile fading. "My mother is dying."

His mother?

Jesus.

Jackson had a grandmother on the Dufort side. That hadn't even occurred to him yet.

"We've been estranged for many years. Her and my older brother. It's a long story, but yesterday, one of my nephews, Logan, phoned to say she doesn't have long. I've called a family meeting for tomorrow. Join us."

Jackson agreed.

"Thank you. For telling me everything," Jackson said, standing to leave.

"I want to see her. Don't make me wait long. I won't wait long," Johnathan said, with a strength in his voice Jackson had not yet heard.

The thing was, the decision wasn't either of theirs. It was Jenna's.

Jackson had no choice but to tell her now, but he would do it calmly, rather than his father turning up in L.A. and freaking the hell out of her.

Thankfully, Johnathan didn't know she was dying. There was no way Jackson would risk her life and share that piece of information with his father.

Did he deserve to know? Perhaps.

But she was *his* mother, and that was far more important in Jackson's mind.

So, he simply nodded and left.

WHEN he got back to the hotel, Jackson found Kristen stretching out on the white linens like a lazy cat.

His kitten.

She slowly opened her eyes.

"Good morning, gorgeous," Jackson said, leaning against the doorjamb.

"Hey." She yawned, then smiled smugly.

Yeah, he'd pleasured his woman well.

Well, his woman for right now. A woman he'd love to keep pleasing, if she didn't live so fucking far away. Pushing that thought away, Jackson focused on spending a beautiful day on the water with her.

She blinked and half sat up. "Why do you look like you've done something I should know about?"

He grinned.

"Because I have. Get dressed," Jackson said, kneeling on the bed to kiss her.

"Coffee first. Then I can function," she said, rolling over and tucking her hands under the pillow.

Kristen spotted the time on the clock and bolted upright.

"Holy shit. It's ten o'clock," she cried as he rang room service and ordered her a coffee.

CHAPTER FIFTEEN

Kristen stepped onto the enormous Dufort superyacht and glanced around.

Everything was pristine. White walls, white leather seats, silver railings, and whitewashed, pale timber deck floors. Along the side of the boat—she'd seen as they boarded—was the metallic Dufort logo. And of course, the name of the craft was *The Dufort*.

Not exactly creative.

Typical boys.

But the rest made up for it. Even from where she stood, Kristen could see luxury at every point.

The captain greeted them and explained there were four decks, a helicopter pad, and multiple dining areas. They could explore as the staff serviced their every need.

Kristen smiled, thanking him, as Jackson handed the man an envelope. She'd never felt like more of a fraud. Her, on a superyacht, on a date with a gorgeous man? In New York City.

In what universe did that even happen?

"I paid fifty-five dollars for the cruise tonight," she said, turning and finding herself in Jackson's arms. They were standing on the bow after dropping their bags and waiting for the crew to take them out.

"Did you?" he said, his lips stretching into a smile. "I hope this will be tolerable for you today, then."

Pressing her lips together to keep from smiling, she finally got control, then huffed. "I'll try to enjoy it. You really are horrible to be around. Annoying at best. Intolerable when you start talking about yourself so much."

Jackson pulled back an inch. "I talk about myself?"

"Not really," she admitted. "But I wish you would more. I like learning more about you."

The yacht began to move, so they headed inside where drinks and nibbles were being served.

Just for them.

Kristen suddenly felt something she'd never felt with a man. Special.

Jackson told her Fletcher had organized it when they'd spoken on the phone that morning. "He also invited us to an event tonight. I want to go, but only if you'll come with me."

"Don't you want to spend time with them on your own?" she asked, wanting to give him space to get to know his family.

She had secretly been hoping he didn't, knowing she only had one more night in the country. Tomorrow night, she'd be heading to the airport and flying home.

"I have the rest of my life to get to know them," he had said, taking her hand and lifting her fingers to his lips. "You, on the other hand, I only have two more days with."

She'd smiled when his eyes met hers.

"Okay. I'll go. It will be nice to see Olivia too."

Kristen wondered if he'd miss her when she left. Every moment she spent with Jackson proved just how amazing he was. It was becoming harder and harder to ignore her growing feelings for him.

Not just because of the way he was spoiling her.

Not because he made her feel like the most beautiful woman on the planet.

And not because the way he fucked her was incredible beyond words. Although that certainly contributed a lot.

No, it was in the little moments. Like the way he had just ordered her a Monte Carlo, knowing she didn't want any fruity cocktails or champagne. She liked her whisky.

Jackson paid attention.

To her.

It was in the way his body navigated to hers, no matter where they were standing or sitting. Like he was protecting her.

Owning her.

Claiming her.

How he slept with his arms around her all night long, placing kisses in her hair and on her neck periodically while they slept.

How he let her run her fingers over the tattoo on his chest, and when their eyes locked, he gazed at her like she was the eighth wonder of the world.

Kristen had never had a man make her feel special.

Yet she did.

It was the most wonderful and terrifying feeling. Because she was leaving him.

How did one bask in the wonder of it all, knowing they had to leave? Perhaps it was the temporary nature of their short affair. Or perhaps Jackson was the most amazing man she'd ever met.

Or worse, would ever meet.

She had to forgo fantasizing about being loved by him forever and force back all thoughts of what it would be like to be pregnant with his child. Kristen had to enjoy the remainder of their time together.

Two days, one night.

This was enough.

If she was falling for him, she was going to just let it happen.

Hearts could heal.

How did the saying go? It was better to have loved and lost, than to never have loved at all.

So it must be true.

THE sun sparkled off the water as the huge craft sailed past the high-rises of Manhattan. The waves slapped against the side, and birds squawked, flying overhead.

Jackson ripped off his top and stretched out his bare legs as he lay down on the deck. Beside him, Kristen was in a bright red bikini and white sheer coverall, big sunglasses, and a floppy hat.

Kevin had replied, saying the meeting had been rescheduled, so the risk Jackson had taken had paid off. One he still wasn't regretting, as he took in the sexy body next to him and what he had planned for tonight.

Still, it had been a stupid business move, and he hoped there would be no repercussions.

"Well, so much for my normal-person tourist experience," Kristen said.

"Normal person?"

She dropped her glasses down her nose. "Normal, like yellow cabs, long queues, crowds, pretzels. Not dinner at The Plaza, staying at the Waldorf-Astoria, and a private superyacht."

Jackson smirked, then turned his head back to the sun.

"I can ask the captain to turn around, if it's so horrible," he said, reaching out and taking her hand, entwining his fingers in hers. Touching her constantly seemed to be an addiction.

Which meant a detox was on the way when she flew home.

"I'll survive," she said, a smile in her voice. "What I won't survive is winter in New Zealand when I get home and having to drive myself around."

Jackson snorted. "I drive in L.A."

He opened one eye when he felt Kristen turn on her side. One of her hands landed on his chest, and a shiver of arousal ran through his body.

There must be rooms on this boat.

If she kept touching him like that, he'd scoop her up and go find one.

"You do? Let me guess…A Maserati. No, a Tesla," she teased.

Jackson closed his eye and, as seriously as he could, said, "I'll have you know, I drive a Honda."

Silence.

After a moment, he turned his head back and couldn't help but laugh at her expression.

"I know this is a trick. Does Honda make a luxury car I don't know about?" she asked, pulling out her phone to Google.

Jackson sat, nudged her onto her back as she giggled, and then climbed over her.

"It's a motorbike, my little kitten, and a sexy one, just like you." One he'd love to have her straddled on, then wrap his body around as they flew along the highways in Los Angeles.

Kristen's eyes widened. "I love motorbikes."

Of course, she did.

God, she was killing him. If she got any more perfect, he was seriously going to consider kidnapping her.

"Perhaps you can visit L.A. next time, and I'll take you for a ride," he said.

As a shadow crossed her eyes, he immediately regretted it.

Damn.

He hadn't meant to go there.

"This was a once-in-a-lifetime vacation for me. Even though I stayed with Harper," she said softly, and he could see the blush on her cheeks.

Embarrassment.

God, he didn't expect her to pay. In fact, paying for her to fly out would…What was he doing?

Then he heard himself say, "I'll pay for your flights."

Shit.

Wasn't this just four days? Then…what? A relationship at a distance?

Is that what he wanted?

Kristen shook her head, and a sadness crept inside his heart, darkening the sun around them.

"Forget I said anything." He leaned one of his elbows on the deck to the side of her head.

Kristen chewed her bottom lip. He ran a finger over it, getting an awkward smile from her.

"Let's just enjoy what this is while I'm still here," Kristen said.

He nodded. "Absolutely."

She reached up, and he met her with his lips, letting her relax back down as it deepened. It was only at the sound of a throat being cleared that he broke away.

"Lunch is served, when you're ready," one of the young crew members said, then disappeared.

A light breeze hit the deck, and Kristen's hair flapped around them as he stood and held his hand out to her. He'd agreed, but he was starting to wonder if letting Kristen walk out of his life completely was something he was capable of. Jackson wanted to take her to the Bahamas, or Hawaii, or the Caribbean, and show her the world. To enjoy more of her, including her gorgeous body and smart mind.

So maybe, just maybe, he didn't want it to end when she flew home.

Did she?

New Zealand might be on the other side of the world, but it wasn't on another planet. It was an eleven-hour flight from L.A. Money wasn't an object for him, so if she was open to a long-distance relationship, he could fly her over frequently.

Christ, how had he gotten to this place.

Look at her, you idiot. She's beautiful. Inside and out.

Except she'd put up a hard brick wall at the mention of her visiting again.

Which meant he had work to do, if he wanted to see his little kitten again. If there was one thing Jackson was good at, it was achieving his goals.

You are going to be mine, little kitten.

Where those goals led them, he would deal with later. For now, he was finally starting to accept Kristen was more than just a fleeting woman he enjoyed sleeping with.

As they stepped into the cabin, Kristen flicked her long hair over her shoulder and gave him a sexy smile.

Their lunch was laid out on the table. Jackson popped a grape into his mouth and chewed. He'd never taken no for an answer before, and he wasn't going to start now. Especially not when it came to Kristen Holle.

She was fast becoming his favorite thing.

CHAPTER SIXTEEN

Kristen stood with her head hanging, the four showerheads streaming hot water over her body.

God, it felt good.

A day on the water, with all the fresh salty air, always left her feeling sated and relaxed. While she'd love to curl up on the sofa and snuggle with Jackson all evening, they had an event to attend.

A fancy new bar in SOHO was opening.

Olivia and Fletcher would be there, so she was looking forward to seeing them one last time.

Even though she knew Daniel had secured them the table at The Plaza, there was no way she could be sure Mr. Secret had told his wife. So, she'd texted Harper and told her she was seeing Jackson so she didn't hear the news thirdhand.

Just be careful Kris, was her only response.

I am. We're just having fun and he apologized, she'd replied back.

All of which was true.

Except the *just* part.

Kristen *was* having fun with Jackson, but it had shifted to being more.

Their day on the water had been so romantic. They'd eaten constantly, lay in the sun talking, laughing, and just kissing and holding hands.

When she'd returned from the bathroom at one point, making her way along the hallway, Jackson had reached out of one of the rooms, making her scream and pulling her inside. Then, he'd kicked the door closed and slammed his mouth down on hers until she moaned.

He'd lifted her, placed her on the bed, pulling her bikini bottoms off, and feasted on her pussy. While the boat gently bounced along the waves, she had clung to his hair and cried out his name.

Her life was horrible.

Simply horrible.

Joking aside, Kristen let a wobbly smile hit her lips as the water continued running over her.

Time to get real.

Maybe Jackson was really just another dumb guy. Holiday romances were, theoretically, just a really long first date. There was no reality in them. There were no chores or real-life issues to deal with.

If they lived in the same town, perhaps he'd be late, or snore—which made no sense since he didn't, but she was digging for dirt. Then, a sense of FOMO created a desire that would dissipate once it was over.

If she was available to him, he might just end up one of those men who didn't want to commit. Plus, he was younger and unlikely interested in settling down yet.

Except…why had he offered to fly her to Los Angeles? Her heart had slammed into her chest when he'd said that. Worse, she'd nearly said yes.

Kristen flipped her head back and began to shampoo her hair.

Aside from her parents' position on the matter, she couldn't. Jackson was the hottest, nicest—and yes, richest—man she'd ever dated. Having a long-distance relationship with a man who turned heads everywhere he went asked way too much of her. She wasn't confident enough to believe he would be loyal when they were apart. Kristen would always be wondering what he was doing. Or rather, who he was seeing.

Or that he would end it when he met someone local.

The chances of a distant love affair working out were so low, she knew it wouldn't be worth the risk. She'd just get hurt.

And yes, she'd promised her parents she wouldn't pull a *Harper* on them and move to the U.S.

Rinsing her hair, then washing her body, she stepped out of the shower and covered herself in one of the large, thick white towels.

Jackson walked in and wrapped his body around hers, his mouth lowering to her neck. Glancing up at her in the mirror, he asked, "Feeling better?"

She nodded. "Much. I was expecting you to join me."

"I had some calls to make," he said, his hands on her hips, turning her around to face him. He kissed her softly, the warmth of his lips more seductive than usual. "I really don't feel like sharing you tonight, so let's not stay long."

Her heart blossomed. She nodded and smiled.

Rich desire poured from his eyes as his arms tightened around her. "I don't ever want to share you, if I'm being honest."

"Jackson…"

His mouth covered hers again, then she was lifted, and her legs wrapped around his body.

"Quiet. Let me make love to you." He stepped out of the room and dropped her on the bed, nudging her backward as he tugged the towel loose.

"We'll be late."

"Good," he replied thickly. "Spread open for me, kitten."

Her heart hammered against her chest as she felt the now-familiar ache race through her body. Her nipples hardening, her core clenching.

Jackson dropped to his knees as her thighs opened. He kissed his way along the inside of one of her legs, then swapped to the other one.

"Oh God, you tease," she cried, arching up.

"Patience," he growled, blowing on her pussy.

She let out a muffled moan.

His fingers traced around the edges of her bikini line, over her abdomen, and then her breasts. He pinched one.

Then she felt his tongue lap at her.

"Christ," she cried, arching.

Then he lapped again. And again. Until he was strumming her clit and sucking her flesh.

"Oh God, oh," she groaned.

"That's it, baby. I want you wet for me," Jackson said between licks. "Nice and wet so I can slide in deep and fast."

The filthy way Jackson spoke to her just added to her arousal. Kristen wanted to be everything he wanted her to be. She wanted all of him.

And more than anything, she loved that he took pleasuring her so damn seriously.

Jackson lifted her legs and laid them over his shoulder, taking her whole clitoris in his mouth and sucking hard as two fingers entered her.

She let out an unholy sound.

As she came, Jackson continued swirling his tongue around her swollen flesh.

Then he stood, his eyes connecting with hers, and a chill went through her.

Jackson undid his trousers and yanked off his top, and there he was, in all his naked glory. Tanned, layers of muscles, and those long dark lashes lowered, barely hiding those glowering predatory eyes.

Like he wasn't yet finished devouring her.

Climbing up onto the bed, he repositioned her with such ownership of her body, it made her heart flutter.

"I'm going deep," he said gruffly. "You ready for this, kitten?"

Kristen had no idea why he called her that, but it had started to become their thing. She nodded with a mumble of something, an indecipherable word, even to her.

"I'm going to fuck you so hard you will never question who is inside of you. Or who you want inside you ever again."

Oh God.

Kristen swallowed.

"This body is mine. For tonight, for two more days. This body is all mine. You hear me?" he growled in such a primal way she began to tremble.

With desire.

"Yes," she said, running her hands over his pecs as he lowered over her.

His mouth claimed hers. Hard.

When he released her, his cock was in his hand, and it was pressed at her core.

"Condom," she gasped out.

"Shit." Jackson reached over to the bedside cabinet and got one out of the drawer. He snapped it on. Then he was back, a half-smile on his lips. "I'd give anything to feel your hot, tight pussy around my cock, bare."

Her entire body reacted, thrusting up into his, the head slipping in.

"You want me, sweetheart?"

"Yes." She nodded.

One hand slid under her hip, and he nudged in.

"Then take me, take me all," he cried and thrust the rest of the way in.

All the fucking way.

"Goddddd," she cried, gripping his biceps. Kristen felt the whole thick length of him inside her.

"That's it, baby. Fuck." He pulled back and then thrust again.

The hotel bed banged and squeaked as they fucked, clinging to each other, like their lives were relying on it.

Jackson pulled out, flipped her over, slid his hand under her stomach, and lifted her hips.

Then slammed into her again.

"I'm going to fuck you from every angle so I can remember this when you leave," he said, his voice labored. "So *you* remember this."

Oh God.

She would.

Kristen would never ever forget this. Or him. Or the way he made her body tremble and fly to the moon in complete and utter surrender and pleasure.

Reaching around, he pinched her clit, and she screamed.

"Tighten baby. Fuck my cock. Take my come," he ordered. Then his hand was on her breast, squeezing, as she contracted her muscles.

That was when he spread her legs and slapped her pussy.

Holy motherfucker.

"That's it, baby. You like that."

"I…I don't—"

He slapped her again.

Fuck.

She did like it. Her body began to orgasm on the spot. Kristen pressed her face into the linens and cried out.

"Fucking hell. Oh fuck," Jackson said, his hands landing back on her hips and digging in hard. "I'm coming, baby. Fuck, Kristen, shit!"

As his cock swelled inside her and her own orgasm pulsed through her, she felt a tear slip from one eye.

How would she ever meet another man like this?

One who could pleasure her in the way he did.

One who treated her like a damn princess.

A queen.

Not because of his wallet, but the way he looked at her.

Like she was his.

CHAPTER SEVENTEEN

"**J**ackson Wiles and Kristen Holle," he said to the security guy, and the rope was lifted for them.

He folded the cuffs of his black Armani silk shirt up his forearms and straightened his Phillipe Patek watch, then took Kristen's hand and led her inside.

"Wow," she said, pressing her body against his.

Jackson wrapped his arm around her possessively. It had taken all his control to not say anything about the black dress she'd put on tonight.

As in, "Over my fucking dead body you're wearing that."

Or…"Technically, is that even a dress?"

Hell, he'd grown up in L.A. He should be used to women dressing so minimally. But when she'd walked out, he'd stood, frozen.

The black fabric, which covered her ass, hung so low down her back it was nearly illegal. The front draped as casually across her breasts, like it was just there for a good time, not a long time.

What if there was a breeze?

Or someone knocked her?

"Is that safe?" he'd ended up asking.

Kristen had frowned. "Is what safe? These shoes?"

God, he hadn't noticed the black stilettos that make her already long, slim legs look fucking incredible.

Maybe they should stay home, he'd thought.

"Do you have a bra on?" he'd asked, to clarify his concerns.

Kristen laughed and spun around. "Does it look like it?"

No. It looked like he'd be punching a whole ton of eyeballs if they even gazed over her body.

Instead, he'd walked over to her and slid his finger down the center of her chest, then nudged the fabric over.

Hello, nipple.

"You want me to fuck you in this club? Because if you wear this, that's what's going to happen," he growled.

Then those green eyes had sparkled with such sexual mischief, he nearly tossed her back on the bed and tied her up.

He should have.

Jackson glanced around. They were standing in the club, just as he'd expected, and men were blatantly staring at her.

Tonight was clearly the night he was going to get arrested for killing someone.

"Stay close," he growled and began to work their way through the crowd.

DREAM was the hottest new bar in New York, and everyone who was anyone was on the list. That meant the place was full of money and high fashion.

And drugs.

The latter, he didn't touch.

"My God, all these women are gorgeous," Kristen said, her mouth gaping at everything.

"You're beautiful. You outshine every fucking single one of them."

She slowed.

"Why are you so grouchy tonight?" she asked, frowning at him.

"Because I hate that you don't think you fit in," Jackson answered honestly. He did hate it because it meant she didn't feel like she fit with him.

And that wasn't true.

He'd just been inside her, and she fit just perfectly.

Too fucking perfect.

"I don't," she snapped. "This is New York. I'm a middle-class kiwi. That woman is wearing a dress that costs nearly twice my yearly salary."

So?

He'd buy her ten if she wanted. A thousand. He didn't care.

Yeah, he was grouchy. But her leaving was starting to fuck him off. Especially after making love to her before they'd left. She was his.

He couldn't shake that feeling, and it was fucking. Him. Off.

Because he couldn't control her. He couldn't keep her. And she didn't want to come back.

So yeah, grumpy.

"I grew up less than middle-class. Now, I could buy this bar tonight and throw it in the trash," he said.

"That's a weird thing to say," she replied, giving him an odd look.

"I'm just saying. It's just four walls, people, and music. You fit. If I say you fit, you fit."

"Grouchy," she mumbled, as he laid his hand on the small of her back and continued to move through the crowd.

Then he stopped.

Turned.

Cupped her face.

"I'm sorry," he said, loud enough so she could hear over the music. "I am…This is my world. I want you to feel comfortable. I want you here with me. But if you want to leave, we can leave."

When he went to pull his arm away, she gripped his forearm.

"How are you so amazing?" she asked, and they stood there, staring at one another for a long moment. "You're right. When you look at me like this, it doesn't matter if I'm wearing a ten-dollar dress or a ten-thousand-dollar dress. I feel like I belong. With you."

His mouth slammed down on hers as he tugged her against him. The music pounded around them, but all he felt was her.

Her soft luscious lips, her pulse beating in time with his. *Her soul speaking to mine.*

When they finally pulled apart, he smiled as her glossy emerald globes held his, waiting for instruction. Submitting to him as if she was already his.

"You want to leave?" Jackson asked.

"No," she said in a breathy voice. "I want to dance with you."

Fuck yes.

That, he was totally into.

As long as that damn dress stayed put.

A FEW minutes later, they found Fletcher and Olivia. The two women flung their arms around each other and began chatting away.

Fletcher reached out his hand and, with a strong grip, shook Jackson's. "Glad you could make it, Jackson."

"Thanks again for the invite. And the boat."

Fletcher snorted.

"I didn't break it. It's back in its box," Jackson added. "Fuck, its huge."

The 120-meter superyacht was impressive, but so was the way the captain had navigated the large craft in and out of its mooring.

"So, is this your life? Coming to these events?" Jackson asked, glancing around the room as Fletcher handed him a glass of what looked like whisky.

"Macallan. Eighteen year," Fletcher said, as Jackson lifted it to his nose. "It *was* my life. Now I have a fiancé and stepdaughter, and a little one on the way, we don't go out as often. Or it's a quick pop in after work, then I just want to get home as fast as possible, if I'm honest."

Jackson was beginning to understand why.

He nodded and glanced over at Kristen. who was chatting with Olivia and sipping on another Monte Carlo. Jackson felt a stupid buzz of happiness that he'd introduced her to the infamous drink.

He could imagine feeling like that if he got to keep her.

"What's it like?" Jackson asked, before he could stop the words from falling out.

"Settling down?" Fletcher followed his eyes to Kristen. "Or being in love?"

Love?

No, that wasn't where he was going with this. Or her.

Jackson turned to the bar, shot a look at his half-brother, and laughed. "Yeah, I mean, you look happy. It must be nice. One day, I mean."

Fletcher laughed and slapped him on the back.

"Let me give you a piece of advice. When it happens, don't fight it. And don't fuck it up. I've had my share of women, so trust me."

That was no secret. Most of the world knew Fletcher was the playboy of Manhattan.

Was. Obviously, past tense.

His conquests were infamous.

How long he'd been in love with Olivia, no one knew, but they'd worked together for longer than they'd been engaged. No doubt, there was an interesting story behind that.

"When the right one comes along, you'll know. Admitting it before you lose them is the difficult part," Fletcher said, letting out a dry laugh.

Jackson turned. "You nearly lost Olivia?"

They both watched the women as Fletcher nodded.

"Her and Sammy. They're a package. I love that little girl and her mother with every fucking thing I am," Fletcher admitted, with such intensity it nearly bowled him over.

Jesus.

Jackson knew this conversation was going somewhere and began to get uncomfortable. Not just the conversation, but where his mind was going.

Kristen's eyes lifted, and she smiled at him. He shot her a smile, then glanced away.

Shit.

Was he…? No.

If he couldn't keep her—and all signs pointed to him not being able to, at this point—then he needed to guard his heart. There was a lot going on in his life right now, and it was important to focus. He'd put his business aside for a few days for her, and that had to be enough.

Now, it looked like he was gaining traction with his family. Being here tonight with Fletcher was a great start.

Then tonight, while Kristen had been in the shower, he'd called his mom. Jenna said she was tired, but the doctor had said she was doing well.

It had to stay that way.

At least until he got home and spoke to her. He wasn't going to do it on the phone. But Johnathan would push to see her, and so he had a week to calmly tell Jenna what he'd discovered.

If she reacted badly, he would tell Johnathan to stay away. Or fucking move her so the man couldn't find her.

Jackson wasn't above doing anything to keep his mother alive.

"I didn't realize this was a family get-together," a voice behind him said, as Addison went flying past and Kristen threw her arms around the woman. "Oh my god. I'm so glad we got to see you again before you leave," Addison cried.

People needed to stop talking about her leaving.

"Hey, bro," Fletcher said. "I invited Jackson. Thought you weren't coming?"

Jackson turned.

So that was why he got the invite? Hunter still hated him, clearly.

"The girls texted. I was forced," Hunter said.

The corners of Jackson's lips twitched, but he hid it as he lifted his whisky.

Hunter stared at him. Jackson drank his drink while holding the man's gaze. He wasn't going to be intimidated.

"So, can't find any dirt on you. Either you are the boy genius you say you are and have covered your tracks. Or…"

"Or I'm some government spy hoping to, what? Commandeer hotel rooms for UN officials?" Jackson asked, laughing.

"I have some theories," Hunter said, lifting his chin at the barman. "Macallan and a Cosmo."

Jackson glanced at Fletcher, who shrugged.

Addison danced over and took her drink. "Hey, Jackson."

He smiled at her as she went back to the girls. They headed onto the dance floor. His eyes followed Kristen, watching as she began to move her hips and laugh.

"Daniel know you're with that girl?" Hunter asked, taking a long draw on his drink.

Without taking his eyes off her, Jackson said, "It's none of Daniel's business. And trust me, she's not a girl."

She was a woman.

Five years his senior. Well, four years and nine months. Was that a concern for her?

"Well, I see you're fucked," Hunter said, and Fletcher spat out his drink.

"I was working up to that but, yeah. That," Fletcher said, grabbing a napkin off the bar, laughing.

Jackson glared at the two men. His brothers.

"What the fuck are you talking about?"

They both burst out laughing.

"You going to tell him?" Fletcher asked.

"Hell no. This is way too much fun to watch. Like a car crash," Hunter said. "If only Daniel was here. Words I never thought I'd say."

Fletcher laughed some more, throwing his head back.

Jackson let out a growl and decided to ignore them.

He turned back to Kristen.

"Absolutely fucked," Hunter said, snickering. "Glad I came now."

Fucking idiot.

Jackson continued to ignore them.

He knew what they were getting at and, frankly, didn't like the implication of their words and that he would fail.

No. He had to decide if he did want to keep Kristen. And admit his feelings. Because he wanted it as much as he was fighting it, and that was twisting him around in circles.

First, he needed to know what she felt.

Then, if she had the same feelings as him, they needed to decide what this meant. Money might not be an issue, but did he really want a long-term relationship? With someone who lived so far away?

With a woman who could tear his heart out and toss it away if she decided to change her mind once she got home and reconsidered?

A man dancing near the girls bumped *accidentally* into Kristen. *Asshole*. She turned, and he smiled at her.

No fucking way.

Jackson's body moved before he realized what was happening. A strong hand gripped his arm.

"Watch," Hunter growled in his ear. "She's turned away from him."

"Let go of my arm," Jackson hissed, and the sound even freaked him out. It was dark and deadly.

Hunter held onto him for a split second longer, then released him.

"One wrong move, and that woman will kick your ass clean across the country, my friend. I just bought you some time to get your inner wolf under control."

Wolf?

Jackson narrowed his eyes.

"You want to claim her. Own her. You need to find out what she desires. What she wants," Hunter said, nodding to Addison. "You think I got a woman like that by flying in half-assed?"

Fletcher cleared his throat.

"Okay, fine. I did a little and totally fucked it up. But I quickly learned."

Jackson watched Kristen turn from the man and then continue dancing with the girls.

She lifted her arms and swayed to the beat of the music. Like a sexy goddess.

"I don't want to own her," Jackson said.

"Yes, you do," Hunter replied. "Men like us don't do anything else."

Men like us? What did that mean?

Dufort men?

Jackson shook his head. "Just because I'm your half-brother doesn't mean we're the same."

Hunter took a sip of his drink, his eyes holding Jackson's for a long moment.

"It's nothing to do with the Dufort bloodline." He shot a look at Fletcher. "I'm talking about dominant alpha-type men. All four of us are controlling bastards, but I see the fire in the way you watch her. I know that look."

Jackson watched Hunter slide his eyes over Addison's body, and it all clicked into place.

When he turned back to his brother, Hunter nodded.

"Dominance, brother. You are more like me than I want to admit. Fucking typical," Hunter said, shaking his head and sipping his drink again. Then he asked, "You ever been to a sex club?"

Jackson shrugged. "Once."

He couldn't believe he was having this conversation, but now he was, he could see the same thing in his brother. The desire to own the woman they…liked.

Or loved.

Whatever.

"Not my scene, but no judgement," Fletcher said, turning to get them more drinks.

The sex club had been an incredible experience. What he'd seen had been some kinky shit.

Some of it turned him on. Some of it didn't.

Finding a woman to experiment on, not pay, was another thing. Paying for sex did not work for him. That was a turn off.

"You ever want to go again, here's my club," Hunter said, slipping him a black card with a single name and number on it. "There's a criteria for joining, but your first visit is open."

Jackson stared down at the card. "You own a sex club?"

"Officially, no," Hunter said, then a dark look filled his eyes. "Though, I'm sure *you* would find it if you went digging. Fucking hackers."

Jackson smirked.

He tucked the card into the pocket of his Armani pants.

"Some of it was hot," Jackson said finally. "Not sure it's a lifestyle thing for me, but you're right. I want to dominate her. I'm holding back."

"Don't," Hunter said. "You want to keep her, claim her. If not, let her go."

Jackson didn't bother answering. Simply nodded.
Hunter was right.
He had to decide.

CHAPTER EIGHTEEN

Jackson walked over to the dance floor, slid an arm around her back, and spun and dipped Kristen, dropping his mouth on hers.

Kristen giggled.

"Hard to kiss you when you're laughing, sexy kitten," he growled playfully.

She pressed her body to his when he straightened her, and he felt like he'd won the lottery. Like every man in the club was rich with envy.

"You're gorgeous, do you know that?" He took her hips, moving them on the dance floor.

Kristen smiled, and he knew she was blushing. He shook his head and let out a small laugh.

"How can you be shy about a compliment like that when I've had my face between your legs?"

"Jackson!" She laughed. "You and your naughty talk."

"You love it."

Her eyes dropped. "I've never met a man like you. My boyfriend's weren't as…nice as you."

Nice? Who the hell were these assholes she was dating?

"Maybe you could be a nun," he teased, knowing he didn't want her being with another man but him.

Kristen laughed. "Pretty sure I wouldn't qualify."

When the song ended, they returned to the bar. Jackson ordered shots.

Tequila.

"This is a bad idea," Kristen said. "I'm flying tomorrow."

"It's a great idea. I haven't seen you drunk since the night I met you." He winked, handing her a shot glass. "Let's get a little tipsy."

"Just one, then," she said.

Kristen held the glass to her lips, then reached out and tapped it against his glass. "To a holiday romance I wasn't expecting, with an incredible man."

"To the sexiest woman I've ever laid eyes on," he purred, winking at her.

They shot back the smooth Clase Azul Tequila.

Kristen did a little dance on the spot. "Holy shit, that burns."

He laughed and ordered them another one. After that went down, she leaned her hip against the bar.

"I have a confession."

Ah, Tequila. It was like a truth serum.

Jackson's lips twitched. "My evil plan is working."

"Stop. Let me say this," she said, slapping her hand against his pec, and he grabbed it, holding her hand against his black silk shirt.

"Okay, go."

"I kissed you. That night. In the cab," she said, nodding.

His smile grew. "I know."

Kristen shook her head. "I was so embarrassed. I thought you were going to kiss me, but then you began to speak, and oh God—"

"Sweetheart. I wanted to kiss you about one thousand times before that," Jackson said, taking her by the hip and pulling her tightly against him. "Why do you think I kissed you back so hungrily?"

Kristen tiptoed up to his mouth as he lowered to hers.

"See, now we're in sync." His hand slid down to her ass, cupping it.

"Hey, lovers," Addison said, leaning into them in a drunken way. "Kris, time to powder our noses."

Olivia stood a foot behind her, rubbing her growing belly.

Jackson released Kristen. "Go. But come back to me quickly," he whispered into her ear.

Kristen grinned and left with the girls.

When he turned back to his brothers, they were both wearing shit-eating grins.

"Don't say a word."

CHAPTER NINETEEN

"**O**kay, first. Holy crap. Jackson," Addison said as they walked into the restroom and stood in the short queue.

"If anyone isn't urgent, can you let the pregnant lady go first?" Olivia called out.

No one moved.

"Typical," she mumbled.

"I know, I know. He apologized," Kristen said, "At *The Plaza*."

Both women raised their brows. Even the lady in front of them turned and gave her a look that said she was impressed.

"Dinner?" Olivia asked.

Kristen nodded. "Dinner."

"Okay, that's smooth," Addison said, as they took a step forward.

"Plus, you know, it was all about meeting his family. I get it. The Dufort's are intimidating. A big wealthy family. Which you both know. So, imagine how he felt."

Addison tucked her purse under her arm. "I guess. It's not like you can be all, '*hey, I'm, like, your son.*'"

Kristen knew she would understand.

"I'm proud of Fletch for reaching out. Family is important to him," Olivia said, dancing on the spot, clearly about to burst. Then she turned to Addison. "Did Hunter get the message about their grandmother being unwell?"

Kristen frowned.

"What grandmother?" she asked. There had been no grandparents at Harper's wedding, nor had she ever heard anything about one.

Addison nodded. "Yeah. Apparently, Johnathan is estranged with his mother and brother. And she's sick. He's estranged with his niece and nephews as well," Addison added. "That's sad, although I'm not surprised, if I'm honest. Johnathan is a polarizing character."

Wait. What?

"There are more Dufort's?" Kristen gasped.

The two women nodded.

"Yes. Logan, and I don't know the other two names," Olivia said. "Johnathan has asked us all to go to brunch tomorrow morning to discuss it."

Oh.

Kristen chewed her lip as they all took another step forward. The queue shortening.

"Thank God. I'm going first, in case there's any confusion," Olivia said, now bouncing up and down.

What did she do?

If Jackson hadn't gotten an invite to the brunch, she'd have to say something to him. She couldn't *not* tell him. Kristen didn't want him hurt like that.

He had a right to know his entire family.

Perhaps he'd been invited and not mentioned it to her. Which she would be fine with. But if not…

"Do you think you could…"

Olivia glanced back at her.

Kristen didn't want to cross the line, but if she could just do this one thing for him. "Could you make sure Jackson is invited? Maybe speak to one of the guys?"

Addison scrunched up her face. "I don't think we should get involved."

Kristen let out a sigh.

"I know. But…" If they could just understand… "His mom is sick, and he's trying to find where he fits in the world. Now the man he thought was his dad has died. This is important to him. He deserves to know he has a grandmother and see her before she dies too."

"Oh, I didn't know. I'm so sorry," Olivia said.

"Yeah, that's horrible. Is she seriously ill?" Addison asked.

Kristen nodded. "Cancer."

Olivia bolted toward the cubicle as soon as it became free, nodding. "Leave it with me. I'll do my best."

Addison shot her a smile. Kristen felt a weight lift off her shoulders, knowing these two knew the situation and would be able to support him when she left.

In twenty-four hours, Jackson Wiles would be a holiday romance. Someone she once knew.

A memory she would hold onto forever.

Her heart felt heavy, and tears prickled in her eyes. Brushing the sadness away, she just wanted to race back out into the club and throw herself into his arms.

And tell him to never let her go.

But cancer was a fucking bitch, and she could never do that to her parents.

Not that he was asking her to stay.

Or that she could.

But for a moment, it was just nice to admit to herself she really, really like Jackson.

Maybe even a bit more than simply *like*.

Shit.

KRISTEN followed the girls back out into the club. As they turned the corner, she spotted Jackson, standing with his brothers. All of them looked like something out of a dark mafia novel.

They were all in black. Tall, solid, and muscular, with dark thick hair and eyes blazing with desire for the women walking toward them.

Including Jackson.

For her.

Ugh. She wanted to keep this man.

How was she going to go back to her life and just forget all of this? Simply wake up, drink her smoothie, drive through boring rush hour traffic, walk to her store, and start preparing bouquets.

With no Jackson.

There would be no gruff, "Good morning, sexy," greeting and morning sex. No gorgeous man standing behind her, brushing his teeth as she did the same, almost losing his brush as he grinned at her.

No one squeezing her ass every two or three minutes of the day. She slapped him each time, but as it turned out, she loved it.

And that accent of his.

How was she going to survive without hearing that smooth purr of his deep voice right beside her, in her hair.

His lips on hers.

On her neck, her belly, her nipples.

Between her legs.

Or his eyes, those rich sexual eyes following every step she made.

Even now.

"You were gone too long," Jackson growled, tugging her against him. Then he stilled. "What's wrong?"

"Nothing."

"Don't lie. What is it?"

His entire body had stiffened, and he looked around for some invisible enemy. She lay her head on his chest.

"Fuck, Kris. Tell me. I'm ready to break a neck or something."

She felt his strong arms wrap around her as she laid a hand on his thick bicep.

"Nobody has hurt me," she said, letting him lift her chin. "Well, except myself."

"Explain," he growled again, quieter this time.

Kristen let out a sigh, reaching to run her fingers over his scruff.

"I'm going to miss you. That's all. This time tomorrow, I will be boarding my plane."

The muscle in his jaw twitched. "I know."

Darkness swirled in his eyes as they stared at one another.

"Bro," Fletcher said.

Jackson drew his eyes away from her and glanced over her head. "Yup?"

"Has dad texted you about brunch tomorrow morning?" Fletcher asked.

Kristen had to give it to Olivia. She worked fast.

"Yes."

"Make sure you go."

Jackson glanced down at her, then back at his brothers, nodding. "I will be there."

Kristen smiled.

Well, at least she was leaving knowing he was making good leeway with his family.

When his eyes returned to hers, she sighed. Kristen didn't want him worrying about her. Or making a drama about her leaving. They had always agreed it would only be four days of sexy fun.

"Sorry, I think I'm just drunk and emotional. Stupid Tequila," she said.

He let out a type of masculine groan that ripped right through her body, heating her from…well, her lady bits and beyond.

"No, baby, you're not. And we're going home," he said thickly.

A shiver ran through her as he ran his hand down her bare back, sliding under her dress as he turned her from the crowd.

They said their goodbyes and promised to see them all at brunch tomorrow.

CHAPTER TWENTY

Jackson held Kristen's hand tightly as they drove back to the hotel.

If he could just freeze time…

The way she'd looked at him when confessing she would miss him had hit him right in the chest, creating a tight feeling that wouldn't ease. He'd hoped she was feeling something deeper, and now—*thank you, fucking Tequila*—she had shown her cards.

It was clear as day in her eyes when they were making love, but lust was a liar at times.

Now, he knew.

Love?

Yeah, it was. He wasn't just fucking her anymore. Maybe he never had been.

The powerful sense of protectiveness that had hit him when she'd returned from the bathrooms had felt like a knife stabbing him. It overtook any common sense he had. How the hell did he protect her when she was halfway across the damn world?

Answer: he couldn't.

So that was a problem.

One he was intending to resolve.

Kristen had been such a trooper, acting like she was fine with leaving, but he knew she wasn't.

As she had given the big, "I'll probably never see you again," speech to the girls while hugging them, Jackson had told her adamantly she was coming with him to brunch.

The girls had all shared a strange look, one he didn't care to translate. Women had their own language, and that was fine.

He now had a goal.

As the driver sped through Manhattan traffic, at a mighty five miles an hour, he glanced down at his girl.

"Do you want to stop anywhere? See anything?" he asked softly, his voice thick.

She shook her head.

"Want to buy anything? It's your last night," Jackson said. Whatever she wanted, he'd make sure she got it.

"I know it's my last night," Kristen snapped quietly. "You don't need to remind me."

Fuck.

"Baby." He reached around and pulled her onto his lap.

She tucked her head under his chin and clung to him.

Goddamn the stupid time. *Stop, you fucker.*

"What do you want to do? Anything. I'll make it happen," Jackson said thickly. "Please, baby. I don't know what to do."

He heard the sniff and lifted her chin. A tear slid down her cheek.

"I'm just drunk."

No, she wasn't. Well, yes, she was, but that wasn't causing her tears.

Jackson smiled softly. "You know I'm going to fucking miss you too, right?"

She nodded. Then shook her head.

"I don't want to regret this. I've been happier the past few days than…maybe ever," Kristen said.

Holy shit, she was killing him. Because the truth was, so had he.

"I want to take you somewhere. Then we'll go home," Jackson suddenly said.

Her eyes widened. "Where?"

"Somewhere you have to go before leaving New York. It's U.S. law. We don't let people leave unless they've been." He kissed her nose, smirking.

It was spur of the moment and cheesy, but Jackson hadn't been to this tourist spot himself, and there was only one person on Earth he wanted to do this with.

Right fucking now.

"Color me intrigued," she said, climbing off his lap.

Jackson gave the driver new directions and then sat back and clutched her hand again. They'd just driven past the Flatiron building, so it didn't take long, once they turned onto Fifth Avenue, to reach their destination.

It was only midnight, so they still had two hours. Jackson climbed out, reaching for Kristen's hand.

"Where are we?"

"Come," he said, leading her into the lobby of the Empire State Building.

"Oh. Oh!" she gasped.

He watched her take in the ornate gold walls, monuments, and the U.S. flags, while he purchased their tickets.

"It's so…dramatic."

Jackson sniggered.

They waited patiently for an elevator, then began the long ascent to the 102 Floor. While she leaned against him, tucked under his arm, Kristen read all the paraphernalia on the walls of the elevator.

"So, fun fact," he said. "The Empire State Building antenna is struck by lightning around twenty-five times a year."

Her eyes widened.

"Don't tell me that. With my luck, it will be tonight," Kristen gasped.

He snorted.

"Okay, how about this one, then. This building is Uber's most demanded address in the entire United States."

Jackson might have Googled these facts when looking at things to do while she was in the Hamptons. Was he optimistic then? A little.

"That's kind of impressive," Kristen said, as the doors opened.

Jackson stood, letting her step out of the lifts first, waiting for her response. Yet his own eyes lifted and took in the view.

It didn't matter how many times he'd seen images online or other friends' social posts; the impact was nothing short of spectacular. He'd spent weeks in New York City already, and yet from this height, it was hard not to feel like the world was your oyster.

Or that people were just tiny specs of dust in this huge universe.

Jackson reminded himself of the luck he'd had so far in his life. A great education. A loving mother. Intelligence and tenacity that had contributed to him creating a business he loved working in, which provided a wonderful lifestyle and opportunities.

Kristen walked slowly over to the floor-to-ceiling glass windows and silently stared out across Manhattan. When he walked up behind her and stood with his hands in his pockets, she leaned back into him. As if it was the most natural thing in the world to do. Like they were connected.

Jackson's heart missed a beat.

His entire body reacted, his temperature hitching up a notch and his cock twitching.

"Spectacular," she said with a sigh, and he drew in her honey vanilla scent, trying to commit it to memory because, as determined as he was, he couldn't be sure he'd be successful.

In business, yes.

In many other areas of his life, yes.

With this beautiful woman from the other side of the world? No. Jackson wasn't confident, and he knew, outside the bedroom, he couldn't control Kristen.

They stood there for a long while, looking at all the famous iconic spots and reveling in the starry night and lights of the city.

A plane appeared in the sky.

"My God, we're higher than the aircraft," Kristen gasped quietly. "I'm so glad we came." She turned, and he slipped his hands out of his pockets and laid them on her hips. "Thank you for bringing me. I'm sure it's boring for you, being American."

Jackson's lips stretched into a smile. "Sweetheart, this is my first time. I wanted to come here with you so we could experience it together."

A little gasp left her lips. "Really?"

"Yes, really." He smiled, knowing the moment was perfect.

Jackson slid a hand into one of his deep pockets and pulled out a velvet pouch. A dark blue one.

Kristen's eyes dropped, then shot back to his sharply.

His heart pounded in his chest, and he could only imagine the emotion burning in his eyes as she looked at him questioningly.

Kristen swallowed.

"When I first met you, you took my breath away," Jackson began.

Her eyes began to glisten.

"I know you think I took advantage of you, and perhaps on some level, I did, but the truth is, it wouldn't have mattered who you were. When those beautiful green eyes met mine from across the room, I was hooked."

"Jackson, you don't—" She began to say, but he quickly tipped the item out into his hand and took her wrist.

"Wear this every day. Remember me when you look at it. Know that you'll always be in my heart," Jackson said, his throat tight. "Always."

He wanted to ask her for more, but he wasn't sure, really sure, it was what she wanted. Tonight was their last night, and he was going to make sure it was special.

Not ruin it with discussions of what could be. Or worse, her rejecting him.

Tonight, they were together, under the Manhattan skies, standing above the world and staring down.

"Oh my goodness," Kristen said, watching as he put the emerald and diamond bracelet on her arm.

Jackson had seen it the day he'd purchased her DIOR dress and knew she had to have it. Harry Winston had taken a chunk of his cash, and he'd been happy to hand it over.

Especially watching her eyes fly open as the three carats of diamonds and green gems sparkled under the night sky.

"This is...beautiful...Too much. It's..." Kristen started up at him, her mouth gaping like a fish. "Are you sure about this?"

He let out a laugh.

"Did you not hear what I just said, little kitten?" He took her face and softly kissed her at first, then as her arms wrapped around him, it deepened.

God, he didn't want to let her go.

Not tonight and not tomorrow.

How had this happened?

When they parted, he wiped a tear away from her cheek and smiled at her. Her beauty glowing and filling him like a super nova.

"I wish..."

"What do you wish?" Jackson asked quietly, their eyes locked.

She swallowed again.

"I wish I could stay. With you," Kristen said softly, vulnerably.

"I know," Jackson said, even though he hadn't been completely sure. But God, it was incredible to hear her say it.

Hope sprung inside him.

"I'm glad you didn't stay away," she added, and the air was thick with unsaid things, promises waiting to be made, love waiting to be invited.

Jackson felt his patience slipping. He was a man who took control, but every cell in his body was telling him to wait. To not push.

Fuck, he hated this.

"Shall we go back to the hotel? I'm going to take my time pleasuring you tonight. All night," his voice thick.

"Promise?"

"Sweetheart, I swear on my life." Jackson winked, lightening the mood because, otherwise, he might seriously start saying things neither of them were ready for.

They walked around the observation deck, taking in the panoramic views, then caught the elevator back down. His driver out on the street was waiting for them when they stepped out of the building.

KRISTEN couldn't stop staring at her bracelet on the drive back to the Waldorf-Astoria.

Well, that wasn't entirely true. Her eyes had darted from the bracelet and up to Jackson's beautiful face. It was like she was trying to commit every detail to memory. His expression could only be described as intense and wild. Like he was ready to explode and ravish her at the same time.

His eyes gleamed with desire and more.

It was the *more* that surprised her.

Kristen was expecting Jackson to grab her the moment the door closed behind them, but he didn't. They walked into the bedroom, his body close behind hers, then slowly, he placed his hands on her shoulders.

A shiver went through her.

His lips gently kissed her neck and made their way down her back. Her dress slipped to the ground, and she was unaware of how he'd undone it, his mouth distracting her.

"I'm going to need complete and absolute control tonight," Jackson growled low.

Her throat hitched.

"Can you give me that?" he asked.

"Yes," she whispered as a moan slipped out when he cupped her breast.

Then his hand was sliding between her legs, under her panties. "Legs apart, kitten."

She did as he said and reached behind, grabbing his thighs for some sort of stability. Kristen felt as if her world was tipping.

Thick skilled fingers slid inside her wet folds as he groaned into her ear, nibbling on it and sending her pulse skyrocketing.

"I'm going to taste you as you fuck my cock with your hot mouth," Jackson said, moving her to the bed. "Take off your lingerie and climb on the bed."

He removed his fingers and undid his shirt as she turned to watch him.

Because watching Jackson Wiles get naked was a gift all on its own.

His Californian tanned skin, large chest, and muscular arms were an aphrodisiac on their own. Those thick powerful thighs were bared next as his pants dropped to the floor.

And commando.

Her core clenched as his cock slapped against his stomach, his eyes waiting for hers to lift.

But Kristen was licking her lips.

Then his hand was on it, stroking.

"On the bed kitten. My patience is thin. You'll get a taste very soon," he said.

Fucking hell. No one had ever been this way before. The dirty way he talked, the total dominance. It was sexy as hell, and she was pretty certain she would hate sex with anyone else for the rest of her life.

Climbing on the bed before she got her ass slapped, she watched Jackson grab a condom and throw it in the center. Then he kneeled on the bed and took her lips. Hard, deep, and passionately as he cupped her ass, squeezing. He pulled them down onto the cover, and her body lay over his.

Between them, his hard erection pulsed.

"Sit up," he said, taking her breasts in his hands as she did. He flicked her nipples, and she rested her hands on his pecs. "So gorgeous. So damn reactive. Look at these hard peaks."

Her hands ran over his solid muscle, and she tried not to reach and slide his cock inside her. Kristen was getting her cream all over it as she wiggled.

"Now let me taste you," Jackson said, lifting and spinning her so her pussy was over his face.

"Oh God," she said as his hands gripped her ass and he spread her wide. "Oh, my fucking yes, do that."

His tongue licked the length of her. The entire length. Her ass puckering at the sensation.

"Oh shitt," she cried, her body pressing into his face.

Kristen's trembling hands landed on his thighs.

"God, you are delicious. Wet, hot, and fucking delicious," Jackson said. "Put your mouth on me, kitten, and go slow. We have all night."

She wasn't sure she would last all night, but then again, he had surprised her all week, so if there were five orgasms awaiting her, then who was she to fight it.

Leaning, she grabbed his shaft and stroked. His head already leaked pre-cum. Her tongue darted out and lapped at it.

As he moaned, his teeth clamped around her clit.

Kristen cried out.

"Mouth on my cock. Now," he growled, nipping some more.

Bending down as Jackson began lapping with speed, she took him in her mouth. Thick throbbing cock filled her while she sucked and rocked against the pleasure at her core.

Was it supposed to be this amazing?

Her body shuddering. Her heart open and feeling wild. Her mind obsessed with the man underneath her.

She was terrified and unable to stop.

He had taken control—of every part of her.

Jackson spread her cheeks wider, and his thumb pressed against her hole. The rear one, and she naturally pulled away.

"Kitten," he growled. "You can stop me, but you know the drill."

Right.

If she stopped him.

It was over.

"I want all of you. Every inch. Every orifice," he grunted, licking and sliding his fingers inside her.

"Oh fuuck," she said, letting his cock slide out of her mouth.

Faster, he pressed them in and out, as his thumb and tongue continued to tease her ass.

Kristen gripped the head of his cock and resumed the blow job.

"God, baby. That is…fuck yes. Suck harder. Yes," he cried.

Then his tongue was back on her clit, and he sucked and lapped with an unnatural speed. Her mind departed. Her body shuddered and exploded into a million stars.

"Come baby," Jackson cried, continuing his sucking, lapping, and fucking her pussy with his fingers.

She came off his cock again and began to cry out. "Jackson, oh God, God, God."

Before her convulsions were over, he had her flipped around, straddling him once more. A condom wrapper ripped, and somehow, she felt the strength to sit on her knees while he sheathed himself.

Then those fiery eyes of his were locked to hers.

"Take me inside you, beautiful," Jackson said, guiding her onto his thick hard cock.

Kristen slid down, his hands around her waist as she held his biceps. The intense connection between them skyrocketed. His eyes burned with an emotion she'd not yet seen, and she knew hers were doing the same.

They said nothing, their expressions rich with desire and need, yet their silence said a million things.

So much more than they had dared to share.

Kristen began to move, her mouth sliding open, her panting loud in the air. His moans of "yes" and "fuck yes" blending with the sounds of their bodies' pleasure.

Jackson sat up, taking her mouth in his, their tongues wild and licking. Uncaring about getting it right. He nipped her, then moved to her neck. Then he took one of her breasts, and his thumb pressed harshly against a nipple.

She gasped, the friction against his body on her clit raising the stakes.

"Oh God."

"Come here," Jackson said, lying back down, pulling her body with him. "Eyes on me as you come."

She wasn't sure she could again.

Not so soon.

God, she'd been wrong.

His hand slid around her body, stretching her cheeks wide, and one of his fingers pressed on that sensitive hole again.

Kristen stifled a loud groan.

Unsure but wanting to please him. Her eyes locking with his.

"Trust me, kitten," Jackson said.

Kristen knew it was an order, which was hot as hell—she loved his dominance—but there was a hint of question.

Could she?

Her body was pressing into his finger, wanting more. It was new. That was all. The sensation out-of-this-world erotic.

She nodded.

As Kristen rode his shaft, her clitoris rubbing against his body, Jackson pressed a finger in her ass. Pleasure unlike anything she'd experienced before ripped through her body.

Her body locked.

Jackson took over with his one free hand, moving her body and milking the orgasm from them both as his hips lifted to go deeper.

He cried out, "Kris, fuck, fuck," and some other incoherent words.

Then, as she collapsed on his chest, he wrapped his arms around her tightly, his lips against her neck, shudders from both their bodies continuing like aftershocks of an earthquake.

An hour later, Jackson was inside her again. This time, she was under him, and it was slow, lazy, and their orgasms had them arching into one another.

Finally, as the early hours crept closer, Jackson tucked her against him, laying a leg over her. "We should sleep."

Moonlight threw shadows around the room, allowing her to see his face. He wiped the hair from her damp forehead.

"So beautiful." His voice a soft growl.

"Thank you," she replied, when what she really wanted to say was, *Damn you, I'm in love with you.*

How was she going to go back to her life and just forget him?

After tonight, there no forgetting this man. A connection so deep had formed between them, and yet, he said nothing.

Kristen wasn't mad. If anything, her heart felt full but heavy. How could she regret this incredible experience?

"Don't think, baby. Just sleep," he said, kissing her with what felt like the most precious love, until they literally passed out.

CHAPTER TWENTY-ONE

When her mobile phone lit up from beside the bed, Kristen reached for it. She figured it was around four in the morning.

After that spellbinding kiss, Kristen thought she'd crash all night, but her brain had woken her up, and she'd been lying there, overthinking her entire life, for the past hour.

Harper.

Hey babes, how's tourist life? You fly home today, right? Your today. It's only 11pm here in Hawaii.

Kristen turned her head.

Jackson was lying on his back, his gorgeous muscular chest on display, with the sheet bunched over his groin, his arm underneath her.

He never *not* touched her. They were always connected, even in sleep.

She smiled softly.

He was so damn gorgeous.

And sexy.

And incredible.

Kristen gently moved and climbed out of bed, tiptoeing out to the living area of the hotel room. She stood staring out the window with her arms crossed, her mobile phone clutched in her hand.

Today was departure day. She was heading back to New Zealand and leaving Jackson.

Her heart felt heavy.

She'd enjoyed New York far more than she thought she would. At first, it had been a culture shock. Auckland was a busy city but nothing compared to the *Big Apple*. The energy had hit her the moment she arrived.

It wasn't just that. So much had happened while she was here.

Getting to know Olivia and Addison and forming genuine friendships with them. Harper's bachelorette party. Their wedding weekend in the Hampton's.

Meeting Jackson.

Falling in love with Jackson.

Kristen drew in a bumpy breath and played with the dazzling diamond and emerald bracelet on her arm.

She had.

She was one hundred percent in love with a damn American.

Dad is going to kill me.

Kristen knew after their dinner at The Plaza—heck, even before then—she liked him. A lot. But she never expected to fall in love with him.

Or this quickly.

She'd tried very hard to keep a barrier up, but it was like they fit together like two pieces of a puzzle. Even while trying not to bond with him, she had.

Lying awake, she had questioned every single feeling. A four-day romance was hardly real life. So was it actually possible to fall in love with someone? To really fall in love under these circumstances?

At home, he probably left the toilet seat up or squeezed the toothpaste tube all the wrong ways.

Or threw wet towels on the ground.

Worked long hours or cheated on his girlfriends.

The fact was, she didn't know him in his real life, so how could she claim to love him? She knew Jackson in New York City, who was wining and dining her. Impressing her. This was a dream, a romantic bubble, they were living.

No laundry.

No bills.

No real life challenges.

Not that Jackson had any problem paying bills, but that wasn't the point.

Still, her heart pounded away as she remembered all the ways he touched her. The way he gazed at her when he thought she didn't know—then she'd catch his eye, and he'd hold hers, sending shivers through her body. He'd look away as if he too was struggling with the intensity of their connection.

Except when they made love.

Even when Jackson was rough, or domineering, the blaze she saw in his eyes told her everything; this wasn't a holiday fling for him either.

He wanted her.

Yet, he'd said nothing more after asking her to visit LA. Then again, why would he? She had shut that conversation down.

Plus, Kristen lived on the other side of the world. Being together would mean frequent travel, or a life commitment because of visa requirements. Neither of them could even consider that discussion right now.

It was way too intense. And insane.

Then, there were their family situations. She couldn't leave her parents at this point in their life. They were too old and frail.

Jackson was trying to piece his life together after losing the man he had thought was his father and meeting Johnathan Dufort. Plus, Daniel, Hunter, and Fletcher.

Now, there was a dying grandmother, an uncle, and three Dufort cousins.

It was a lot.

Kristen knew she had to go home, back to her life, and carry on. Her heart would heal. She would slowly forget him,

Then one day, meet someone else.

Her heart and throat tightened at the same time. She uncrossed her arms and swiped to open her text from Harper.

Yes, flying home tonight. How's the honeymoon?

It's so romantic. But, hey, not to stalk or anything but the security system says you haven't been home. Are you staying with Jackson?

Kristen smiled to herself. She'd told her she was seeing him but not staying with him.

Yes. It's been an amazing four days. I'm…going to miss him.

Like how much?

At least a whole bottle of whisky and two tubs of ice cream.

Shit.

Kristen let out a sigh.

I'll be okay. Work will keep me busy.

…

She heard the sheets rustle.

Gotta go, Harp. Love you. I'll message when I'm home. X

Love you back x

When she went to turn, the warmth of Jackson's body surrounded her.

"What's wrong?" his gruff, deep voice asked.

Kristen turned in his arms and tossed her phone on the sofa, her palms landing on the smooth skin of his pecs. "Harper was messaging from Hawaii."

"That's not why you are awake," he said intuitively, brushing her hair from her face and kissing her forehead. "Talk to me."

She blinked and held his eyes.

Even though they were dark with sleep, that same blazing emotion was there, and she tried to figure out what he might be thinking. Neither of them were willing to open up, and perhaps it was for the best. She'd been over it a million times. There just wasn't the option for them to be anything more than what had been.

"Just reflecting on my holiday, and I guess I couldn't sleep."

"I'm offended. I thought I had devoured you enough for at least a week's sleep," he replied, a twitch in his lips.

"Oh, you did. Maybe even two." She smiled as he pulled her against his chest, his beautiful body fitting perfectly with hers, his constant erection snug between them.

The worry in his eyes still there.

"I'm okay. I get a little nervous before flying, that's all," she said, not completely lying.

Brushing his hand over her hair, he kissed her gently. "In the morning, we'll upgrade you. I want to know you're taken care of."

Be still, my breaking fucking heart.

She didn't try to stop him. Kristen knew it was Jackson's way of showing he cared.

"Thank you," she whispered, giving him a sad smile.

"We'll take your bags with us to brunch, then we can spend the day together and head to the airport after."

She was going to miss this.

Jackson loved making plans, being in control, and while she was used to being independent, a part of her loved letting him take care of her.

No man had ever been as thoughtful or protective as he was. Or sexy. Or funny.

Or just…everything.

"Okay," she said, pressing her lips together.

"I wish I could read your mind," Jackson said. "I wish you'd tell me what you are thinking.

Kristen considered him for a long moment, then said, "Trust me, you really don't."

Because if one of them said what they were thinking, it would only spoil their happy ending.

A sad happy ending, but it was better to leave wondering if maybe it could have been, than to hear that it never could.

Wasn't it?

CHAPTER TWENTY-TWO

Kristen snuggled into Jackson as the driver pulled up to the restaurant where they were meeting the Dufort's.

Jackson wasn't yet comfortable calling them his family, even though he had, and they were. It was taking some adjustment. Plus, he felt this immense disloyalty to his mother, even though he deserved to know his father and half-brothers and be in their lives.

There was a lot going on.

The government meeting had been rescheduled, and now he had to make sure they had a very impressive and solid presentation when they delivered, to make up for the reschedule. He was well aware his decision to reschedule might have been a life changing, stupid decision.

But Jackson was also quietly confident they could pull it off and wow them with his tech. He trusted his team. More than his cock right now.

Still, as he held Kristen in his arms, he found it hard to regret the extra time with her.

Meanwhile, today was about saying goodbye, when every cell in his body wanted to keep her. He was trying to hold it together, but he wasn't sure he would make it to the end of the day without telling her how he felt.

Was he even capable of standing in the airport and watching her walk through the gates?

Fucking doubt it.

Despite their night together, she hadn't opened up about her feelings, and that fucking hurt.

He had to tell her.

Letting her fly home and not telling her he loved her was stupid. If what he felt for her was even a small percent of what he believed she also felt, he was hoping she would be open to being a part of his life.

How and what that looked like, he had no idea, but life without Kristen? No.

Nope.

This was unexpected.

He hadn't been looking for a girlfriend or relationship. Fuck, he was pretty sure this thing between them was far greater than that.

Jackson had told her his biggest secrets. He wanted her in his bed every morning when he woke up. He wanted his mouth on her, his cock inside her.

Her. Not any other woman.

Nor did he want to find himself wondering if some random asshole was touching his woman. Because at some point, Jackson had decided Kristen was his.

When the car stopped, he tilted her chin. She smiled.

"This won't take long, then I'll have you all to myself again," he said, kissing her lips.

She pressed hard into him, and their kiss deepened.

"Jackson...," she said, then glanced away.

"Say it," he growled softly.

She shook her head and wiped at her eyes.

Goddamn her.

"Kris, fuck. You're killing me, sweetheart."

The driver got out.

Jackson locked the doors with the button, knowing the driver would notice and give them a minute.

She sniffed. "I'm sorry."

He turned her face to his again.

Then words from deep inside fell from his lips, like he didn't have a choice in the matter.

Kristen had to know how he felt.

"I'm falling in love with you," he said, holding her chin.

A small gasp left her lips as her eyes widened.

"Oh,"

"Tell me you feel it too," he said, their eyes locking as the world around them vanished. "Say it, Kristen."

She nodded, and a tear fell.

Thank fucking God.

His heart burst open as he caught the tear and felt his face break into a smile the size of Texas.

"Yes, but…"

"Okay. Stop," Jackson said, kissing her. "Let's just enjoy this moment. Without overthinking the future. I love you. You love me. Holy shit."

"I do," Kristen said with a teary smile. "Damn you. Did you plan this?"

He kissed her again, grinning. "I can assure you, I did not plan this."

He glanced out the window toward the restaurant. "Maybe we should cancel. I want to drag you back into bed and show you how much I fucking love you. For hours. All day. Then kidnap you or something."

She giggled, sliding her fingers over his scruff. "No. It's just breakfast. But let's do that afterwards. I don't want to go anywhere. Just be with you."

His heart felt like it exploded open with love for this woman.

Kristen hadn't said no to the kidnapping, so that was good. Jackson pressed a hard kiss against her mouth, then they climbed out of the car.

"We won't be long," he said to the driver.

"Yes, sir. I'll stay close."

KRISTEN ate the last mouthful of her eggs Benedict as the Dufort family sat discussing the health of the grandmother they barely knew.

Jackson leaned in his seat, his arm hanging on the top of her chair.

"Let me get Daniel on the line," Johnathan said.

Next minute, the newlyweds filled the screen, which he propped up against a glass water bottle.

Kristen waved at Harper.

They looked tanned, with palm trees swaying in the background, the sky a beautiful bright blue.

"That's not our hotel," Fletcher said, leaning closer to the screen.

"We're on Maui," Daniel replied. "I'm not having my honeymoon at a Dufort hotel."

"Correction. *You* said we should. *I* said no," Harper said, raising her brows at him with a healthy dose of sass.

Olivia caught Kristen's eye, and they both smirked.

Hunter barked out a laugh. "Why am I not surprised."

Daniel slid an arm around Harper and covered her mouth with his palm. Harper began to giggle, and then they kissed.

Ah, love.

Jackson tickled Kristen's shoulder with the hand wrapped around her. She turned to him, and he winked. Damn him, always making her blush.

But he loved her?

Loved.

L O V E.

Him. Jackson Wiles. Gorgeous, tall, sexy, amazing and…lived in L.A.

But she'd think about that when she got home.

What this meant for them, she didn't know. Instead, following his orders, she was basking in the glow of falling in love.

Wow.

She dropped her hand to his leg, and when his muscle tensed, a desire to be back in the hotel rushed through her.

They shared one more longing glance.

"Right, let me get everyone up to date, as we have some new members of the family," Johnathan said, glancing at the women around the table.

And her.

Kristen blushed again.

Jackson's fingers pressed into her, and a feeling of belonging to him began to cement into her heart.

"My mother is dying. Close to death, from what my nephew, Logan, told me during his call," Johnathan said.

"Logan is the eldest, right?" Fletcher asked.

"I remember him. We met when I was young," Daniel said.

Johnathan nodded. "Shortly after that, I had an argument with my brother, and in a nutshell, I have been estranged from my family since."

Some argument, Kristen thought.

"Logan reached out, believing we should know she was at the end of her life. Which I am grateful for," Johnathan added.

Jackson continued to rub Kristen's arm, as he always had from the moment they'd met. Now, it felt familiar and comforting.

"I want you all to have the option to visit her before she dies. Her funeral will be in Manhattan, and she will be buried with my father in the New York Marble Cemetery."

Kristen glanced around the table.

Daniel and Harper had a quieter discussion on the phone, as everyone in the restaurant began to discuss it.

Kristen felt a little like she didn't belong here but wondered how Jackson was feeling. Not wanting to pressure him, she just sat quietly.

"You should go, Hunt," Addison said, dropping her hand onto his arm.

"How long does she have?" Hunter asked.

"Could be days, or weeks. It's not months," his father replied. "They live in Philadelphia, so it's only a few hours' drive, or you can train."

Fletcher snorted.

"I could train," Hunter said.

"You'll take the chopper," Olivia said. "Be honest."

Kristen sighed. "I'm going to miss that helicopter. You guys are so lucky."

The table went quiet.

"Oh. I didn't mean anything by that. It's just…never mind," she said, feeling suddenly embarrassed.

Their wealth was never something they were shy about, so she wasn't sure why they had gone silent.

"I get it, girl," Addison said, winking.

"You're coming back!" Harper said through the phone.

"Damn straight, she is," Jackson agreed, and she shot him a smile, leaning into him.

It was the first sign they both wanted to continue seeing each other, and a shiver of excitement ran through her. Despite all the reasons why not, her heart wanted this man.

"Are you going to visit her?" Hunter asked Johnathan.

Johnathan sipped his coffee, and Kristen could tell he was buying himself time.

How long had they been estranged?

What a tricky situation to be in. Kristen felt for him, even though she was sure there would be a very interesting story behind the break in the relationships.

"I'm not sure. But all of you should go. I'm sorry I haven't been more proactive in encouraging you to know your grandmother. Or your uncle and cousins, for that matter. It was wrong of me," Johnathan admitted.

"Is it just old age?" Olivia asked, leaning back in her chair to rub her pregnant belly.

Fletcher ran his hand over her hair and kissed her head.

Kristen smiled at them. It was like she was aware of love everywhere. Could she have this with Jackson?

Leaving felt so much harder, now they had confessed their feelings. All she wanted was to get back to the hotel and just bask in these delicious emotions.

"Cancer, I believe," Johnathan answered. "But likely a bit of both at her age. She's eighty-five."

"Damn cancer," Addison said. "Your mom has it too, Jackson. Is that right?"

Kristen felt the blood drain from her face.

Jackson's arm stiffened against her body, then slowly slid away.

Her mouth went dry.

The world froze as she felt Jackson move further away. She turned, and his face was like stone.

"What!" Johnathan said, dropping his cup into the saucer with a bang.

"Fuck," Jackson muttered, rubbing his forehead, then he shot her a look that began to shatter her heart.

No.

God, noooo.

"Jenna is dying?" Johnathan said again, louder. "You lied to me."

Jackson cursed, and his chair creaked as it moved even further away from her. His face pale, angry. His jaw taunt.

"Jackson," she said, reaching for him, but his dark eyes warned her away. Her hand dropped.

Then he was confronting Johnathan.

"No. I didn't tell you. There's a difference," Jackson said firmly, his voice a growl.

Johnathan slid his chair back.

"How bad is it?" he demanded. "How. Bad. Is. It?"

Jackson stood. "Stop. Do not do this."

"Oh God. Jackson, I'm sorry...I—" Kristen groaned, reaching for him again.

He stepped away and glared at her. "How could you? I fucking trusted you. How…God."

Tears prickled at her eyes, her heart thundering in her chest as her world began to crumble.

"What's going on?" Harper cried through the phone, but Johnathan grabbed it and ended the call.

Oh fuck. What had she done?

Kristen stood and reached for her coat on the back of her chair. He was going to bolt, and when he did, she was going with him.

Jackson ran his hands through his hair, his face staring at the floor, shaking his head.

Then he cursed.

"Don't even try to stop me, son," Johnathan said.

"He's 'son' now?" Hunter asked, and everyone ignored him.

"Sorry. Shit. I'm sorry. I didn't know it was a secret," Addison said, throwing her hand over her face.

"Do not do this, Johnathan," Jackson growled, lifting his face to his father. "There's a reason Jenna doesn't want to see you. Doesn't want me to know about you. She's very sick. Going there could trigger her illness."

Both Addison and Kristen gasped. She felt like she was going to throw up.

Fletcher stood. "Okay, calm down. Dad, you need to listen to Jackson. If she is that ill, you can't just show up in her life again."

Johnathan glanced around the table.

"I've given you boys my life. I tried to stay with your mother, and it was impossible. Jenna is the love of my life. Every day for over twenty-four years, I've questioned. I've missed her," Johnathan declared. "None of you have the right to stop me. Not even you, Jackson."

Addison was hanging her head in her hands, with Hunter rubbing her back. Kristen wrapped her arms around herself and began to tremble.

"Jackson," she said quietly, and he continued to ignore her.

"You'll kill her," Jackson growled. "Fuck, fuck!"

She took a step closer to him, her hand reaching out. Then his eyes met hers and flashed with anger and pain. She dropped her hand.

"Don't," he said. Then he blinked, and she saw for a split second a mix of the love he had for her…and regret.

Then it was gone.

Jackson turned to Fletcher. "Come and get her bags. I'm catching a jet home."

Then he turned and walked out of the restaurant.

KRISTEN stared at the doorway, let out a sob, then crumpled to the floor.

CHAPTER TWENTY-THREE

"Stay in touch," Addison said, hugging Kristen for the third time.

"Let her go, Addy." Hunter gave Kristen a shake of his head. "She knows you're sorry and didn't mean to cause all of this."

Kristen nearly laughed at his lack of diplomacy.

"Can you spell it out a bit more so I feel even *more* guilty? Gah," Addison growled, releasing her.

"I didn't…Christ. Sorry," Hunter said, rolling his eyes. He pulled Kristen in for a hug. "Jackson will come around. Give him time."

Kristen nodded and let out a little laugh. She knew she looked a mess. Her eyes were red, her nose swollen.

She didn't care.

Kristen didn't care about much right now.

It felt wrong checking into first class, which Jackson had paid for. It felt wrong being here without him, saying goodbye. Or whatever would have happened, if she hadn't been so stupid and shared his secret.

Neither she nor Addison had meant any harm, but their actions had caused it.

Guilt plagued her, but she wasn't sure she deserved to be completely shunned, her bags dumped on the sidewalk and just left like that.

Not after declaring he loved her.

If this was love, she was done.

It had been chaos after he'd left. The men bringing her bags in, the girls dropping to the ground to collect her.

Her sobs.

Johnathan apologizing, then abruptly leaving. His phone to his ear, supposedly to call Jackson's mom. Or, if Fletcher was right, he'd be on his private jet and in the air within the hour.

Which was why Jackson had bolted.

Kristen knew as well as anyone that family was important, but his response had been cruel and thoughtless.

Is that all she meant to him?

Harper had rung insistently until she'd stopped crying enough to answer, then she'd gone into the bathrooms and told her what had happened. Addison never left her side.

"He said he loved you?" both women cried.

"I said it back. I do. I love him," she mumbled, a little embarrassed now. After all, this was the second drama, and they didn't know him like she did.

Or *thought* she did.

"How could he just walk out and leave me like that?"

They had been silent.

"It's my fault," Addison said, shaking her head. "I can't believe the mess I've caused."

"Addy, it was a genuine mistake. Jackson didn't need to overreact. But in saying that, we don't know the full story," Harper said. "Clearly, there's huge history between Johnathan and Jenna. You might just have to be patient…or—"

"Don't say it. I already know," Kristen said. "Forget him. Story of my life."

More tears had flowed.

Eventually, Addison and Hunter had taken her back to their place, where she'd lain down and slept fitfully for a few hours.

Emotionally, she'd been drained.

Was still drained.

Kristen tugged her handbag up onto her shoulder and grabbed the handle of her carryon. She smiled sadly at Hunter and Addison. "Thank you for dropping me off."

"Safe flight," Hunter said, draping his arm over Addison shoulder, which just sent an arrow of pain through Kristen's heart.

Jackson should be here, hugging her, wrapping his arm around her. But he had chosen his actions, and she had to accept that old adage, actions speak louder than words.

Kristen gave them a sad smile and walked through the gate. This wasn't at all how she envisaged leaving the United States, but here she was. Heartbroken.

Twenty-three hours and one stopover later, she landed in Auckland. Then burst into tears.

CHAPTER TWENTY-FOUR

Jackson stared out the window of the private jet he'd rented. Fortunately, he'd been able to bring his flight forward, after planning to fly out the next day.

He didn't own one like his father and brothers, yet, so had no idea if Johnathan was already on his way to L.A.—able to get in the air before him—or simply planning to call Jenna.

Or if the man would do as he asked and leave sleeping dogs lie, so to speak.

Shit.

Shit, shit, shit.

Jackson had called his mother and gotten her voicemail several times. Which wasn't unusual. She slept a lot.

Visions of Johnathan turning up on her doorstep and causing her undue stress, worsening her conditions, plagued him.

And guilt.

Why had he not just waited?

It had been twenty-four years. Did he need to meet his damn father now?

Don't go digging up ghosts.

Fuck!

This wasn't how he wanted to tell Jenna about what he'd discovered and been doing the past few weeks.

Jackson tossed back his whisky.

His third.

Arriving drunk wouldn't help anyone. He stood, got a bottle of water out of the fridge, and ordered something to eat. Then he shot back a forth whisky after his meal and tried to fall asleep.

Jackson couldn't do anything right now, and he was haunted by those piercing green eyes and the intense pain within them.

I love you.

No. He couldn't focus on that—on her—right now. He had to keep his mother alive. But Jackson knew, if he thought too hard, he might tell them to turn the plane around.

In the end, he did sleep. But it was fitful, and when he woke, he felt like crap.

One look at his phone and he swiped to clear all the messages from Kristen, his stomach lurching as he did.

Jackson knew he had lost her.

She wouldn't forgive him for this.

He wasn't sure *he* could forgive her. No matter what happened in the next few hours or days. She had broken his trust and shared the one secret that could put his mother in her grave.

WHEN he arrived back in L.A., he got the driver to drop him at home first. It was closer and allowed him to drop his bags off.

Jackson showered, had a quick shave, and then grabbed the keys to his black Maserati.

He had lied to Kristen. Well, not entirely. He did own a Honda motorbike, but he also owned two vehicles: a Maserati and a red Tesla.

As the garage door rolled open, he looked at the empty seat beside him and felt a pang in his chest.

Kristen could be here with you, asshole.

He pressed down on the gas and reversed out, ignoring the heavy feeling, then sped to his mother's house. When he arrived, a dark SUV was parked outside.

Johnathan was already here.

He wasn't surprised.

Don't go digging up ghosts.

Bile rose in his throat.

Jackson eyed the dark SUV as he jogged up the path, spotting a driver behind the wheel tapping his fingers to whatever song he was listening to. Then Jackson was at the door and wondering what shitshow he was going to find himself in—his mother furious, or reacting to Johnathan's visit.

It wasn't like she would keel over, but the stress would take its toll, and he was furious with Johnathan's selfishness.

Knock, knock, knock, knock, knock.

His blood pumping, Jackson paced back and forth on the doorstep. When no one answered, he knocked again.

Finally, he heard the locks clicking.

His mother opened the door and glanced at him with disappointment and what looked like sadness.

Goddamn.

Jackson pulled her into his arms.

"I'm sorry, Mom," he said, wishing he could turn back time.

And never meet Kristen?

Focus, man.

When he released her, Jackson tilted his head to see further into the house. An impossibility because of the layout, but he still tried.

Jenna shook her head. "Jackson, I told you not to do this."

"I know, but he's my father, Mom."

"Come inside." She sighed, and he followed her through the house. In the same living room he had grown up in, there sat Johnathan Dufort.

"Hello, Jackson," the man said, his face now calm but fierce with confidence in his decision.

Asshole.

"I fucking asked you not to do this," Jackson growled, crossing his arms.

Johnathan stood and walked to Jenna's side, like they were partners in crime. Well, he didn't give a fuck. The man had totally disrespected him and ignored his wishes.

Great start to their relationship.

"There was no way I couldn't come," Johnathan said. "An army couldn't have stopped me from being by your mother's side. *She* couldn't have stopped me."

As Jackson watched his mother lift her face to the tall, wealthy man beside her, he saw something he'd never seen before.

Love.

Not the love of a mother, or daughter. Or friend.

True love.

Jenna loved Johnathan Dufort. There was absolutely no mistaking it. The well of tears in her eyes, the blush on her cheeks—he recognized that from…

Her.

The woman he'd just lost.

At least your mother is alive and well.

"Jenna is the love of my life and has been since the moment I saw her," Johnathan said, wrapping an arm around her shoulders. "I'm not leaving her this time. You are mine, Jenna, until your last breath."

Jesus.

His mother swallowed, letting her tears flow, and then Johnathan pulled her into his arms.

Well, shit.

CHAPTER TWENTY-FIVE

Kristen sat in the heavy traffic, tapping her fingers against the steering wheel. Being back on the other side of the world—and therefore car and road—was weird, even after only a few weeks of being away.

It was funny how the brain adjusted.

Which meant she would get over this heartache quickly, right?

Good try, sunshine.

She lifted her smoothie out of the cup holder in her car and took a long sip.

Jetlag and a broken heart were a bitch when combined. Add broken sleep and the fact it was freezing cold in Auckland, and Kristen wanted to curl up in a ball and hide from life.

She'd been home a few days but was still not acclimated, the seventeen-hour time difference hard to adjust to.

Plus, she'd been crying her heart out.

Last night, she'd decided to give up messaging Jackson. He hadn't replied, and each rejection stabbed her in the heart deeper.

Kristen had never been in love before. Not like this.

Damn him for pushing her to open up and say those three stupid words. She understood him being mad and upset about his mom, but completely ghosting her was cruel and unwarranted.

Why wouldn't he let her explain?

Why couldn't he just yell at her, or have it out with her, then focus back on what they had built over the past few weeks.

Harper had called, and they'd Facetimed for over an hour, talking it through until they were both exhausted.

"What has Daniel said?" Kristen had asked.

Harper sighed and dropped her chin into her hand. "He's withholding judgement and said he won't take sides. Not until they find out more about how sick his mom is. Or what the real story is between Johnathan and Jenna."

Kristen respected that, despite how broken she felt.

"That's nice of him, I guess. I might be angry, but I want Jackson to have support," Kristen said, spinning the diamond and emerald bracelet around on her arm, doing exactly what he'd told her to do—think about him. "Guess I better get over it. When you have kids, he'll be an uncle. He's not going anywhere. So, I suppose one day our paths will cross again."

That reality had been a hard pill to swallow, but it was true. Jackson wasn't just some guy she'd never see again. Her friendship with Harper was lifelong, and Jackson was Harper's brother-in-law. Any big events in her life would include him in one way or another.

Fact: she would see him again.

One day, he would get married and have a family. She would meet his wife and children. With her luck, she'd probably still be single.

Her phone rang, snapping Kristen back to the present and the traffic around her.

"Hey," she said, pressing the button on her steering wheel to put the call on speaker.

"Hey, Shrimp," her sister Karen said, yawning. "How's the jetlag?"

The stupid nickname had been given to her when she was an infant. Something about her mom craving seafood and her being a tiny baby. No matter how hard she'd tried over the years, they wouldn't drop it.

Thankfully, her friends thought it was stupid and hadn't adopted it.

"Crappy. Why are you awake?" she asked, glancing at the clock. It was seven thirty in the morning.

"Your niece called from London and got the time mixed up." Karen sighed. Her daughter, Selena, was overseas in Europe on a working holiday. It was a thing a lot of young kiwis did.

"Let me guess. She's drunk in a pub somewhere." Kristen glanced at the clock. Morning in New Zealand meant evening in London. "Eight at night. That's totally pub o'clock."

"Don't have kids, Kris. Honestly, it's like ripping out your heart and throwing it into the crowd so people can just toss it around and crumple it."

She snorted.

Except Kristen *did* want to be a mom. More than anything. With thirty looming and yet another relationship failure under her belt—this one lasting barely five minutes—Kristen was starting to think she'd never settle down and have kids.

At least Harper was married.

"I need a sperm donor for that, and so far, the only ones I meet are assholes," Kristen said, noting she had moved onto the angry stage of the grief cycle.

Except Jackson wasn't an asshole.

Nor was he hers.

"Come for dinner tonight. Mom said you were sounding depressed," Karen said.

Ugh.

Kristen wasn't going to tell her sister about Jackson. She'd only get a lecture about the statistics of holiday romances not working out. Karen was like a second mom because of the age difference. She loved her, but right now, Kristen didn't want to hear it.

"Post-holiday blues. That's all," she muttered.

There was silence.

"You know, you *could* do the sperm-donor thing. Don't wait if you do want kids, Shrimp," Karen said, suddenly surprising her.

Kristen stared at the road, blinking.

"Heavy conversation for this early in the day, sis," she replied after a moment. "I'll visit on the weekend. I need to catch up at work, as today's my first day back."

She also wasn't sure she wouldn't burst into tears and tell her sister everything.

They agreed to lunch on Saturday. When she ended the call, Kristen drove into her designated parking spot and shut off the engine.

Back to work. Back to her life. Just as it was before she had met Jackson.

Except now, she felt different.

Now she could close her eyes and feel his touch. Feel his mouth on her neck, his lips on hers. His fingers gently running over her skin as he sat next to her. His thick cock inside her, claiming her as his.

Yet, he hadn't.

Yes, she'd made a mistake, but his reaction was nearly as bad. If Jackson could turn his back on her in such a dramatic, cold way, then he didn't love her.

That was the hardest thing of all to accept.

He'd lied.

Jackson Wiles *did not* love her.

She caught the tear slipping out, drew in a long shaky breath, and got out of the car. As she had a million times before, she opened up the shop, turned on the lights, and began pulling out all the ribbons and materials her and the team would use to make today's bouquets.

Out back, boxes of flowers had been delivered, as they were daily, and she began to carry them in.

Tina arrived, muttering a welcome back and saying it was her time for a holiday.

Sally, their junior assistant, arrived next. She was a little bouncier but after a, "How was the Big Apple?" and a few *wows, sounds great,* they got on with their day.

As they did every day.

Kristen slid a white rose into the bouquet she was building and added two peonies, then wrapped the organic woven material around it and selected the natural-colored string to hold it together.

This was her life again.

Her holiday was over.

It was time to make some decisions on how she moved forward because she knew, deep in her heart, she would never hear from Jackson again.

CHAPTER TWENTY-SIX

Jackson shook the man's hand. "Thank you, Stanley. We look forward to hearing from you."

Kevin opened the door to the boardroom and then walked the four government officials out to the elevators.

Their presentation had been over two hours long, with questions. And there had been plenty. This was, after all, a very important decision for the military to make. Which is why they'd flown from Washington to see their operations, rather than asking the Appopolis team to go to them.

Jackson was confident they'd given it one hundred percent.

"Good job, guys," Jackson said to three of his team, who were packing up their laptops and turning off the screens.

"When do you think we'll know more?" Jerry, their Chief Robot Whisperer, asked.

Jackson had let his team create their own job titles and was still regretting it. In another company, the guy would be called their Chief Systems Engineer. Still, it created a sense of fun and freedom Jackson wanted in the culture of his organization. Life was serious enough as it was.

"It could be weeks," Jackson replied, sliding his hands into his pockets, when Kevin walked back in. They shared a look as the team emptied out of the room.

"I'm happy," Kevin said.

Jackson nodded.

"No one else has the coding and skills for that technology, so as long as they're happy with everything else they see, with us, I'm quietly confident we have a very strong chance," Jackson said, rocking on his heels.

And he meant it.

With his skills and the technology they were building, he was sure they were ahead of the game in the industry.

Appopolis was now internationally known for its supply of high-tech capabilities. They were prepared and set up to use the coding he had created in products to help the government step further into modern warfare technology.

Kevin leaned against the long cabinet by the wall. "We'll need more people. A *lot* more."

Jackson turned to stare out the glass windows.

It was a sunny afternoon in Los Angeles. The city he'd grown up in. Aside from his years at Brown, he'd lived in L.A. all his life.

"Whether we get it or not, we need to expand," Jackson said. "You've been pushing for the last twelve months for this, and you're right."

When he looked back, Kevin was nodding, the pen in his hand tapping on his chin.

"The sales team have reached their targets this month. By double. Again. We need to move now before we burn our people out. Before we start losing them," Kevin said.

Jackson didn't believe he'd lose them. Anyone who jumped ship wasn't smart enough or passionate enough to be part of a leading, cutting-edge tech company. But he valued his people and agreed they were all working extremely hard. Too hard.

To get the best out of people, you had to provide a nourishing place to work and be aware, before they were, when burnout could happen.

It was one of many reason's Kevin was his CEO. First, he had selected a normal fucking job title, and second, he was a people leader.

A people motivator.

What was a company if it didn't have people?

Just an idea. Or a name on the door.

So, Jackson was listening. Even if Kevin had been on his case for months.

Then hadn't been the time. Now it was.

As the founder and director, it was Jackson's job to trust his instinct more than the people around him. He'd learned early on in business that one of the tricks to staying at the top was knowing when to grow and when to tighten the purse strings.

Economies went up and down. Opportunities came and went. Partnerships thrived and broke down.

In life and in business.

His mind flashed to Kristen, but he pushed it aside.

Again.

Night after night, he'd tossed and turned, unable to get her off his mind.

Worrying. Second guessing.

Going over and over everything that had happened since he flew out the door in New York.

So much had happened in the past week that he'd kept busy, but that didn't mean he'd stopped thinking of her. Not for a second.

Jackson cleared his throat.

"Put together a proposal, and we'll go through it at the management team meeting on Friday," Jackson said. "Expect some ideas from me...but I'll save those for Friday."

"Jesus, Jackson. Don't throw me any curve balls," Keven groaned.

"You can handle it, buddy," he said, laughing and heading out the door as he slapped Kevin on the shoulder. "I'll be out of the office the rest of the afternoon."

He had a family dinner to attend tonight.

With his mother and Johnathan.

After being asked to give them a few days to talk, they had booted him out the door. Not before he'd made sure Jenna had taken her meds and Johnathan was well aware of her doctor's orders to keep her stress free.

Something he'd happily rubbed in.

"I am fine," his mother had insisted. "Your father and I need to talk. Go home. I'll call you when I'm ready to tell you everything."

Fuck, that had hurt.

He'd lifted his brows and looked down his nose. "Mom, you are ill. Very ill."

"Johnathan will make sure I am fine," Jenna had said. "You might be our son, but what we need to say to each other is private."

As much as that had been to swallow, his mother was right.

"I'll make sure she is taken care of and ring you if anything happens," Johnathan said, his voice rich with emotion.

So, he'd driven home, his heart heavy, and sat watching mindless TV while he tried to stop his racing mind.

Kristen had been in the air, flying home to New Zealand. Johnathan and his seriously ill mother were going over old wounds that could trigger her cancer and see her back in the fucking hospital.

He'd scrolled through Kristen's messages and finally deleted them all. She would move on faster if he didn't reply.

The sick feeling in his stomach surely would pass. Eventually.

The next day, he'd received a text to say his mom was tired and needed some rest, then locking in a time later in the week.

Johnathan was still there.

Tonight was the night he got his answers.

JACKSON stepped out of the shower and rubbed his towel over his hair. Standing on the shower mat, he stared at himself in the mirror.

A familiar sense of loss spread through his chest.

He placed a hand on the bathroom bench and stared into the sink, picked up his toothbrush, and ran the cold water.

Then, he was spreading on the Colgate.

He'd begun hating his time in the bathroom. All it did was remind him of that gorgeous woman with those stunning green eyes.

She who shall not be named.

If she'd been here, he would have his hands all over her. He would wrap his body around her, lock eyes until that sexy-as-fuck blush hit her cheeks and she leaned back into him.

Because she always did.

Then his mouth would kiss his way down her neck, and his fingers would reach to slide into her pink wet flesh.

"Fuck," he said, spitting and rinsing.

Kristen had broken his trust.

If it had been Harper she told, he might have understood it a little more. But Addison? Kristen had only known the woman for a few weeks.

Why had she told them such personal information?

Jackson might not have spelled it out and asked her to sign a fucking confidentiality agreement, but clearly, it was personal and sensitive, given the conversations going on with his father.

She should have fucking known.

But goddamn, he loved her.

He craved her, he missed her, he was so damn angry. His body needed her. The animalistic part of him inside was screaming to have her back. To know she was safe. To know she was protected.

To know she was his.

Yet, if you didn't have trust in a relationship, then what did you have?

It was over.

They were worlds apart, and it had to stay that way.

Forever.

He had to move on and forget Kristen Holle.

WHEN he drove up to his mother's house this time, he was calmer but still tense. He parked the Tesla in the driveway and hopped out of the car.

The temperatures were still warm, so he wore long beige shorts, a white shirt rolled up his forearms, and sneakers. He pushed his dark glasses up his nose and walked down the path lined with pruned rose bushes.

Kristen would know their names, along with some random fact to make him smile.

Christ, why couldn't he forget her?

Move on.

Then his stupid brain began imagining her here, meeting his mom and having conversations about plants and probably many more things. They would get along.

And he hated that.

She could have been the woman he married. The woman he loved for the rest of his life. The woman he created children with and watched them run around this house, just as he had once.

The door opened before he could knock.

Johnathan.

"Making yourself at home, I see," Jackson said with a lifted brow as he stepped inside.

There was no point pretending he was okay with this. He wasn't.

Despite his undying love for his mother, Johnathan had flown across the country and bowled up, not caring what his appearance back in her life would do to her health. God knows what sort of stress this little reunion had caused her.

They might have appeared to love each other, but he knew how quickly that could turn. And yes, guilt was pulsing through his veins, knowing he was the cause of it all. He could have let those fucking ghosts just stay dead.

"She's fine," Johnathan said, reading his mind.

"Good."

When he stepped into the kitchen, Jenna was tossing a salad. The doors to the outside area were open, and the smell of the barbeque cooking wafted inside. Johnathan grabbed the tongs off the bench and went outside, giving Jenna a wink.

The fuck?

"Hello, Martha Stewart," Jackson said, dropping his phone and wallet on the table.

Jenna snorted. "Grab a beer from the fridge. Or whatever you want to drink."

He took a long look at his mother and didn't miss the glow on her cheeks, which had been missing for months.

She looked…well.

"Have you been drinking?" he asked.

"Good one," Jenna said. She wasn't allowed to drink alcohol.

Johnathan returned with a plate of steak and corn on the cob, darkened on the grill.

Jesus, it was like the guy had just moved in and assumed the role of husband.

Over Jackson's damn body.

"She got some sunshine today," Johnathan said, dropping the plate on the dining table. "Grab me a beer, while you're there."

Jackson leaned into the fridge and pulled two bottles out. He walked and handed one to him.

"Let's sit. Eat and talk," Jenna said, carrying the salad over.

Feeling a little bit like he'd stepped inside the *Pleasantville* movie, Jackson decided to play the game. If it kept his mom happy, then he'd do it.

So, he ate, told them about the potential government contract, leaving out all the top secret details, and how they were getting ready to expand.

"I've got some great business consultants, if you want someone to go over your plans," Johnathan offered.

"I'll see how I go," Jackson said.

The last thing he wanted to do was commit to anything when it came to his birth father. Regret for going to New York was still racing through his veins, despite this happy family game they were playing.

His eyes landed on a plaque on the wall, two tiny silver footprints embedded on it. A reminder of one last secret left unspoken.

Jenna caught him and pressed her lips together.

Shit.

Jackson's eyes widened. "I didn't…Not that, Mom."

That was one secret he never spoke about. Not to anyone.

"Johnathan knows about Jessica," his mother said, her eyes lowering as his own widened.

Jessica was his twin sister. She had been a stillborn, having died in his mother's womb a week before he'd been born.

It was a strange feeling he'd always carried with him. Never feeling fully complete. Wondering if it had been him who'd killed her.

Something he'd once voiced, and his mother had shut him down immediately, while Trevor had mumbled, "Probably."

Asshole.

"Can't believe we had a daughter," Johnathan said.

"Nearly." Jenna played with her fork, which was lying on the table, and Johnathan reached out and took her hand, squeezing it.

His mother saw his cynical questioning gaze and slightly moved her hand.

"I understand you know what happened up until the point I told John I was pregnant with you and your sister," Jenna said.

John.

"He told me." Jackson nodded. "But he also said he was in love with you. So why did you stay with Trevor?"

The two of them shared a look.

"A lot happened after that moment. I'm going to tell you things about your father—"

"The man who raised me. He wasn't my father," Jackson said firmly.

Jenna nodded.

"He was never kind to you. And there are reasons," Jenna said, sighing.

Johnathan cursed and emptied his beer. One glance across the table and Jackson nodded, knowing Johnathan was asking if he wanted another.

Hell yes.

It sounded like he was going to need one.

As the man walked to the fridge and retrieved the bottles, his mother continued.

"I'd had morning sickness. Trevor had worked it out," Jenna said as the beer was handed to him. "We were unable to conceive. He'd been tested and learned he was infertile and never told me. So, when he suspected my nausea was pregnancy, he hit the roof."

"He knew you were having an affair," Jackson said, gritting his teeth at the idea of Trevor harming his mother.

Jenna nodded.

"I'd been photographed with John, so he connected the dots."

"You should have fucking told me, Jenna," Johnathan said, standing beside her chair but staring out the window.

Obviously, the two had spent days talking about it, but Johnathan was still coming to grips with what had happened. It must have been hard, after two and a half decades.

His mother gave him a sad smile across the table. "It gets worse, darling. I don't want you to hear this, but you deserve the truth. I loved Johnathan. I still love him." She glanced up at the man, and he smiled softly back.

Jackson stared between them. Seeing them together was so surreal. Until a few months ago, he thought the two were strangers. Johnathan was a hotel mogul, not the man barbecuing with his mom.

Or making bug eyes at her.

Yet here they were.

"If he wasn't dead, I'd fucking kill him," Johnathan said, and Jackson raised his brows.

"What did he do?" he asked, his eyes darting back to his mom.

"It was one of the worst nights of my life. He confronted me and said he'd go to the media and record company," Jenna said. "At the time, Johnathan's business was growing, and he had three little boys and a wife. I'll be honest, I wasn't sure if he would leave her if this all blew up publicly."

Johnathan cursed.

"I was pregnant, vulnerable, and a public figure," Jenna said. "Trevor said he could overlook my affair if I stayed with him, and everyone believed the child, children, were his."

"Really? He hated me," Jackson said, shaking his head.

"Because you look like me," Johnathan muttered, and Jenna nodded her agreement.

In some ways, Jackson understood that, but he was an innocent kid. He hadn't deserved the hate and humiliation the man threw at him. It might have been subtle, but it had gone on all his life.

"After we fought, he left. I went to the record label offices to meet with my manager. I thought if I could talk to them, and tell them, Trevor would have less power over me. Then I planned to ring Johnathan."

His father drew long on his beer. His jaw tight.

Shit.

A cold chill ran through him. Jackson was starting to think he didn't want to hear this.

"When I got there, one of the bands who had signed with the same company were wrapping up after recording. I'm not going to say who, so don't ask me," Jenna said, scrunching her napkin in her hand.

Johnathan moved behind her and laid his hands on her shoulders. Jackson tried to catch his eye, but no one would look at him.

The chill in his blood turned to ice.

"One of the guys, their guitarist, tried to get me to join the party in their room. You know, it might have been the nineties, but there was still a lot of booze and drugs around then," she continued. "But I was pregnant and upset after the fight."

Fuck, this was painful to hear.

Jackson chugged down his beer.

"So, I went out the back near the parking lot to wait for my manager, trying to keep out of the way of the party."

Jackson closed his eyes.

He knew what was coming. It was like he'd seen the movie a hundred times.

This time, it was his mother.

"Don't tell him the details. No son needs to hear this," Johnathan said. "And one day, Jenna, you *will* tell me who it was."

The two men locked eyes, and Jackson nodded.

Whatever it was, he was on team Johnathan when it came to seeking revenge on whatever he was about to learn.

His mother finally met his eyes.

"It wasn't sexual. It nearly was. But he did hurt me. Badly," she said.

Jackson's voice was shaky as he cursed.

"When my manager arrived, he raced me to the hospital, where Trevor met us. I had to stay there for nearly a week to recover."

Fury raced through him.

"Mother fucker," he growled, and for a moment, his mind flashed to Kristen. To the possibility of, one day, her being hurt while he was half a world away.

Fuck that.

"I had a broken jaw, broken arm, and a broken rib," she said. "But the babies were fine, I was told."

Jessica.

When their eyes met again, his mother's lowered. "I've been told it may not be related but…yes, it could be."

"Shit," Jackson cursed. "Who is this asshole? Tell us!"

Jenna shook her head and continued. "After that, the record company dropped me like a hot potato because they were scared I'd talk. My manager had overheard the medical people talking and knew you weren't Trevor's. It was a mess. I was threatened with all kinds of horrible legal stuff."

"I still would have left my wife, Jenna. Nothing would have kept me from being with you."

When she said nothing, Jackson glanced at his father. "Except her. Except Mom not giving you the chance."

Johnathan nodded.

Jackson understood now.

His mother had shut the door and never given him the opportunity.

"There were a million things I could have or should have done," Jenna said. "But all I wanted was my babies to be safe. Trevor looked after me. He wasn't perfect, but he was committed and loyal."

Except he hated me.

"He was heartbroken when Jessica died," Jenna continued.

"That was why you only sent me the photo of Jackson," Johnathan said, and his mother nodded.

"Every day, I looked at our son and thought of you. Every single day," she said, tears gleaming in her eyes.

Jackson's own eyes prickled.

"Jesus, Mom," he whispered, his voice thick with emotion.

"Please forgive me," she said, softly crying. "Both of you. I may not have made the right decision, but I was broken, weakened, and scared. And pregnant with crazy hormones. You were a wealthy man with a family. I didn't have it in me to go through what we'd have needed to do, publicly, after being attacked and losing my career."

Johnathan sat down. "It's probably good you never told me. I'd likely be in prison for murdering that son of a bitch."

Jackson nodded knowingly.

"Ditto."

Jenna frowned at them both. "Which is why I will never tell you. Two alpha men. I don't want to lose you both."

"You won't, Mom."

"I told you I'm not leaving you," Johnathan said firmly, then looked over at Jackson. "I'm taking your mother back to New York with me."

Jackson's brows flew up. "What?"

"I have a specialist there who is the best in the world. She'll have the best care…and as I just said. This time, I am *not* losing your mother."

The stiffness in his jaw and the hard tone of his voice made it clear there would be no budging him. But it wasn't just his decision. This was the last months or years of his mother's life.

He would ensure she made the right decision for her.

Jackson turned to his mother. "And you are okay with this?"

She smiled at him.

"Darling, I have loved this man my entire life. I may not have long, so if he wants to put me up in a fancy penthouse and treat me like a princess while loving me, I am *very* okay with that."

Why the hell was he thinking about Kristen right now?

Again.

The idea of protecting the woman he loved was eating away at his heart. Like he was failing her by not spending his life with her and telling her every fucking day she was the most important thing in the world to him.

Was she?

The more he watched his parents together, their little touches and glances, he saw himself with Kristen. She'd been the one to point it out to him. Calling him affectionate as they sat in Central Park that sunny day.

His eyes drifted outside to the yard, and his brain began spinning.

New York. His mother would be on the other side of the country from him.

No damn way.

"Then I'm moving too," he said. "If this is what you want. Then I'm moving to Manhattan."

CHAPTER TWENTY-SEVEN

Two weeks later

"**A**nd you turn thirty in four months?" the doctor asked, glancing up from his screen to look at her like she was an ancient artifact.

"That's right," Kristen said for the fifth time. Never had she been made to feel more ancient in her life than the last thirty minutes she'd spent in this fertility clinic.

"No partner. You are currently single?"

Jesus.

"Yes." Again.

"So, you'll be wanting donor sperm and eggs?" Dr. Letterman asked, clicking his mouse.

Kristen shook her head once. "I mean… no. I was thinking I would use my eggs and…"

She trailed off and began chewing her nails as the doctor continued talking about how old her eggs were now and the number each woman has and their decline each year, but she wasn't listening.

He'd spent the entire session telling her how difficult it was to get pregnant. Meanwhile, somewhere, someone was having protected sex, and that determined sperm was breaking through the rubber and impregnating the woman.

The population was growing on Earth, not reducing.

It can't be that damn hard.

She wasn't fifty.

"Sorry. Can we just…You've told me all that. I'm assuming you have nice flashy offices and are still in business because it *does* work," Kristen said, lifting a brow.

Or rather because it doesn't, and people have to do it over and over, failing each time.

"Which I'm telling you, Ms. Holle."

"No. You're scaring me. I don't want to hear how shitty my eggs are. How many I won't have. I'm here, trying to be proactive, because I want to be a mother. I'm nearing thirty, not fifty. Can we keep it relative?"

The doctor sighed.

"Yes, you have come in at the right time, but my job is to give you all the information. The good, bad, and the ugly."

They had a stare off for a long moment.

"Where's the good news?" she finally asked.

The doctor sighed and pulled out some brochures.

"Here's the process to freeze your eggs," Dr Letterman said, opening one of them and pointing to the pages, then did the same with another. "This one shows the lifecycle of a woman's eggs. You *have* come at the right time, but if you are serious about having a baby and don't have a partner, then I recommend you get started immediately. Freezing or IVF."

Kristen took the brochures and nodded.

None of this felt natural because it wasn't. She'd never imagined sitting in a medical office, talking about having a baby on her own.

She felt judged and pathetic.

"We have a three-month waiting list. The sooner you decide and book, the faster we can have a baby in those arms. First, we'll run tests to see the quality and quantity of your eggs."

"You can do that?" she asked.

"Yes, we can and *need* to do that," the doctor said, then pulled out a sheet of paper, folding it in half. Never a good sign. "These are the prices. I'm sorry, we don't offer financing, nor recommend you go down that path."

It wasn't like she'd expected someone to sit across from her, congratulate her on making an exciting life decision, and start talking baby names. But nothing about this appointment had been enjoyable.

It wasn't nurturing or caring.

He'd treated her like she was a failure and didn't have the money to afford it. One glance at the prices and it was true. IVF in New Zealand was tens of thousands of dollars each time.

She gulped and said goodbye.

Kristen left the office after paying a stupid amount of money for the forty-five-minute appointment and drove home in a daze.

She dropped her keys on the kitchen bench once she got home and poured herself a glass of whisky. The one she'd purchased from the duty-free shops when she flew back in the country.

Every damn drop reminded her of *him*.

Glancing around the room, she let out a sigh. Life felt so empty. Harper was in Manhattan, the excitement of her move and the wedding now over.

Kristen had been and gone on her holiday, and returned with a broken heart to boot.

Maybe she needed a cat?

Or a goldfish.

Her phone beeped. She ignored it and kept sipping her whisky, wondering what Jackson was doing. It was early morning in Los Angeles. He'd be off to work. Or perhaps he was in some other state or country—he'd shared that he traveled for business.

Harper had told her his mother was fine. She hadn't dropped dead when Johnathan showed up.

Surprise.

She meant no disrespect, but the woman hadn't been on her death bed, yet Jackson had been incredibly defensive and reactive.

And he had walked away from her because of it.

Kristen scoffed and threw back the rest of her whisky.

She dropped the glass on the counter and looked around her two-bedroom house. Kristen had purchased it two years ago. It would be a nice home to have a baby. The lounge was sunny and had a set of double doors which led out to a small fenced outdoor area, which was paved. There was even a grassy area.

The neighborhood was safe.

A school nearby had good ratings.

Her sister lived close by, as did her parents.

Perhaps the doctor was right. If she waited for another few years and it took two or three attempts, which apparently wasn't unusual, her eggs would be reducing in number and quality.

She wasn't going to jump into anything, but the truth was, she had a talent for choosing the wrong men.

Was that going to change?

Or would she be forty and wishing she'd done this a decade ago?

Kristen rinsed her glass and headed to the bathroom for a shower. As the water flowed over her hair and down her face, she let the tears flow.

It was the only place she let herself cry now. Lying to herself that it was the water, not her broken heart that never seemed to heal.

He'd said he loved her.

He had lied.

THE next morning, she was sitting at a café, waiting to meet a friend for coffee. Despite the cold, she was layered up and sitting at one of the tables on the sidewalk.

It was Saturday, and Melanie was always late, so Kristen was scrolling through her social feeds, when her phone rang.

It was a Facetime request. She grinned, answering it.

"Harper Dufort, are you out partying?" It was Friday night in New York. As the screen came to life, she could tell Harper wasn't at home.

"No. We're at some boring event," Harper replied.

"We can hear you!" someone called out.

Kristen giggled. "Was that Olivia?"

Harper rolled her eyes and nodded.

A pang of sadness hit her. She missed them all so much and wished she could be there.

But she was moving on and creating a different life.

Creating life.

"How did it go with the specialist?" Harper asked, taking a step away from the noise.

"Well, he was a bit of a dick, but I got all the information I need," she said, then bit her lip. "I think I'm going to do it."

"Freeze your eggs?" Harper's eyes grew wider. "That's great. Such good insurance for when you meet someone."

She pressed her lips together and shook her head.

Overnight, Kristen had thought long and hard about what the Dick Doctor had said. While he had been harsh, the facts were what they were.

Why wait?

She could freeze her eggs, but with no relationship in sight and knowing, if she did meet someone, it would take a year or two before they decided to start trying, she could start running out of time.

So why wait?

Kristen could refinance her house and get some money out of it. When she'd woken, it felt like the right thing to do.

Even if her heart was heavy.

"No. I'm going to do IVF. Have a baby, Harp." She smiled.

"Shut the front door! Are you kidding me?"

Kristen let out a giggle and laughed. "Yes. No, I mean. I'm going to have a baby. Fuck waiting for a man. I want to be a mom, so that's what I'm going to do."

There was silence as Harper stared at her through the screen. "I hate you are there and I'm here. I need to hug you right now."

Tears leaked out her eyes.

"I'm out in public, damn you. Now my mascara is going everywhere," Kristen said, letting out a little laugh, wiping them with her arm.

"Call me tomorrow. I'll come over and be there when you do it. I can write my books and whatever," Harper said, "Wait, how long does it take? Daniel will probably get pissed. Too bad. I'm your best friend."

Kristen sat back and listened to drunk Harper go around in circles. She also offered to pay for it about three times, before finally, her husband leaned over her shoulder.

"Thought it might be you. Hello, Kristen."

She waved. "Hey, Daniel."

"She's having a baby," Harper blurted.

Oh my god.

Kristen slapped her hand over her forehead.

"Christ. Is it Jackson's?" Daniel asked, his eyes widening and his brows shooting to the top of his forehead.

"No! Shit. Daniel. No. I am not, I repeat *not having a baby*. I am not pregnant," Kristen said robotically.

"Well, that's good to hear," Melanie said, plopping down in the seat in front of her. "Immaculate conception and all that."

Kristen laughed.

Harper, she mouthed, pointing at the screen. "Drunk."

"Ah," Melanie said, ordering their drinks when the server appeared.

"So, you're not pregnant with my half-brother's child. Got it. Fine. I'm out. Harper, we need to get you home. Did you have shots when I went to the bathroom?" Daniel asked.

Harper went silent.

"That's a yes," Daniel, Melanie, and Kristen all said at once.

Harper put her face into the phone, like really ugly close. "Emma is here. We have a book signing next week, so she's staying with us. You should read her books. Superrrr kinky."

"Okay, that's great," Kristen said, looking around and hoping the nearby diners didn't hear that.

"Send me the book details. I need," Melanie called.

Talking to drunk people when you're sober had a short life span. Plus, now Melanie had arrived, Kristen needed to wrap-up this crazy call.

"Call you tomorrow, Harp. And please, make sure Daniel knows I am *not* pregnant. At all. To anyone," she said, not wanting to say Jackson's name, or mention him so she had to explain it to Melanie.

When she ended the call, she let out a sigh.

Melanie lifted her coffee to her lips. "Her husband is seriously hot."

Yeah, he is. You should see his half-brother.

"So, how's work?" Kristen asked instead. Those Dufort brothers were not going to be on today's topic of discussion.

She was moving on.

CHAPTER TWENTY-EIGHT

"Well," Kevin said, lifting his bourbon to his lips, "I think it's a great space. If you're happy, I'll follow up on the paperwork and get it all signed."

"Smart man," Hunter said.

Jackson swirled his whisky around in his glass and leaned back in his chair. Being back in New York was fucking with his brain.

Everywhere he looked, all he saw was Kristen.

In fact, he thought he'd seen her at least ten goddamn times in the past twelve hours since he'd landed. If she was going to be anywhere, it would not be in the Cloud Bar at the SoHo Dufort Hotel, where he was sharing a drink with his CEO and Hunter.

Just then, Fletcher and Daniel walked in.

"Two whisky's on the rocks, thank you," Daniel said.

"I'm not drinking," Fletcher growled.

"Bullshit. You aren't drinking when Olivia is around. Anyway, she's the one pregnant, not you." Daniel shook his head like the guy was an idiot.

"It doesn't work that way," Fletcher replied, calling out to the waiter. "Make mine an H20 on the rocks."

"Just say iced water." Daniel rolled his eyes.

Jackson laughed into his drink.

"Why, when it irks you so much?" Fletcher then turned to Jackson and smirked. "Welcome back to the Big Apple, bro."

Jackson shot his whisky back. "Thanks. I've missed all the bickering."

"Really?" Hunter asked, frowning.

"No." Jackson laughed.

Fletcher sniggered, and Jackson then did a round of introductions for Kevin.

"Nice to meet you. So how was the office space?" Daniel asked, looking between Jackson and Kevin.

"It's great," Kevin replied. "A bit big right now, but we're in growth mode, so in two years, it will be perfect."

Jackson would sign it off.

Plus, he'd found a penthouse five blocks away from the office, so he could easily walk to work if he so chose. It was only ten minutes or so from his father's.

And now mother's.

Jenna had put her house on the market, and Johnathan had her moved to Manhattan a few days later. She was meeting with the specialist next week.

It was amazing how your life could change in an instant, with one decision.

Just as his had with one decision to walk away from the woman he still fucking loved.

The drinks arrived, and Fletcher lifted his glass in the air. "Cheers. Here's to the success of your super-secret contract with the military."

Three days ago, they'd been advised they were the successful supplier. The details were highly confidential, but he could share that the military branch of the U.S. government was his client.

That was about it.

They'd been pushing for information but knew he would never spill. He'd learned that his brothers loved to taunt each other.

Now he was one of them.

"Thanks, man," Jackson said, and they all lifted their drinks.

Following meetings with his team, he'd already told them he wanted an office in NYC. Especially after his mother had told him she was moving. Plus, he wanted to spend time with his new family.

The downside, it was bringing back memories of being here with Kristen.

Who was he kidding? He'd not stopped thinking about her. At night, he tossed back far too many whisky's to knock himself out.

That wasn't the only tossing he was doing.

Her face was the only one he saw as his hand slid up and down his cock, then hated himself for it afterwards.

"So, they were long lost loves, huh?" Fletcher said. "Guess it makes sense. The way he was never happy with Mom. And the philandering since forever."

"Says the Playboy of Manhattan," Daniel snorted.

"Was. Not anymore. Pregnant, remember?" Fletcher said, and Kevin, who had kids, let out a laugh.

"For the love of God, Fletcher. Have a drink. You aren't pregnant," Daniel said, shaking his head. "You won't see me giving up the gods' ambrosia when Harper is with child."

Fletcher gave him the bird and sipped his water.

"Is she?" Hunter asked.

Jackson raised his brows.

"Who, Harper?" Daniel asked. "You saw her the other night, right? Drunk."

"Yeah, but I heard you talking about being pregnant," Hunter replied.

"No, that was Kristen. They were on Facetime from New Zealand," Daniel said, shaking his head.

What the fuck?

His blood turned to ice. The hand with his glass halfway to his mouth frozen.

Kristen's pregnant?

Jackson cleared his throat, a frog stuck as he tried to speak. "I'm sorry...did you say...Kristen was...fucking pregnant?"

Daniel dropped his glass down heavy on the table, letting out a laugh.

What part of this was funny?

"Fuck. No. Shit, sorry, Jackson. She's not pregnant. You didn't knock her up," Daniel coughed out.

Jackson's body slowly began to relax. His shoulders dropping, his heart still thundering.

Kristen pregnant?

What if he *had* knocked her up?

What if it was true—even if it wasn't.

How would he feel about that?

The image of her with his baby in her belly hit him like a ton of bricks. Worse, his heart sped up even further with *desire.*

He fucking wanted it.

Obviously, that was the most ridiculous thing in the world.

Wasn't it?

"Jesus, don't scare the guy to death," Hunter said.

"Who's Kristen?" Kevin asked.

Jackson liked to keep his private life separate from work. Kevin had become a friend of sorts, but he'd talked to no one about Kristen.

Why?

Probably because it was hard for even him to reconcile what he'd done. How he'd left her.

"By wife's best friend," Daniel said, shooting Jackson a glance. "You know what women are like. They're talking babies. Her friend is doing IVF."

The hell?

Jackson began to cough and choke on his last sip. He thumped his chest and stood.

"You good, man?" Hunter asked. "I thought things were—"

"Yeah." *Cough, cough, cough.* "I'm…Excuse me," he said, standing and heading to the men's room.

IVF?

What the hell was she…?

It's none of your business.

Kristen is having a baby. Another man's baby. Okay, fine, a sperm donor. Maybe. Perhaps she knew someone who was donating.

Oh goddamn it. Now his brain was in overdrive. Jackson felt completely powerless. He pushed open the door and let it slam behind him.

Jackson stared in the mirror at himself.

What the hell was he doing? He'd walked away from her. She could do what she wanted.

She's mine.

Nope. You gave up that right when you drove away, asshole.

Jackson began to pace.

Why was she doing this? She was only twenty-nine. Not even thirty yet. Kristen had told him she wanted to be a mom one day, but he didn't think she was in this much of a hurry.

What if she'd been pregnant with his child? Would she have told him? Was that why she was calling?

No. Too early.

Or was it? What if she was and this IVF was a cover story?

He should call her.

Jackson pulled out his phone.

No, don't.

He paced some more.

Call her.

As he swiped his phone, the door opened, and Daniel walked in, crossing his arms across his crisp white Armani shirt, and leaned on the wall. "I'm a fucking idiot."

"Ahh, okay," Jackson replied, wishing Daniel would just fuck off while he had a mental breakdown.

Instead, he just waited.

"You're in love with her," Daniel said, or rather stated, as if it was news to him. "I didn't see you guys together while I was on my honeymoon, but now, it's clear as day."

"Was," Jackson said.

"Sure. Looks exactly like past tense." Daniel laughed.

"You just threw me, that's all. I'm, ah, happy for her. Having a baby is good. Yes, good. She wants that."

Daniel shook his head, still smiling. "You having trouble getting those lies out there, little brother?"

Asshole.

Jackson let out a groan and sat on the edge of the basin, not giving a fuck that his Tom Ford pants were going to get germs and shit all over them.

"Fine. I'm still in love with Kristen," he spat out, then lifted his head to stare back at Daniel. "But it is past tense. She broke my trust. Trust is vital in relationships."

If anyone understood that, it would be Daniel. The man headed up a billion-dollar empire.

"So is forgiveness," Daniel said. "She made a mistake."

One that could have cost my mother her life.

"A big mistake," Jackson said.

"Was it, though? Seems like it's turned out pretty well for your mom. And before you call me an asshole and say anything about the money and my father, I don't mean that," Daniel said, lifting a hand. "The two of them are happy."

That wasn't what Jackson would have said.

His brothers needed to stop with the money talk. His fortune had changed dramatically with the military contract. But even then, he'd been worth many millions beforehand.

Fucking billionaires.

Now he was one of them.

"She had money. I provided everything she needed," Jackson stated.

"Except romantic love."

"Dude, obviously." He frowned.

"Don't be a dick. I mean, what Kristen did led to them being together. Something you were too scared to risk. Have you given her the chance to explain?" Daniel asked.

He hadn't.

Jackson hadn't wanted to hear her voice—a lie, he was dying to—and then have to say goodbye again. Because she had broken his trust by sharing a private conversation they'd had. Nothing would change that.

Jackson shook his head.

"You might want to. In fact, I know you won't. You're as stubborn as our father," Daniel said. "So, I fucking will. Kristen told the girls that night at the bar because she wanted to make sure you were invited to the family breakfast. None of them knew you had already been invited."

Jackson blinked.

"She wasn't gossiping about your life. Kristen was recruiting the girls to get Hunter and Fletcher to invite you along."

"Why would she do that?" Jackson asked, shaking his head in disbelief.

"Harper said it was something about making sure you were part of our family before she left New York."

Fucking hell.

"Look, I'm not good at this shit, but you do know that girl loves you, right?" Daniel said.

Jackson nodded.

"Then what the fuck are you doing, standing here, while she is getting hormones and shit injected into her so some other guy's sperm impregnates her? If that was Harper, I would be kicking down doors," Daniel growled.

Goddamn it.

I'm a fucking idiot.

"If you love her, get your stubborn ass across the Pacific Ocean," Daniel added.

Jackson drew in a long breath and let it out. "Trust me, in my head, I am already there."

CHAPTER TWENTY-NINE

Daniel hung up his phone as Harper and her author friend, Emma, walked into the bar. He'd just arranged for his private jet to take Jackson on a little flight across the world.

What an idiot.

Still, he'd been the same. Under different circumstances. But less of an idiot, obviously.

"Hey, gorgeous. Hi, Emma," Daniel said as Harper planted a kiss on his lips.

"Hey." Emma dropped her shopping bags down and flopped into a chair. "Did you know your wife is a professional shopper *and* an author?"

Daniel shrugged. She could spend every cent he had, as long as she remained in his arms. Or his lap, he thought, as she plonked down on it.

And instant erection.

"I'm still teaching her how to spend money," Daniel said, wrapping his arm around his wife and kissing her neck.

"God. You guys are such juicy content for my next book," Emma noted, grinning.

Daniel let out a dry laugh.

"What are you wearing to the book conference? We'll need to get comfortable shoes," Harper said, then glanced around the table. "Wait. I thought Jackson was going to be here?"

"He's…had to disappear," Daniel said, knowing he was going to get his ass kicked for the little white lie.

Hunter shook his head at him across the table.

But Jackson deserved the chance to surprise Kristen before the girl gang, as he'd named them, got involved.

His phone rang.

Logan. His cousin. Johnathan had given them all his number after updating them about their grandmother.

Daniel shot Fletcher a look across the table and lifted his phone to his ear. "Daniel Dufort."

"Daniel, it's Logan."

Obviously.

"I'm in the city. Can we catch up?" Logan said.

"Is it anything confidential?" he asked, catching Hunter's narrowed-eye look.

"No. More a pre-funeral chat. To break the ice," Logan said, his voice as gravelly as Daniel's.

"We're all at the SoHo, down in the bar. If you're free right now, it's a good time to catch us all. My wife is here too."

"Perfect, see you in ten minutes," Logan said, ending the call.

His brothers looked at him.

Daniel put his phone down on the table and another call came through. When he got off that one, he updated them.

"Logan is popping in for a drink. You'll get to meet him before the funeral," Daniel said.

"Should I go?" Emma asked, tugging her long brunette hair around to one side of her neck. "Sounds like family stuff."

Harper glanced at him in question.

"No, I think he just wants to connect so it's less awkward when it happens," Daniel said. "If there's anything confidential, he'll know not to say anything in public. Logan is a businessman. He knows the drill."

"He's in the liquor industry, right?" Harper asked, tugging playfully on his tie.

She was going over his lap tonight for this public teasing. He gripped her fingers, and she gave him a knowing smile.

Witch.

"Logan is the CEO of Dufort Wines and Spirits. They're the biggest liquor distributor in the U.S, and they move bottles internationally," Daniel said.

"Logan Dufort. I knew I knew that name," Emma said, clicking her fingers.

"Do you, now?" Logan said, walking up behind her.

Emma jumped and let out a little embarrassed noise as she blushed.

Harper snorted.

Daniel lifted her from his lap as he stood and greeted his long-lost cousin. "Nice to see you again, Logan."

"Daniel," Logan said and began introducing himself to Fletcher and Hunter.

The apple didn't fall far from the tree. Logan was a few years older than him, just as tall, wide in the chest, and eyes that said he was hiding a few secrets. His suit expensive. Ermenegildo Zegna, by the looks, and a nice-looking timepiece on his wrist.

"This is my wife, Harper."

"Nice to meet you," Harper said, reaching out her hand. "This is my friend, Emma."

"I'm no one. Ignore me," Emma said, waving her hand out.

His cousin glanced down at the author like he was hungry as hell.

"I doubt that very much," Logan said, drinking her in like a long glass of rich whisky. "How about you tell me how you know me."

"Book research," Emma replied, and Daniel spotted the heat on her cheeks.

Logan's eyes shot up.

"For a romance novel," Emma said. "I write sexy smut books."

"Is that right? So, did I get the girl?" Logan asked, a sparkle in his eyes, while the rest of his expression remained serious.

The guy had broody perfected.

Harper shot a glance up at him, and Daniel lifted a shoulder, trying not to smile.

Emma was in New York for a book conference with Harper for another ten days. He didn't know her very well, except she was a successful author and lived in Chicago.

And wrote dirtier books than his wife.

Which he wasn't allowed to read.

Emma lifted her drink to her lips. "I haven't finished the story yet, so we'll just have to see."

Oh, Christ.

Harper was going to single-handedly matchmake the entire Dufort family.

CHAPTER THIRTY

Kristen stared at her phone like an alien was about to jump out of it.

Jackson.

He'd finally called her. Why now? What did he want?

More importantly, should she find a trash can or toilet? Because she was about to barf. Her stomach was churning in reaction to seeing his number.

What. Did. He. Want?

Of all nights to call her. She'd just been on a date. It had been horrible.

Todd.

Todd, the farmer from the Waikato region. All night, she'd had to listen to him talk about milking cows and udders and stuff about hay. She was not a farm girl. Or a morning girl. That was one match that was never going to happen.

Then, when she'd gotten in her car to drive home and pulled her phone out, she'd seen Jackson's missed call.

Her heart had leaped out of her chest.

She was surprised it wasn't lying on her damn lap, pumping away.

What a night.

Her ex ringing and her date terrible.

Kristen had only gone because a friend of a friend had said they'd be great together. It had been a blind date. She'd decided to go as one last hurrah before diving into the IVF program.

Kristen would start next week.

It was going to be intense, but when she finally held the baby in her arms, it would be worth it.

What she was going to tell her family was another thing. She could tell them it was a one-night stand. Would that be better than telling her elderly parents she'd had to pay to have a baby because she was crap at relationships?

They were a generation that wouldn't understand.

They were also at the tail-end of their lives, and she was creating hers with every decision she made. So, worrying about what they thought was something she wasn't willing to do.

Kristen knew them. They would love her child, after the shock of there not being a father. The rest she would figure out.

So, the date with Todd had not convinced her there was hope doing it the natural way. Not that he knew he was responsible for the huge decision in her life.

She turned on the car and began the drive back to her house, across town.

Ringggg.

Jesus.

Jackson again.

Kristen shook her head, gripping the steering wheel. She wasn't answering.

What the hell could he want after all these weeks? She was tempted to answer and give him a piece of her mind, but she was tired.

Todd wasn't getting a second date, and she was done trying all those online platforms and being setup by friends. She needed a good sleep, and then she'd do some more baby planning. Maybe even start looking at how she'd decorate the baby room.

Probably not a good idea to get ahead of herself, she thought.

Kristen turned onto her road and slowed as she approached her driveway. She pulled in and parked around the back of her house. The neighbor's cat rolled onto its back on the driveway as she walked back up.

"Hey, Tiger," Kristen said, crouching to give its tummy a rub. "You should get inside. It's chilly out."

As if agreeing with her, the cat leaped up and ran across the lawn to its home.

"Good kitty," she said to no one, then turned to walk up her path.

Kristen let out a scream.

A man in a long black coat, dark pants, and shirt stood on her doorstep. He stepped out into the light, and her mouth dropped open.

Suddenly, two neighbor's lights turned on, and her head swiveled as they both called out to her.

Gathering herself, Kristen responded, "Sorry, possum. Gave me a fright."

"Damn rodents," Mrs. Robinson muttered and closed her door, waving. Possums were classified as a pest in New Zealand.

The other neighbor disappeared.

Kristen turned back and stood frozen, staring at the man.

"Are you going to say hello?" Jackson asked, digging his hands into his coat.

CHAPTER THIRTY-ONE

Jackson stood on Kristen's path, watching as she stared back at him. From the fifteen or so feet between them, Jackson didn't like what he saw in her eyes.

Sadness.

Hurt.

Emptiness.

Was she pregnant already? He ran his eyes over her body.

It was winter in New Zealand, and she looked gorgeous all wrapped up. She wore a red dress under a navy coat and matching shoes. Her hair was curled, and she had full make-up on.

She'd been out with a man.

Fucking hell. But he had no one to blame but himself. He had let her go.

His chest tightened, his fists clenching with the need to claim what was his.

Mine.

But he had some work to do. She deserved yet another damn apology from him, and Jackson wasn't convinced he had much of a chance with her, after walking away like he had in New York.

Yet he'd flown across the world to try his damnedest.

Well, Daniel had flown him across the world. The Dufort jet was parked at the Auckland Airport, and if he had his way, it would be flying them both back to New York when it departed.

He wasn't leaving without her.

Jackson loved Kristen, and his life felt incomplete without her in it. He'd been ignoring it, but during the flight, as he began to understand what she had done and lower his defenses, it became suddenly and strikingly clear just how much he had been faking it the past several weeks.

He wanted his kitten back.

The government contract was the biggest success of his career, and yet when he went home at night and turned on the lights, staring at his empty luxury house, it was empty.

Even if it *had* been filled, Jackson wanted to share it with Kristen. To see the pride in her eyes. To go out and celebrate with her.

Only her.

It was always only her.

"What are you doing here?" she asked, pulling her coat around her tighter.

"What do you think I'm doing here?" he asked, taking a few steps.

Finally, she snapped out of her shock and let out a long sigh. She stormed past him.

"Wasting your time, that's what you're doing. Go home, Jackson," she snapped, pulling her keys out of her bag and attempting to unlock the door.

She dropped them.

Picked them up.

Dropped them again.

Jackson walked up behind her, reached around her calmly, and took the keys from her. With his hand on her lower back, he moved her to the side and unlocked the door.

She glanced up at him as he handed her the keys.

"I messaged you one hundred times," Kristen said, clutching the keys and not moving.

"Seven times," he said, clenching his hand so he didn't reach out and cup her face.

"That's six too many." Kristen glanced inside her house.

"I deserve that," he replied, dying to touch her. "Can we talk inside?"

"No."

"Okay."

"Go home," she whispered, her eyes slowly lifting to his. But he saw the pain. He saw the unrequited love she felt. But it wasn't.

"No," he replied, and this time, he *did* reach out and run the back of his fingers gently over her cheek.

Her lips parted, then pressed together.

"I can't do this, Jackson. You should have called from the States. Or messaged. Turning up like this is too much." Kristen moved back an inch.

"Well, that was sort of the plan. You would've ignored me." The corner of his lip twitched. "Which you did."

Her eyes roamed over his face.

"Are you here on business?" she asked, mistrust rich in her eyes.

"If getting you back is business, then yes."

"No. No. No." Kristen pushed past him and walked inside.

He stood on the doorstep and put his hands in his coat again. Turning to face her, he waited for her invite inside.

"No," she said again, her hand on the door.

"Then I will go sit in my car until you're ready to speak with me." Jackson nodded to the black SUV across the road.

Kristen glared at him, took in the car, and looked back at him.

"Fine. Do that." She shut the door.

Jackson smiled.

Good for her.

But he wasn't giving up that easily.

CHAPTER THIRTY-TWO

"Fuck, fuck, fuck, fuck, fuck," Kristen muttered as she walked down the hall to her bedroom.

Jackson Wiles was in New Fucking Zealand.

Here.

Oh my fucking god.

Her blood was pumping at an unnatural speed, and she was sure she was going to have a heart attack. Kristen dropped her bag on the chair in her bedroom and tiptoed over to the window.

"Why am I tiptoeing?" she growled. "Ugh."

Moving the curtains slightly, she looked across the road. Jackson was climbing into the SUV, and she watched him recline the seat and get comfortable. Then, the internal light of the vehicle faded.

Pfftt.

He'd last five damn minutes without his fancy penthouse and room service.

Stupid rich people.

She wasn't letting him inside. She wasn't going to let him back into her life. She most definitely was *not* going to kiss him.

Nor was she going to let herself feel the love she knew still existed and risk getting hurt all over again.

Beep, beep.

She jumped.

Shit.

Jackson. *I'm not leaving.*

You will, she replied.

Kristen sat on the end of her bed and chewed her thumbnail.

What if he needed the bathroom?

Should she take him a blanket?

Kristen stood and paced.

This was what he wanted. No, she wasn't going to bend. He could have apologized any time within the past few weeks, but she had not heard a single word.

I'm sorry.

Thanks. Okay, bye.

Kristen frowned at herself.

That was childish.

But the thing was, seeing him again was messing with her body and mind. The need to throw herself into that strong thick chest of his and feel him wrap his big arms around her was overwhelming.

The small touch when he took the keys had sent an electrical charge through her that was still buzzing. His familiar woody scent making her warm at her core.

Goddamn him.

How could she hate him and want him at the same time?

No, she didn't hate him. He was still as gorgeous as she remembered. Not that she'd forgotten. She'd stared at his photos a million times as she'd cried and yelled at the screen.

One minute with Jackson and she'd felt a million things she'd never felt after a night with Todd. Not at all.

God, even those determined eyes of his, the way his lush lips had a hint of smile and a lifetime of pleasure promised on them, created a heat through her.

If getting you back is business, then yes.

Why now?

There was no way he was in love with her. A man didn't do that to a woman he loved. Perhaps a stupid man…

What if…

Stop. Do not go there, girlfriend.

Did she really think he was here to whisk her away into the sunset and live happily ever after?

I'm such an idiot.

She couldn't get involved in a long-distance relationship with him, or anyone, if she was going to have a baby.

Not *if*. She was.

It was better if she shut that door and moved on. Completely. Jackson needed to do the same.

Decision made, Kristen stood and walked to the curtain again.

He was still there.

She needed time to gather her thoughts, so she had a quick shower and changed into a pair of jeans and a sweatshirt. Pulling on some thick socks, she walked into the kitchen and put the kettle on.

Then texted him.

Come inside and let's talk. Then you can leave.

Two minutes later, she walked to the door and opened it. Jackson was standing there, waiting.

He stepped inside.

She closed the door.

When she turned around, she bumped straight into him. Jackson encircled her with his body, and she melted into him.

Fail.

Just this once, she promised herself, as his warmth and energy filled her with everything she had been needing and missing since leaving NYC.

THANK God, Jackson thought, as he held Kristen in his arms again. It was as if the universe had turned a light on, and everything felt bright again.

He closed his eyes and nuzzled into the vanilla honey scent of her long soft hair. The knowledge she was safe and that he could stand here and protect her was the most primal feeling he'd ever felt.

Jackson loved her so fucking much.

Except she didn't know it.

He wasn't going to let her make a damn baby with any man, sperm donor or otherwise. If anyone was putting his sperm inside this woman, it was him.

His woman.

This was going to be the presentation of his life. The most important contract he'd ever win.

Hopefully.

Kristen pulled away, her eyes meeting his for a quick moment, then dropping.

"Would you like a drink? I'm making a hot chocolate," Kristen said, her feet padding along the floor in her socks.

It was incredibly cute.

"Do you have whisky?" At her glance, he grinned. "Of course, you have whisky."

"Not the fancy stuff you have," she said, opening a cupboard and pulling out a bottle and glass for him.

She was right.

It wasn't the fancy, or even half-decent, stuff.

Jackson looked around her house. It was modestly decorated. A sofa and two armchairs facing a flat screen TV on the wall, paintings, a dining table, and chairs in the corner, which led to the kitchen.

Photos of her and friends.

He recognized Harper.

Potted plants and soft furnishings. Cushions in warm colors against the natural tones. A throw blanket on the sofa and a book on the side table, which hinted to how she spent her spare time.

Jackson pulled off his coat and dropped it on the back of the armchair. That's when he noticed it.

Beside her laptop on the coffee table were fertility brochures.

Shit.

How far along in the process was she?

Kristen walked out of the kitchen with her hot chocolate and a glass of whisky, handing it to him.

"Sit," she said, pointing to a chair.

He took the glass, his fingers brushing hers, and their eyes locked as that same desire ignited.

When he sat, Jackson went straight for the jugular. It was unplanned, but it just fell out. Mostly because he'd been brewing on it since returning to his car.

"You were on a date tonight," Jackson said, his voice gruff.

Her brows lifted, then narrowed. "Yes."

Clenching his teeth, he nodded, then took a big gulp of the cheap whisky.

Jesus, mother of Mary and all the saints, it was terrible.

He cleared his throat multiple times, and Kristen tried to hide her smile. It was the first hint of happiness on her face he'd seen in over a month. God, he missed it.

His own eyes lit up.

"If I need to drink bleach to make you happy, I'd consider it," he said, dropping the glass on the table in front of him.

Her smile faded.

"Fuck, Kris. I'm sorry. I should never have walked away at breakfast." He raked his hand through his hair. "I lost my mind."

Kristen shook her head.

"Look, I get it. Your mom is sick. I should never have told Addy and Liv. I was just trying to help, but that's no exc—"

"I know what you did. Daniel told me. I'm a fool," Jackson said, interrupting her. He wasn't here for her apology.

Kristen sipped her drink.

"What did you think was going to happen by coming here, Jackson? Because honestly, I can't go back. You hurt me." She placed her drink onto the table. "Fool me once, shame on you. Fool me twice, shame on me. We've been down this road before."

Jackson stared at her a long moment, his brows lowering. What was she talking about? They were two different situations.

The first time, she'd thought he was using her to get to his family. He hadn't. Jackson had genuinely liked her. The open door to the Dufort's had been the cherry on top. They'd been over this.

This time, he'd run in fear, back to his mother.

Fuck that.

He was clearing this up, once and for all.

"You have got caught up in a very muddled story. I'm sorry for that. My mother has lied to me my entire life. There was a lot of lies tied to bringing me into this world. Including the fact that I had a twin sister, who died at birth."

Her mouth dropped open.

"She never told Johnathan about Jessica. She never told any of us a lot of stuff," Jackson said, glancing at the whisky and deciding it wasn't worth it. He needed the skin on the back of his throat.

Jackson undid the buttons on his shirt, folded them over his black cashmere sweater sleeves, and pushed them up his forearms.

Her eyes followed his movement, and he saw the desire there.

Hope fluttered in his chest.

"You have a twin?" she whispered.

"Yes. Well, no," he replied, smiling. "I don't know how to answer that. It's not something I've talked to anyone about, except Mom. And now Johnathan."

Kristen shook her head. "Wow."

"Since learning someone had funded my college tuition, and getting a hint that something wasn't right in my life, Mom warned me from asking any questions." Jackson shook his head. "She should have known I wouldn't listen."

"She probably did," Kristen replied, giving him a small smile.

"Yeah." He smiled back, then it fell from his face. "But she had good reason to warn me off. What happened was terrible. She has now told me everything."

Kristen sat listening.

"My point is, it's been a confusing time," Jackson said. "Mom is dying, and I was terrified I was going to lose her and be left alone. Trevor, who I thought was my father, died earlier this year. When I met Johnathan and discovered he loved Jenna, I realized I had opened the can of worms Mom was warning me about.

"He's not a man you can control. I knew I couldn't tell him about her health."

"Fuck, I'm so sorry."

Jackson's eyes lifted to hers. "No. I was wrong."

He opted to take another sip of the whisky.

Regretted it.

"I knew when Johnathan learned about her illness, I couldn't stop him going to her." Jackson shook his head. "I felt responsible and terrified she was going to go into shock and…die. As irrational as it sounds."

Kristen's eyes filled with tears. "You didn't want to lose your mom."

He shook his head and took in a long breath. "If my selfishness in finding my father ended in her dying…"

Kristen moved across the room and crouched in front of him, laying her hands on his thighs. "Oh God, Jackson. I get it." She rubbed her hand on one leg. "Is she okay?"

"She's fragile, but she loves Johnathan as much as he loves her." Jackson cupped her face with his hand. "She's moved to New York. To be with Johnathan."

"Oh," Kristen said, flinching in surprise. "Wasn't expecting that."

His eyes took in her freshly washed face and still damp hair. "You're so fucking beautiful, Kris."

She stood.

"No. I can't Jackson," she said, backing up.

Jackson stood. "Can't forgive me?"

She shook her head. "I do forgive you. But you shouldn't have come here. I've made some big life decisions, and they don't include you. They don't include anyone."

"So I've heard, sweetheart. But I'm sorry, that's not happening. If you're having anyone's baby, it will be mine."

CHAPTER THIRTY-THREE

Kristen gasped. "You know?"

Harper would never have told him. Daniel, on the other hand? No, he was a private person and would know how important this was.

"Daniel let it slip," Jackson said, and she groaned. "I'm glad he did."

Goodie for you. I'm pissed.

"So? You find out I'm having a baby and fly across the world? Why? I'm happy to hear things have worked out with your family, but you treated me very badly. Did you think you would be a donor? Come over here and stick your dick in me?"

Fury raced through her.

How dare Daniel tell him about this. Slip or not.

Yes, she was aware how ironic her anger was.

His brows raised. "I mean, I was hoping that would be in the cards at some point, but first, I need you to know that I still love you. That I will do whatever it takes to apologize and prove to you that I am not living without you, Kristen Holle."

Her mouth fell open.

Was he insane?

Jackson took a step closer, and his hands landed on her hips.

What was happening?

"No," she whispered.

"Yes," he replied, just as softly. "There has not been a day gone by you weren't on my mind. A day where I've wished you were in my bed, my kitchen, my bathroom, brushing your teeth with me."

A little noise escaped her throat.

His hand brushed over her hair.

"I wanted to apologize soon after arriving home, but I think I knew if I spoke to you again, I wouldn't be able to walk away. I was scared. I think I've always known you were it for me." Jackson's eyes glittered in the soft light..

"No."

"Yes, sweetheart. You are mine."

She couldn't breathe.

He wanted her?

Jackson was claiming her.

Then he closed the gap and pressed his warm soft lips against hers. "Marry me. Have my baby. Spend the rest of your life with me, Kristen. I love you."

Marry him?

Before she could answer, he slid his tongue inside and claimed her mouth with such passion and dominance she lost all thought.

What is happening right now?

As always, Kristen's body completely surrendered to his claim, her mouth opening and arms wrapping around him. He lifted her against him.

God, how she had longed for his touch.

To feel his desire, his need, once again.

They lapped at each other's mouths, and Jackson held her tightly against every inch of his body that was physically possible.

When he slid her down his body, she stared up at him. Without shoes, she was a heck of a lot shorter than this tall handsome man.

God, she was going to miss him.

Because she knew this couldn't work.

"I can't," she said, shaking her head. "I can't leave my parents. I'm doing IVF. I'm…"

"Stop."

Jackson picked her up and wrapped her legs around his body. He walked her down to her bedroom, easily finding his way because it was hardly the huge luxury home he was used to being in.

"Jackson."

"Tell me you love me," he demanded.

"You know I do," she said, as he tugged her sweatshirt off.

"Tell me you want to have my baby." He tossed her jeans across the room and tore off his own top.

She stared at his gorgeous, muscular chest, her mouth watering, her core heating as she felt herself get wet. Wet like she hadn't been for weeks.

"Tell me."

Kristen let him undo her bra and nudge her panties aside until she was completely naked. His mouth fell to hers, the kiss far more passionate this time.

Then his jeans disappeared.

"I told you I wasn't leaving. I told you, you're mine." Jackson spread her legs and crouched between them.

Lick.

Oh God.

Another even longer, slower lick, as he held her eyes.

"You want a baby, sweetheart? Let's make the most beautiful damn baby. Two, three. However many you want."

"You are insane," she said, trying to focus.

"Crazy for you." He sucked hard on her clit.

Kristen fell back on the bed and closed her eyes as Jackson demolished her. Her orgasm hit like a thunderbolt. Fast. And out of nowhere.

God, how she had wanted him for so long.

Then he was climbing on her and claiming her lips again. Her hands slid to his chest, then into his hair.

"This isn't real."

"Feel that?" Jackson said, as the head of his cock slid inside her.

She arched, needing more.

"That feel real to you?" he asked, his face inches from hers, their eyes locked. "Tell me you want my babies, Kristen, and that you are mine."

His head throbbed at the entrance of her pussy as they both waited.

Kristen did want him.

She'd always wanted him.

How, she didn't know. There was still so much to discuss, but she loved Jackson Wiles with all she was, and the idea of having his babies made her heart flare to life and nearly explode from her chest.

"Yes, damn you. I want your babies," she cried as he thrust inside her.

Then stopped.

"And me. Say you'll marry me," he growled.

"Not on your life. You have to propose far more romantically than that," she said, moaning and writhing beneath him.

His smile lit up like fireworks. "Done."

Then his cock was pumping in and out of her, her body arching and nipples rubbing against his muscular chest.

"Kris, fuck, you feel incredible," Jackson groaned.

"More, harder. I need this," she begged.

"Clench around my cock, baby. That's, oh God," Jackson cried. "This round is going to be short."

She laughed, then mumbled out another moan as his hand found her clit, and her next orgasm began to build.

This every day of her life?

Yes, please.

JACKSON flipped and lay on his back, pulling Kristen on top of him. Her legs flopped, but he slid his cock inside her.

The connection was important.

"We just made a baby." He grinned.

"Okay, soldier, settle down. It's not that easy," Kristen snorted.

"Oh well, we'll have to keep practicing. Day and night. I'm persistent." He kissed her lips lazily and brushed her hair off her face. "Fuck, I missed you."

Kristen leaned her elbow on his shoulder. "You really want to marry me?"

He quirked a brow. "I *am* marrying you."

"So arrogant."

"We can come back here as often as you like to see your parents," he said, knowing that was important to her. "I'm going to buy a jet."

She reared back. "A what?"

"Plane. Things that fly in the air. Jet." He grinned.

"I know what they are. That's…How?"

Warmth flooded through him as he began to share how he'd secured the contract and the changes he was making to Appopolis.

"New York?" She sighed.

"Sweetheart, this includes you. You'll be close to Harper and the girls. I know you'll miss your family, but I promise you, whenever you want to come back here, you can."

Kristen chewed her lip.

"I do love you. I'm not saying yes because you have to ask me when your cock isn't inside me."

Jackson titled his head. "That's going to give me very limited time to propose because I intend to fuck you every second I can. I want these babies."

Kristen grinned as moisture filled her eyes. "Then consider this a tentative yes. Now, make love to me again. You have a lot of time to make up."

He slapped her naked sexy butt. "Yes, ma'am."

EPILOGUE

One week later

Jackson sat on the sofa with his arm draped over Kristen's shoulder, watching the game on Daniel's big screen.

"So, this isn't anything like rugby?" Kristen asked, and both he and Daniel shot her a frown.

"Oh boy. I'll initiate her, I promise. The answer is no, and whatever you do, never say anything bad about football. Like ever," Harper said.

Emma, Harper's author friend, laughed. "Do you have baseball in New Zealand?"

Harper shrugged and glanced at Kristen.

"I think so. We're not really sports fans," Kristen said.

"You are now." Jackson put his feet up on the coffee table. "Our babies are going to play football and baseball. Also basketball."

Kristen shot him a glance that told him he'd gone a little overboard.

He didn't care. He couldn't wait to be a dad. Jackson was going to be the best damn father on the planet.

"Get her pregnant first, Jackson." Daniel shook his head. "At least you put a ring on it."

Jackson lifted Kristen's left hand and kissed her knuckles, just missing the square four carat diamond.

"He sure did, and very romantically too," Kristen said. "My father is still coming to terms with it, but my mother fell in love with him, so she's talking him around."

"And I'm in trouble," Harper noted. "Oh well, I have my best friend living in New York, so my evil plan worked."

Jackson laughed. "You didn't even know who I was."

"That's what you think," Harper replied, waggling her eyebrows.

"Ignore her. She's writing a thriller and gets like this." Kristen shook her head.

Jackson shot Daniel a look, and he nodded to confirm as Emma laughed.

Wow. That was nuts.

They had stayed in New Zealand for a week, packing up Kristen's things and preparing to have them shipped to NYC, before returning to the U.S.

Her employer had been mad, but he'd dumped a bunch of cash to cover her month-long notice period, and suddenly, the man had been happier.

Funny how money worked like that.

Jackson had had to speed up the purchase of the penthouse, but with Daniel pulling some strings, it had been ready when they landed.

"Tell us how he proposed." Emma put her hand in her chin.

Kristen shot him a grin.

"Jackson dropped to his knees when we were walking through the Waitakere Ranges. It's a beautiful, lush green bush walk. He did it right in front of a waterfall."

"And tell them the other bit."

Kristen snorted. "It was about to rain, and the water spray had created a rainbow. He insists he created it."

Jackson saw Daniel roll his eyes, and he silently laughed, his chest bouncing up and down.

"I didn't see him at first. I was staring at the rainbow and the waterfall. It's so beautiful there."

It was true. It had felt like a million years, waiting for her to turn around.

"In the end, I had to tug on her hand, and when she turned, she was confused. It was pretty funny." Jackson smirked. "When she looked down at me, immediate tears."

"I mean, not immediately."

"Immediately, sweetheart. More water than the damn waterfall," Jackson teased.

"He's an idiot," Kristen said to the girls.

"But you are marrying him." Emma sighed and pulled out her phone.

"She can't escape. I've kidnapped her," Jackson said. "But I said to her, 'You knew I was going to do this,' and what did you do?"

Kristen laughed. "Told him it didn't matter and waved him on."

"Waved. Me. On."

This time, Daniel barked out a laugh.

Kristen grinned at him, knowing neither of them would share the rest. He hadn't exactly prepared what he would say, but the words had flowed.

"Kristen Holle, you showed up in my life at the most ridiculous time. My life was a mess, and I didn't know where I belonged. Or who I was. When I am with you, I know exactly who I am and where I want to be. With you. As your husband."

He had taken her hand in his.

"Will you be my wife?"

Tears had flowed down her face as she nodded and let out the most beautiful word he'd ever heard in his life.

"Yes."

When they'd landed back in the United States, he'd arranged for a jeweler to present them some rings, and Kristen had chosen one they both loved.

He fucking loved seeing his ring on her finger.

And one day, his child growing inside her.

As predicted, his mother had loved Kristen immediately, and the two of them had chatted for hours. Johnathan had, later the afternoon of their visit, surprised him.

"Jackson, I'd like you to take my name."

His mouth had dropped open.

"Trevor was never your father, and you've told me you didn't have a close relationship with the man. So, if it's something you'd like to do, especially before you marry this young lady, then you may."

Jackson had glanced at his mother, and she had smiled.

Then his eyes landed on Kristen's. "What do you think?"

"It's your decision," she'd answered. "But that would officially make me Mrs. Dufort and Harper's sister-in-law, so I'm all for it."

"You are supposed to be excited about becoming my wife," he'd teased.

"Oh, I am, baby. I am." She patted his knee, and his mother laughed.

The two most important women in his life were happy. It had filled his heart as he nodded at his father. "Thank you. It would be my honor."

Johnathan was right about Trevor. He didn't deserve his loyalty.

Cue the happy tears from his mom.

Taking the Dufort name had felt like the right thing to do. Especially knowing his half-brothers had accepted him into the fold. It felt almost natural.

Daniel's phone beeped, and he pulled it out of his pocket, swiping.

"God, my feet are killing me from all this walking," Emma said. "Even with your driver."

"Same," Harper acknowledged. "We need massages. Let's book them for tomorrow. You in, Kris?"

She looked up at Jackson. "Yes. If this guy can handle a few hours without me."

"Nope. I'll die," he said, kissing her lips. "Of course. Can you arrange your car to pick her up, Harper? I will be using ours tomorrow. We haven't organized a separate driver and car for Kristen yet."

"So weird," Kristen said, leaning into him.

"You'll get used to it. You're a rich woman now, baby," Jackson said.

Comparable with his brothers, now he had this contract in place. At nearly twenty-five, he was only just beginning.

"I'll teach her everything I know," Harper said. "It takes some getting used to."

"More book content." Emma rubbed her hands together.

When Jackson glanced at Daniel, he shook his head. "She writes about billionaires. Don't ask, trust me. Do. Not. Ask."

The girls all giggled.

"Anyway. I have news," Daniel said, holding out his phone. "Grandma has passed."

This time, the girls all gasped.

"That was Dad. Logan just messaged him."

Jackson hadn't had a chance to meet his paternal grandmother. Time had been limited, and as much as it would have been nice, Kristen had been his priority.

"The funeral is in a few days. Logan will be arranging everything and coming from Philly tomorrow."

Harper nudged Emma.

"Stop," Emma said and blushed.

Harper giggled. "What? You like him. I can see why. I think he's kind of hot."

"The fuck you do," Daniel growled.

"Not like that," Harper scoffed.

"How else is there to take that?" Daniel asked, glancing at him.

Jackson laughed and pulled Kristen onto his lap. "Welcome to the Dufort family, baby. It's never a dull day."

Daniel grunted.

To read Logan and Emma's spicy romance, go to
www.books2read.com/darksurrender

Or turn the page to read the first chapter now!

Also, if you love steamy paranormal romances check out The Vampire Prince – **its FREE** and is the first book in my bestselling vampire series, **The Moretti Blood Brothers!**

www.books2read.com/thevampireprince

Turn the page to read the first chapter.

CHAPTER ONE

Willow leaned on the counter and slowly counted to ten.

She'd been waiting for the sonographer for over thirty minutes. It was seven in the evening, and as the only person in the waiting room, it wasn't clear why she was having to wait so long.

Her patience was dwindling.

Tap, tap, tap.

Her subtle attempt at getting the absent receptionist's attention wasn't working. This was the last place she felt like being; however, she'd injured her ankle over a month ago, and regular treatments weren't working, so her osteopath had sent her for an ultrasound.

She didn't have a problem with ultrasounds; the problem was the time taken out of her day. With multiple deadlines due, Willow was still learning how to balance her own needs over her well-paying but demanding clients in her new media relations business.

When she'd discovered the clinic was open late, she'd booked a six-thirty appointment hoping to be home by seven where she could heat leftovers and dive back into work.

Yet here she stood thirty minutes later, still waiting. She'd browsed Facebook, put hearts on all the Instagram posts, and sent out a tweet.

"Excuse me," she called out as politely as she could. "Hello!"

The receptionist who had greeted her earlier popped her face around the corner. She held her phone in her hand and looked annoyed at the interruption.

Willow inwardly sighed. The girl was probably making a tick tock, or whatever the kids called it these days. Not that she was old, but yeah, it wasn't her thing.

"Can I help you?"

"Sorry to disturb you"—*no, I'm not*—"How much longer will the wait be?"

Chest heaving, the girl didn't even attempt to hide her annoyance. She walked to her computer and began tapping away with some barely contained huffs. They both squinted as headlights from a large SUV pulled up onto the sidewalk. Willow covered her eyes and looked away.

"Let me see," the girl said once whoever was driving had turned the headlights off. "He should be available soon. We had a delay earlier, which created a backlog."

Willow ground her teeth.

"Oh."

She forced a small smile to her lips, then returned to her seat where she imagined how the conversation could have gone.

Why in the hell didn't you tell me, then I could have rescheduled?

Oh, he won't be long. It's only half an hour.

That's my decision to make. You took that decision from me.

Lady, chill out.

Don't tell me to chill, you tick tocking—

"Oh, they're back," the receptionist said, interrupting her hypothetical argument—which she was winning, by the way.

She *was* winning.

Willow looked out at the big men who had exited the SUV.

"Who are they?"

The men were all dressed in black. Their attire should have made them look like thugs with all that leather and denim, but there was an air of wealth about them. Perhaps it was the big SUV, the quality of their clothes, or the chunky, shiny watches on their wrists.

One thing was for sure—they were all ridiculously good looking, as if they'd stepped off a movie set. Rough but polished.

"I don't know. For the past few weeks, they've shown up religiously every night before heading upstairs to the medical rooms."

Then they did just that. All six of the men walked in a tight group, gathering around one dark-haired man as if they were secret service. Willow wondered if he was a celebrity or politician hoping for anonymity. Or perhaps she watched too much television.

"What kind of treatment do they do upstairs? Cosmetic?" It was a wild guess, but why else would you sneak in for treatment late at night so regularly.

The girl looked away from the testosterone-loaded view and shrugged.

"That's just the thing; no one really knows. Recently they've been working late into the night. It's weird."

Willow stood to watch their progress, taking in their long, confident strides. Outside, the sky had grown dark, but streetlights poured golden light around the area, offering good visibility.

She'd been right—they were all extremely attractive, each of them taller than the average man, with broad shoulders, thick necks, and solid thighs.

"Perhaps they're security?"

"Hmm, who knows?" the girl mumbled as her finger swiped across her phone screen.

"Pretty hot security if they are," she added with a small grin, despite losing her audience.

Suddenly, one man turned his head and looked directly at her. Her heart began pounding in her chest, racing as she stepped back, gasping.

Silver, ethereal-looking eyes seemed to hold her on the spot. His eyes narrowed, yet his gaze didn't feel threatening. As they continued to stare, she felt her body and face heat unexpectedly.

"What?"

What?

The spell broken, Willow's eyes flicked to the receptionist.

"What?" Willow asked back.

"Oh, sorry. I thought you said something."

She looked back at the man whose eyes stayed on her a moment longer before he turned to the man standing next to him and laughed casually, totally carrying on with his life.

Which was fine. Except she was suddenly overcome with a strange and irrational feeling of loss.

"Willow Thompson-Davies?"

She turned abruptly and found the sonographer standing with an iPad in his hand, greeting her.

"Are you okay?"

Willow blinked. "Yes. Oh, yes, I was just...never mind. Hello."

"I'm Mark. Sorry for the wait; it has been one of those crazy days," he said with a grin that had the power to melt panties.

She grabbed her purse and followed him through to the treatment room, wondering if she was being pranked by a relaunch of *Candid Camera.*

She could just see it.

Now we see Willow being greeted by the male stripper posing as a medical practitioner. She does not know the men outside will join him in a moment and do a Magic Mike routine.

"Now, let's get your pants off."

Willow's mouth fell open. Mark grinned again and nodded to the door on her left. "Pop right in there and change into the scrubs."

Her face flamed as she began mumbling words which were not of the English language.

I really need to get laid.

Clearly her mind was in the gutter, and judging by the handsome man's grin, he was enjoying her discomfort.

Thirty minutes later, she followed him back to the reception. Her eyes immediately glanced outside and found her silver-eyed man and one other leaning against a power pole. She hadn't stopped thinking about him during her appointment. The absence of his eyes had left an icy shiver throughout her body that she'd been unable to shake.

He was beautiful, in a dark and dominant way. His hair was black with waves that fell just below his ears, and he had a strong, masculine jaw. Even from here, she could see he hadn't shaved recently, which gave him that sexy edge women loved. She was one of them.

The jacket he wore only emphasized his muscular upper body, and as he dug his hand into his jean pocket, his T-shirt and pants separated just enough to expose an inch of silky olive skin.

She licked her lips unconsciously. His head turned. She couldn't breathe. He held her stare for a moment, then glanced between her and Mark.

She whipped her head around as Mark spoke. He was leaning flirtatiously against the counter beside her, smirking.

"I will send the results to your osteopath tomorrow afternoon. They'll call you and talk through them."

"So, you can't tell me anything?" she asked again, trying her luck.

He shook his head. "My expertise is in taking the images. I leave the diagnosis up to your specialist."

"Not even a hint?" She smiled and lowered her eyelashes. It had been years since she'd flirted, so she must have looked like she had something stuck in her eye.

He laughed, confirming her suspicion, and shoved a piece of paper in her hand. "Not even a hint. Now be gone with you."

"Fine." She laughed, and with one last glance at the receptionist, she hoisted her handbag onto her shoulder and stepped out the door.

Like all street-smart women, Willow pretended not to look at the darkly clad men, but she couldn't help herself. The second man was also large and muscular, but an inch or two shorter. He had a very predatory way in which he held himself, which gave off a dangerous vibe the silver-eyed man didn't have. Or at least not as much. She was certain they were military or security of some kind.

The closer she got to them, unable to reach her vehicle any other way, the louder her heart thumped in her chest.

Around her, businesses were turning off their lights, closing for the evening, but the area was lit by nearby streetlights, so she felt safe enough.

The men may be supersized—and my God, they were, from their heads to their hands, legs, and arms—but that didn't make them dangerous. Heck, she was a sucker for bulging biceps. Usually. Today, her inner voice told her to be wary.

A few steps away now, and she felt a zing rush through her. A ringtone broke the silent tension as "Who Let the Dogs Out" filled the night air.

Willow glanced at the man with the silver eyes, and her heart skipped a beat as the corner of his lips twitched. His friend answered his phone and took a few steps away. Silver Eyes stepped away from the pole and watched her. It wasn't a threatening move, yet it made her tense.

"I won't hurt you," he said.

"No. You won't," she replied, deliberately looking directly into his eyes in warning.

His smile grew, softening his strong jawline and sending warm shivers through her body. Warmth that had no place being there.

"Good girl."

God, he was gorgeous. He was just the right amount of bad boy with a spoonful of class. Now that she was closer, she could see just how well his jeans fit, and that his leather jacket was clearly designer. Before she could help herself, a blush hit her cheeks, and she gave him a shy smile.

Damn traitorous body.

Her blush spread its way down her face, across her chest, and descended to her core.

What is wrong with me?

She felt an unreasonable need for him to reach out and touch her. To touch him back.

If I could just run my fingers over those biceps and through his hair.

Willow scrunched her eyes closed at her desperation. She'd never reacted to a man like this so quickly. God, she needed to get laid.

Maybe if she hadn't been distracted, she would have seen them and been able to avoid the group of kids on skateboards that came flying around the corner. When she attempted to dodge them, she cursed in embarrassment as her ankle gave out. Arms flailing in the air, Willow began to fall, her head hitting the trash can and...

Am I flying?

Large hands caught her and placed her gently on her feet, holding her steady.

"You okay?"

They both looked around at the kids who were rapidly calling out apologies and wisely hightailing it out of there.

Shaking, Willow took a deep breath and ran her hands over her body to make sure her pants weren't ripped.

"Shit, thank you," she said, rubbing the back of her head. There would be a nice lump there soon. "How did you catch me so fast?"

He shrugged. "I work out."

"No kidding," she replied without thinking.

He let out a little laugh as Willow wobbled on her ankle and stepped out of his hold.

"Seriously though, thank you. God, I'll probably need another stupid ultrasound." Willow glanced over at the clinic and cringed. The sonographer was still leaning over the counter, chatting. When she turned back, she found those silver eyes narrowed at her.

"Did that man harass you? I'll—"

"No. Nothing like that," she replied quickly, surprised by his response. "It was just a long wait, and I'm impatient."

He nodded, looking unconvinced.

She wobbled some more. "Hey, listen, I better put this on ice. Thanks for catching me." Willow gave him a grateful smile, straightened her handbag, and began limping away.

"Wait," he told her, barking out the order and surprising her again. "You can't drive like that."

He had a point. She could feel her ankle swelling and her head beginning to pound. Her house was only a few minutes' drive away, but it was still unsafe for her to be behind the wheel.

Willow looked around, considering how safe it would be to leave her car if she ordered an Uber.

"Sure, I'll..." She turned, swayed, and once again, the man steadied her.

"Let me give you a ride home."

What? Oh, hell no.

"No, that's not necessary."

Nor was it wise. Her body, despite the accident, felt like a volcano about to erupt in his presence. Every time he spoke, a vibration ran through her.

"I'll book an Uber." Willow pulled out her phone and wrapped an arm around her middle. Despite the inferno raging within her, she could feel the chill of shock setting in.

The other guy ended his phone call.

"You saving damsels in distress now?" He smirked, then raised an eyebrow as Silver Eyes removed his jacket and laid it over her shoulders.

"I'm giving this *damsel in distress* a ride home. Give me the keys." He held out his hand and tipped his chin up toward the building in front of them. "I'll be back by the time he's done."

He? Who was "he"?

The jacket was warm and had a deliciously masculine scent she wanted to melt into. She let out a little groan, and may have wiggled into it a little. Still, Willow considered herself street smart. She hadn't survived living in Los Angeles all her life by getting in vehicles with strangers.

"I'm not in distress." She shrugged off the jacket and began to hand it back, quietly mourning the loss of the delicious scent.

She would not be accepting his offer of a ride home nor getting in a vehicle with him. He looked like the strong, protective type, but that didn't mean she could trust him. Or his pecs.

He pushed the jacket back in place. "You hit your head and can barely stand up. Let me help you, woman."

Woman?

Oh, so it was like that, was it?

She knew exactly the type of man he was. Protective, yes. But also dominant and bossy. Probably incredible in bed, but a complete control freak outside of it. Unfortunately, she had a love-hate relationship with those kinds of men. They turned her on, but she hated being controlled.

Or have I just never met a man mentally stronger than me?

"Like I said, I'll just book an Uber."

"No, you won't," he growled. Like, an actual growl.

Startled, she looked up from her phone, a chill running through her. "What?"

Something felt wrong.

"It's not safe," he said.

She narrowed her eyes, glanced at his friend, then laughed to lighten the situation. "I don't even know your name. You're a stranger. I appreciate you catching my fall, but I am not getting into a car with a stranger late at night."

Okay, so it wasn't that late, but still. Did this man think she was stupid? This was Los Angeles, for goodness' sake. Getting into a car with someone who looked like he had a gun stashed in those tight, hot pants was stupid and irresponsible.

I don't think that's a gun.

Willow began removing the jacket, but again, he stopped her.

"Frank. My name is Frank."

His friend coughed. She glanced at them both with narrowed eyes. "Your name is *not* Frank." She really hoped she hadn't just offended him. But seriously, *Frank?*

"Okay, fine, it's Brayden. Now you know my name, so let me drive you home."

"So now you're just making up names and expect me to jump in your car? No, nope, nada. Not happening." She stepped away, removed his jacket, and looked around for a place to put it.

"Bray, what are you doing? Let the human go and let's wait for Vincent."

Human? And who was Vincent?

He took the jacket from her, gripping her hand while holding her gaze deeply for a moment. Willow felt mesmerized and frozen. Then he turned to his friend.

"No. Tell him I will see him tomorrow before the sun comes up. I won't need the vehicle."

"Oh, fuck."

The presumptuous, sexy son of a—

"Come," Brayden said, his silver eyes determined as they sparkled in the artificial light.

Her mouth fell open as he reached down and lifted her into his arms with such speed, she never saw it coming.

"What are you doing?" she gasped.

"Close your eyes." His voice was husky as he stared down at her.

"Wh—"

"Close your eyes. It'll be easier."

She couldn't explain why she did, but she closed them, and felt her whole universe shake.

To keep reading Brayden and Willow's (very!) steamy romance in THE VAMPIRE PRINCE for FREE go to:

www.books2read.com/thevampireprince

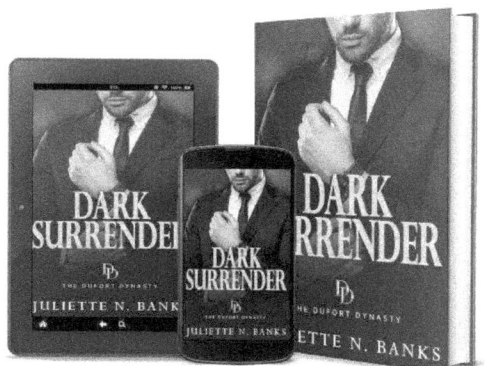

CHAPTER ONE

Logan dabbed his lips with his white linen napkin and placed it on the table beside his plate. The silverware was already discarded to show he had finished his meal, put on by his cousin, Daniel, in the luxurious dining room in his Fifth Ave penthouse.

His chef was incredible.

The simple Chicken Orzo, with fresh green vegetables and warm dinner rolls, had been cooked to perfection. Logan was a bit of a foodie so appreciated a culinary delight when he tasted it.

His eyes lifted and immediately navigated to the sexy brunette further down the table.

Emma.

Romance author and friend of Harper's, who was Daniel's wife. A mouthful, ironically, as he was keen to get his mouth on her. At least, the space between her legs.

Crass? Probably, but he wasn't sorry at all.

Though he should be.

He was in New York City for his grandmother's funeral, not some boy's weekend.

A boy?

Hardly.

Logan stood at six foot three, was wide in the chest, and spent enough time in his home gym that his arms gave his business shirts a run for their money.

Good money, as he had them purchased for him from the likes of Tom Ford and Armani.

Logan was also thirty-four, and the eldest of the Dufort cousins. His brother, Aiden, was thirty-one and his sister, Jessica, twenty-eight.

Daniel, his eldest cousin, had been born just after Aiden, and Logan wasn't sure the exact ages of Fletcher and Hunter because their parents had become estranged at that point.

He knew why.

Logan just wasn't sure if his cousins did.

As a businessman, Logan could've reached out years ago, despite their fathers' broken relationship, but it also included his grandmother. He'd been close enough to her that it wasn't worth creating any animosity.

And life sort of happened.

University. Buying a house. Getting married.

And now fucking divorced.

"So, the funeral is tomorrow," Daniel said, mirroring his actions with the napkin.

"It's at eleven. I got your secretary to put it in your calendar," Harper, Daniel's wife, said. "Are you sure you don't mind me not going? I can, if you want."

Logan watched as Emma lifted the last piece of her chicken to her lips. They parted, and as her tongue reached out and closed around her fork, her eyes met his.

He didn't look away.

Logan wanted her to know he wanted to fuck her.

It was what he did.

Heat warmed her cheeks as she slightly froze, her eyes flaring wide before she glanced down.

Logans lips twitched and threatened to lift into a smile. Something he didn't do very often these days.

"No, you go to your book thing," Daniel said.

"It's not a book thing. It's a book conference," Harper said, shooting Emma a glance. "Thousands of readers will be there to see us. Well, and other authors."

Daniel glanced at him, and Logan could see he was fighting his own smile.

"Book conference. Got it," Daniel said, then Logan watched him turn serious. "David is going with you, so don't fight me on that. He can hang in the back or lift boxes, but he's going."

Harper sighed.

"Who is David?" Logan asked.

"My personal security dude," Harper said, rolling her eyes.

Daniel was a billionaire—the CEO of the global Dufort Hotel chain that his father had built from the ground up. His two brothers also held senior roles in the organization, the three of them holding equal majority shares.

"He's not a dude. He's a former marine with a purple heart," Daniel said, rolling his eyes.

"Oooh hot idea," Emma noted. "Seriously, my next book is going to be sizzling."

Her brows lazily lifted as he pressed the wine glass to his lips. He'd brought the *Edmond Vatan Sancerre Clos le Neore* with him tonight. Not that Daniel couldn't afford it, but it was a good drop and a perfect paring with the chicken.

"Is this my book?" Logan teased.

"It's not *your* book. I was just googling wealthy, um, businessmen in the liquor industry, and your name came up." Emma blushed brighter and tried for a lighthearted laugh.

Failing.

She was impacted by his presence, and he liked that. He wanted to unnerve her.

Logan was an asshole like that.

And women liked assholes. Whether they admitted it or not.

Except perhaps his ex-wife. Apparently.

Harper smirked at her friend across the table.

"What?" Emma asked, looking a little annoyed.

Rattled.

Heat settled in his groin. Not that his cock wasn't wide awake. The woman was wearing a dress which emphasized her more-than-a-handful breasts and slim waist. And with her long hair twisted into a bun, he'd imagined at least twenty times how he'd pull it out and fist it while he tipped her head back.

Before she dropped to her knees.

Harper lifted a shoulder, and her grin widened.

Oh Jesus. No.

If Daniel's wife was thinking about matchmaking them, she was going down the wrong path.

Logan fucked.

He didn't date.

And he certainly wasn't getting married again.

Logan needed to clear this up. Especially if the chemistry between them continued to increase the way it was. This was the second time he'd seen her in as many days.

"Well, as long as it's not a happy ever after, then you are on track," Logan said, shifting his weight in his chair to be more relaxed.

"Why do you say that?" Emma asked, defiance in her eyes.

"Because men like me don't have happy ever afters. We have pleasure. We have power. We have control." Logan tossed back the rest of his wine. "Love? No."

"She writes kinky stuff, so you'll be well represented." Harper laughed, lining her discarded cutlery on her plate. "Now, who's for dessert?"

Kinky?

Jesus, his cock twitched in his pants.

That was right down his alley.

Eyes locked on Emma's, Logan shot her his darkest, most sultry look. "Oh, I'm most definitely up for that."

The way she slowly swallowed, her throat bobbling, told him she understood exactly what he meant.

What he was offering.

Logan had a few days after the funeral tomorrow to spend in NYC before returning to Philadelphia. He'd already learned she was in town, visiting from Chicago, for a few days for the book conference.

"Emma?" Harper said. "I know Daniel will."

The brunette cleared her throat. "No, thanks. I'm not a sweet tooth."

Oh, but I bet you are sweet.

Logan was looking forward to tasting her.

ALSO BY JULIETTE N. BANKS

Visit www.juliettebanks.com to get all my books!

THE MORETTI BLOOD BROTHERS
Steamy paranormal romance
The Vampire Prince - **FREE**
The Vampire Protector
The Vampire Spy
The Vampire's Christmas
The Vampire Assassin
The Vampire Awoken
The Vampire Lover
The Vampire Wolf
The Vampire Warrior
The Vampire's Oath
The Vampire's Fate

THE MORETTI BLOOD WOLVES
Steamy paranormal shifter romance
The Claimed Wolf - **FREE**
The Alpha Wolf

THE DUFORT DYNASTY
Steamy billionaire romance
Sinful Duty - **FREE**
Forbidden Touch
Total Possession
Desire Unbound
Dark Surrender
Ruthless Temptation

REALM OF THE IMMORTALS
Steamy paranormal fantasy romance
The Archangel's Heart
The Archangel's Star

REALM OF THE IMMORTALS
Steamy paranormal fantasy romance
The Archangel's Heart
The Archangel's Star

LET'S STAY IN TOUCH

To receive information about my new or upcoming releases, new series and free giveaways join my **VIP BOOKCLUB.**

Sign up at

www.juliettebanks.com

Also, if you love my books, you are invited to join my VIP readers group on Facebook. It's a private R18 (and FUN!) space to talk about all my series and these sexy book boyfriends.

www.facebook.com/groups/authorjuliettebanksreaders

Ingram Content Group UK Ltd.
Milton Keynes UK
UKHW010638050623
422889UK00001B/145